# PRAISE FOR CHRISTIE CRAIG AND DIVORCED, DESPERATE AND DELICIOUS!

"Christie Craig delivers humor, heat, and suspense in addictive doses. She's the newest addition to my list of have-to-read authors....Funny, hot, and suspenseful. Christie Craig's writing has it all. Warning: definitely addictive."

—*New York Times* best-selling author Nina Bangs

"Readers who enjoy Jennie Crusie and Janet Evanovich will fall head over heels for *Divorced, Desperate and Delicious*, a witty romantic adventure by debut author Christie Craig....A page-turner filled with humorous wit, sexy romance and just enough danger to keep you up long past midnight."

—RITA Award-winning author Dianna Love Snell

"Suspense and romance that keeps you on the edge of your seat...until you fall off laughing....Christie Craig writes a book you can't put down."

—RITA finalist Gemma Halliday

# CAUGHT!

"Fabio!" the voice called. "Mama's tootsies are cold. Not to mention other body parts."

The dog barreled around the shed, bouncing and barking, his red cloth horns flopping. The footsteps drew nearer. Chase braced himself. Damn, he didn't want to do this. Involving a civilian meant trouble.

"For Pete's sake, come on. Let's—" The brunette's mouth fell open. Her pale blue eyes grew wide as quarters.

Chase registered her features. Damp black hair dangled in ringlets just above her shoulders. His gaze lowered. While her height was average, nothing else about her fit that description. Breasts, body, curves. Her shirt was pulled taut, and he could read the words printed in large black letters across the front: *Divorced, Desperate and Delicious.* He didn't know about the rest, but he recognized delicious when he saw it.

# Divorced, Desperate and Delicious

# Christie Craig

LOVE SPELL  NEW YORK CITY

LOVE SPELL®

December 2007

Published by

Dorchester Publishing Co., Inc.
200 Madison Avenue
New York, NY 10016

ISBN 10: 0-505-52730-8
ISBN 13: 978-0-505-52730-1

The name "Love Spell" and its logo are trademarks of Dorchester
Publishing Co., Inc.

Printed in the United States of America.

10 9 8 7 6 5 4 3 2

Visit us on the web at www.dorchesterpub.com.

# ACKNOWLEDGMENTS

Writing can be a lonely business. However, I'm fortunate to be supported by a cast of characters:

My mom, who always tells me how proud she is and keeps me laughing at her stories of accidentally stealing cars and hitching rides with ice cream trucks. (Where else would I have learned humor?)

To Bob, Mom's husband, who is still trying to teach me to drive around the block. (It was a confusing block.)

My dad, who swears he's entitled to half my royalties because I inherited my art of "making up crap" from him. (Well, he is a contractor.)

My supportive husband—model for all my heroes. (I told him you wouldn't buy that.)

My son, who actually loves that his personal experiences are fair game. (I couldn't make that stuff up.)

My daughter, who tolerates my taking pictures of her feet for my Web site. (Don't ask.)

My son-in-law, who, as far as I know, has only denied knowing me twice. (My daughter chose well.)

My writing buddies, Jo Anne & Colleen, who listen to me whine and seldom hang up on me.

My Old Timers lunch bunch, who tolerate my endless chatter about writing, and love me in spite of my being the youngest.

My critique partners, Jody, Suzan, Nancy & Teri, who work diligently at getting the Alabamian out of my dialogue. (Their support is priceless—but I ain't giving 'em a raise.)

[continues on the next page]

To Faye, a cowriter on our nonfiction book, a critique partner from hell, and a sister in all my crimes. (She denies any affiliation with this book unless it gets good reviews.)

My police advisor, Lt. D. R. "Duke" Adkins Jr., HPD, who tolerates questions like, "What kind of gun would have a barrel about the same size as a super absorbent tampon?" (Thanks, Duke!)

My agent, Kim Lionetti, who admits I scare her but hasn't fired me. Yet.

My editor, Chris Keeslar, who wasn't sure about *my* definition of a thingamabob and can't understand how my heroine could spend $500 at Victoria's Secret but bought my books anyway.

To editor Leah Hultenschmidt, who threatened to buy me if Chris didn't, and to the amazing Dorchester team who make me look good.

# Divorced, Desperate and Delicious

# ONE

Detective Chase Kelly stared into the nose of a .45 semiautomatic, his mind desperately seeking a way out. "Has anyone ever told you that you have anger issues?"

Had it been a lowlife perp with his finger on the trigger, the situation might have been easier to swallow. But it wasn't a perp. He forced a calm that he didn't feel into his voice. "You should see someone about this."

Zeke Duncun, his partner for the last two months, nudged Chase with the gun. Chase bumped against the steel ledge of the bridge. A good forty feet below, the slow ripples of the lake splashed against shore. He stared in the direction of the '61 Bellaire Chevy parked a half block down the street, which had brought him to death's door. Hip-hop music blared from the souped-up Chevy's stereo. Big Bruno, the driver, a known street dealer and all-around bad guy, danced outside it, his feet shuffling to the beat, his head bobbing in and out like a turtle.

Chase motioned toward Bruno, hoping to buy a few more minutes to figure out how to get his ass out of this jam. "Such talent and he's wasting his life selling drugs. What gives?"

"Where's the damn book?" Zeke asked, the sun glinting off his receding hairline.

*What book?* Chase mentally filed that piece of info to consider later. "Now you're gritting your teeth. That's another sign of rage syndrome."

The barrel pressed cold against Chase's temple. Panic roiled in his stomach, hitting a ten on the Richter scale of serious emotional upheaval. He didn't have time to analyze it. Nor would he give Zeke the pleasure of seeing his fear.

Zeke's nostrils flared. "Wanting to die is one thing, but you disappoint me. I thought you'd at least care about your fellow officer Stokes. All it took was one bullet."

"He ate my last cherry-filled donut last week." Chase shrugged, appearing cool on the outside, but inside . . . If Stokes was really dead, he had two little boys who, thanks to Zeke, would grow up without a father. "And you know how much I love those donuts." It took everything Chase had not to go for Zeke's throat, rip out his vocal cords, and tie them in a bow around his freaking neck. Chase resisted, knowing Zeke wanted him to lose control and make a foolish move so he could find the motivation to pull the trigger.

Chase, on the other hand, needed just a few sane seconds to make sure the move he made *wasn't* foolish. He needed a plan that excluded the lake below, a bullet, or another confrontation with dancing Bruno. The big man had given Chase a few solid blows to the ribs while forcing him into the car earlier. What Chase needed was to reach the gun Bruno had overlooked, the one strapped to his ankle.

Zeke sneered. "You know what they'll say, don't you? You were just another Houston cop gone bad. Lost your wife and your sense of justice. And I'll be the guy who took you down after I saw you kill Stokes. Of course, I'll take it hard."

"Do you grind your teeth at night, too?" Acid burned Chase's stomach. "That's bad for your overbite."

"You think you're funny?" Zeke jammed his gun into Chase's cheek. "Laugh if you want, but I've already set this up. After an anonymous tip, the captain found that missing cocaine under your bed. I was told by IA to bring you in. What a pity that you turned on me and I had to shoot." Zeke's mouth pinched and creased white. "I can make this easy or hard. What do you want? I let Stokes go fast. One to the heart was all it took."

Chase held out his hands, hoping his rage didn't make them tremble. "Can you give me a second? I just hate making spur-of-the-moment decisions."

A glint of hundred-proof evil flashed in his partner's eyes. Time had run out.

Chase knocked Zeke's hand to the right. The gun fired, the bullet shattering one of the Chevy's headlights. Bruno's dance routine ended. "My car!" All three-hundred-plus pounds of the man came barreling at them. Thankfully, Bruno danced better than he barreled. The man ran like a drunk elephant.

Chase slammed Zeke's wrist into the bridge's steel rail. Seeing his gun hit the pavement brought a flash of relief, then Chase spotted Bruno digging into his pants. The man had either serious jock itch or his own gun, and Chase would put his bet on the gun.

Without enough time to go for his own weapon, Chase shoved Zeke down and took his only out. Not one that he felt particularly happy about either. He dove off the bridge, and the hot pain of a bullet exploded through his shoulder right before he smacked into the water below.

# TWO

"Mother, I'm standing here wearing nothing but a towel and I refuse to discuss my sex life with you!" Lacy Maguire's grip on the purple phone tightened. Why had she answered the call? She could still be chin-deep in jasmine-smelling bubbles, drowning her frustrations and watching on her tub's DVD player The Little Mermaid peeping at Prince Eric.

"We're not discussing your sex life. *You* don't have a sex life," her mother said, her tone a mix of humor and snideness.

"I'm not talking about this." Lacy glanced at the flat-screen sixty-inch television left on for the cat's entertainment. While the TV remained on mute, an anchorwoman stood in front of the local police station and a picture of a man's face, not an altogether unpleasant face, took up half of the screen. The words *Armed and Dangerous?* appeared beneath the picture. Lacy started to hit the volume when she heard frantic barking in the backyard.

"It's not natural!" her mother insisted.

5

Neither was talking about sex with her mother. Lacy attempted a conversational U-turn: "I got a post-card from Mimi." Then she tugged the towel higher around her breasts and peered out the window at the gloomy February day. The song "Grandma Got Run Over by a Reindeer" played over her home sound system.

Pressing her nose against the cold glass, she spotted her poodle/Boston Terrier mix running in circles by the shed. "Mom, Fabio is having a fit in the backyard. I should go see what he's terrorizing. It could be another rabid raccoon."

"It's probably a stray cat. And you *can't* adopt another one. You know what they say about a woman with more than three cats."

"What do they say?" She jumped at the change of subject. Pulling at the door, she grunted when she realized the deadbolt was locked and her keys were in her purse. Dropping onto her hands and knees, she slapped open the doggy door. "Fabio, come here!"

Her mother's high-pitched voice carried through the line. "Any woman with more than three cats is destined to be an old maid. The fact that you named that mutt 'Fabio' is proof that you need a man in your life."

"I can't be an old maid. I'm divorced." *Just like you. Like I swore I'd never be.* Lacy mentally pushed the delete button on that thought and poked her head out the doggy door. A cold, rain-scented wind whipped her hair into her eyes. "Fabio, come to Mama!" The dog, his Velcroed reindeer horns sagging, shot her a glance but continued to howl and run in circles. Whatever he'd found, pride echoed in his bark.

Lacy nudged the phone back to her ear just as her

mother said, "Of course I remember. Why do you think I'm calling you? I know how hard ex-anniversaries are to take."

Lacy began backing up, wishing she could reverse time. Five minutes back and she would never have answered the dad-burn phone. Five days back and she'd have never agreed to do the Christmas card photo shoot for the Pet Magazine Group. Five years back and she would have never married Peter.

Finally drawing her head out of the doggy door, she plopped down, the hardwood floor cold on her naked rear. "Mom, can I call you back later?" *In a couple of years, maybe?*

Her mom kept talking. "It usually takes me about a month to rebound. And the best—"

"With six ex-anniversaries, that means you're depressed half of the year. Why, it barely gives you time to hunt down your next victim. I mean husband." Lacy frowned, knowing the comment would bring repercussions. Her mother's "divorce record" had *sensitive subject* stamped all over it. But so did Lacy's non-sex life.

"Don't get cute with me, Lace! Is that Christmas music? Are you doing a Christmas shoot? Are all photographers weird? Tell me you didn't put up a tree this time. Why couldn't you be something normal? Martha's daughter works at Wal-Mart and she has a sex life."

"I'll put my application in tomorrow. Sex is a nice company benefit." Lacy glanced down the hall where the reflection of Christmas lights danced against the wall. It was a prop. And the music and candles, well . . . it put her in the spirit. "Do you ask everyone about their sex life?"

"No! She just happens to be pregnant." Her mother's voice mingled with another bout of Fabio's serious come-see-what-I-found barking.

"Mom, Fabio needs me. Gotta go. Kiss-kiss." She mimicked her mother's voice.

"Don't you dare hang up on me, Lace! I'm not—"

Lacy hung up, risking her mother's wrath. Karina Callahan, mother to one, a divorcée to six and counting, considered hanging up on someone a federal offense. She had left a couple of husbands for that very reason. No doubt, Lacy would pay for the crime later, but right now she had a dog situation, her naked buns were drawing a chill though the rest of her body, and today was her fifth wedding anniversary. Or it would have been, if eighteen months ago Peter hadn't decided to play Pin the Secretary to the Elevator Wall.

Scrambling to her feet, she tossed the phone on the blue recliner. The chair, equipped with a massager, heating pad, and a mini refrigerator, had been the only thing she and Peter had fought over in court. She'd been determined to keep it, not because she liked it, but because Leonardo, Samantha, and Sweetie Pie did.

Peter liked it, too, but he had his secretary to keep him massaged and hot.

She glanced up just as Leonardo, her red tabby, sashayed into the room. His Santa hat cocked over one ear reminded Lacy that she needed to finish the shoot. She would have been done by now if Samantha hadn't gone on modeling strike and taken refuge under the bed, sending Lacy to hide her frustrations in the tub.

Leonardo balanced on his hind legs, sending the hat's white puff ball dangling around his stiff whiskers. He eyed the phone in his chair and cut his accusing green gaze to her.

"Sorry." Lacy grabbed the phone and tickled the cat's chin.

Fabio's ear-piercing bark drew Lacy's attention again. She dropped the towel and the phone in a different chair. Naked, she skirted around the coffee table and opened a gift bag containing an oversized pink T-shirt—a Valentine's gift from her friend, Sue.

After donning the Pepto-Bismol-colored shirt, she found her keys, unlocked the door, and darted out to rescue Fabio's latest victim. Probably another Texas-size cockroach. Fabio took pride in his roach conquests. And at these sizes, he had a right to be proud.

Big Bruno heaved in a gaspy breath. "You don't think I killed him, do you?"

Zeke gritted his teeth and stared out at the bank of the lake. They'd walked for almost an hour and found nothing. Bruno, holding his side, wheezed and huffed. How was it that he could dance for hours, but after walking a mile, he couldn't breathe? Zeke curled his hand into a fist, wanting to hit something. Wanting to hit Chase Kelly.

"I sure as hell don't want to go down for killing a cop. I got"—Bruno inhaled deeply—"plans, you know. A talent scout is coming to Houston next week for that new reality show. I got a spot to perform. If I make it, I'll be on . . . TV and everything. I'll go straight then. No more illegal crap. Did—"

"Shut up!" Zeke swung around. "And stop breathing like that!"

"Have a 'tude, man," Bruno said, and swiped at the sweat dripping down his dark brow.

Thirty degrees and the man was sweating. Zeke's patience teetered on the edge. In a few more months, he would have been out. Retired with honors, and almost enough money to make the last twenty years worth the effort. But no! Things had to get screwed up. That damn snitch had to start nosing around. And he'd given Kelly enough evidence to ruin everything.

"He's not here." Bruno picked up a rock and flung it into the water with a splash. "I bet the fall killed him. Probably hit his head on a rock. I don't think my shot got him. Like I told you before, I don't mind wounding someone, breaking an arm or a leg, but I don't kill folks. Especially not cops."

"Where's his damn body, then?" Zeke spit out.

"Maybe it got caught on the bottom."

Zeke dragged his fingers through his thinning hair. His hands shook with rage. "No!" He kicked at some loose rocks. "Chase Kelly is a lucky son of a bitch. He made it out alive, and damn it if he didn't get away."

"But he's not here," Bruno whined. "And he's shot. Just how far could he get?"

Zeke looked down one side of the waterway and then the other. Chase Kelly could take him down. He couldn't let that happen. "We've got to find him. He's got to die and he's got to die today."

"Fabio, come here, boy."

Chase heard the voice and knew he should try to run. Only, it hurt too much to move. It hurt to breathe. It hurt to live. But then, he'd already made that choice, hadn't he? He'd chosen to live.

Oh, he'd denied it at every mandatory shrink visit

he'd made in the last two years. Denied it to Jason, his ex-partner, who'd gone ape on him because Chase took so many risks.

In truth, he hadn't set out to get himself killed. Not to say that if the opportunity had knocked, he wouldn't have invited it in to discuss things over a beer. Yet when the Hereafter stared him in the face, he'd found something in himself he'd thought had died along with Sarah: his will to live.

"Fabio!" the dog's owner called out again.

Picking up a rock, Chase tossed it toward the yapping dog. The ugly mutt looked like that *Star Wars* character Yoda, but with reindeer horns and a perm gone bad.

Grimacing, Chase stood. The last thing he needed was to have to explain himself to some civilian. If what Zeke had said was true, the local news would have Chase's face plastered on TV screens across Texas.

Sucking air into his battered lungs, he knew he needed to contact someone, but who would believe that Zeke, a twenty-year HPD veteran, had gone bad? Hell, Chase still had a hard time believing it.

His gaze zipped around the property. The slight clearing in the pine thicket had a storage shed that backed up to a house and looked promising. He needed a place to catch his breath—a place he could think things through, away from the icy wind. He needed to figure out what damn book Zeke wanted.

Chase eyed his bloody shirt. The bullet had only grazed his shoulder. While it hurt like hell, the bleeding had stopped. Still, he could use a painkiller. His entire body throbbed from his leap off that bridge. Or was it from Bruno's fist? Running his hand over his ribs, he didn't think any were broken, but they sure as hell felt loose.

"Jeez." He almost tripped over his own feet. Having been undercover for almost a week, he'd hardly closed his eyes. And for the last hour he'd pushed himself harder, running on a tank of adrenaline that had just run dry.

Hearing approaching footsteps, he started to move. His pain shot from high to higher. Staggering behind the shed, gun in hand, he collapsed against the splintery planks of the small building.

"What is it, Fabio? Don't get your outfit dirty."

The cold wind slapped against Chase's lake-soaked clothes. He listened and mentally created a mug shot of a person who would own such a strange animal and would dress it in reindeer horns in February. Christmas, maybe, but February?

"Fabio, I don't need another cockroach in my collection." The voice and footsteps sounded too young to belong to the blue-haired old lady he'd conjured up in his mind.

Chase's knees buckled. The cold nipped at his bones. He leaned harder against the shed wall. Now wouldn't be a good time to pass out. The dog's owner would probably call an ambulance and the police, and he'd be stitched up and hauled off to jail before he could say uncle.

No, before he faced his fellow officers, he needed to think of a way to prove his innocence. Or rather, a way to prove Zeke's guilt. Zeke wouldn't take him down without a fight.

"Fabio!" the voice called. "Mama's tootsies are cold. Not to mention other body parts."

The dog barreled around the shed, bouncing and

barking, his red cloth horns flopping. The footsteps drew nearer. Chase braced himself. Damn, he didn't want to do this. Involving a civilian meant trouble.

"For Pete's sake, come on. Let's—" The brunette's mouth fell open. Her pale blue eyes grew as wide as quarters.

Chase registered her features. Damp black hair dangled in ringlets just above her shoulders. His gaze lowered. While her height was average, nothing else about her fit that word. Her big shirt hung, but swayed enough to give him an idea of what was below. Breasts, body, curves. At the end of that shirt extended a pair of *nice* legs.

As she danced from one bare foot to the other, the edge of her shirt flipped from side to side. He swallowed, his interest level climbing. And his reasons for not passing out were now altogether different.

His eyes stayed focused on the hem of the shirt. Was she naked beneath—? She squealed and yanked the hem down to mid-thigh. With the shirt pulled taut, he could read the words printed in large black letters across the front: *Divorced, Desperate and Delicious.*

Chase blinked. He was shot, wet, cold, and beat up, but he wasn't dead, and he recognized delicious when he saw it.

# THREE

"Oh, God!" The brunette focused on his gun. Dropping to her knees, she snatched up the dog. "Don't shoot! He doesn't bite."

Chase realized that the gun did point at the dog and now at the kneeling woman, who clutched the Yoda-like creature to her breasts. Turning the gun away, he pushed himself off the wall. "I'm not going to shoot. I need your help."

She zeroed in on his shoulder, where his tan T-shirt had grown dark with his blood. Then her gaze zipped to his face. "Oh, God!" she repeated again, and her expression washed white.

The last "Oh, God," told Chase that she recognized him. Yep, his face had been plastered across the news, all right. Double damn.

"Are you alone?" Pain vibrated his voice.

"No! My husband is here." Her eyes went wide again, then darted left as she tucked a strand of hair behind her left ear.

He reread the word "divorced" on her shirt. As

an undercover cop, he appreciated poor lying skills in a person—it made his job a hell of a lot easier. "Get up."

She rose to her feet, keeping the squirming dog cuddled in her arms. "Why don't I close my eyes, turn around, and you disappear? Then I'll pretend I never saw you."

"You would do that?" He studied her, wanting to believe it.

Her eyes widened and cut left again. "Of course."

If ten different kinds of pain didn't grip him in its clutches, he would laugh at her inability to lie. Hell, if not for the pain, he wouldn't want to leave. His gaze swept over her again. At least he had her pegged: a very gorgeous, slightly nutty divorcée, who mostly told the truth—or did a terrible job of it when she did lie.

"Let's go inside." Forgetting he held the gun in his hand, he motioned for her to move.

"Please, just leave." Her voice wobbled.

Dragging air into his battered lungs, he considered doing just that. But his next step flung him back against the wall of reality. He wouldn't make it a block before the cops arrived. Then he wouldn't have a chance in hell of proving he wasn't involved in killing Stokes, or that he hadn't taken the drugs from that bad bust that he and Zeke had worked a month ago. But damn, why hadn't he ever suspected Zeke of taking the cocaine?

"I can't leave," he told her. "Look, I know you're scared and you don't believe me. You'd be a fool to believe me. But I'm not out to hurt you. I don't care what they're saying. I've been set up, and . . . Shit, I'm not guilty."

Her slender throat bobbed up and down as if she attempted to swallow his words as the truth. One glance into her terror-filled eyes told him she hadn't been able to pull it off.

"Let's go inside." This time he motioned with his hand instead of the gun. "You're safe with me, I swear."

She took a step back, stumbled, and almost fell. Normally, he would have jumped at the chance to wrap his arms around someone who looked like her—someone who he was sure was naked aside from her pink shirt. But after being beat up, shot, and leaping off a bridge, jumping was damn near impossible. He waited for her to right herself, then nodded toward the house. "Come on."

Her gaze cut to his bloody shirt as if she wondered what chance she'd have at overpowering him.

A tad worried about those chances himself, he squared his shoulders. Pain filled the pit of his stomach. He refused to flinch. "Move." He had intended to sound gruff but regretted it when fear masked her expression.

Chin high, she started walking. He stayed hip-close, in case she tried something. When she opened the back door, he shoved his foot in the doorjamb. She tripped over him in a last-ditch effort to lunge inside and lock him out. Forgetting his bruised ribs, he caught her. The breath-hitching pain dragged a growl from his gut. The dog echoed an angry version of the same sound when Chase latched on to the woman's elbow. Not wanting to add dog bites to his list of injuries, he released her.

Twisting around, she glared at him. Her eyes

widened. Anger smoldered in her baby blues. Before the smoldering flared into action, he nudged her inside. Following, he shut the door, never taking his gaze off her. Until he convinced her he meant no harm to her or that strange dog, she wasn't going to be a willing hostage.

"Sit down." He pointed at the white leather sofa. When she obeyed, he inventoried the room. Sofa, chair . . . in the corner of his vision he spotted something moving. Chase wrenched around and confronted a large red tabby wearing a . . . Santa cap. His panic lessened, yet his curiosity zapped into high gear.

He blinked, looked again. The Santa cat gave him a slow once-over; then as if finding him boring, the feline went back to his nap. Chase became aware of the tune, "Jingle Bells." His next breath caught the scent of gingerbread and pine—Christmas.

He raked a hand over his face and continued to survey his surroundings. An extremely large, space-age-looking television played silently in one corner of the room, while an antique grandfather clock hypnotically ticked off the seconds in another.

Stepping to the New Age-looking recliner, he leaned against it for support. He'd never seen such an eclectic mix of stuff. The sofa looked expensive and modern in style, but the pale blue chair looked antique, and in need of a reupholstery job.

His knee bumped the side of the odd recliner and it came to life, humming and vibrating. Chase flinched. The feline Santa raised its head, meowed as if in appreciation, and snuggled deeper into the chair. Christmas music played. "Jingle all the way . . ."

Chase arched an eyebrow at the woman. The dog,

sitting in her lap, shook its large head and nearly lost its reindeer horns.

"You do know it's not Christmas?" he asked.

Ignoring him, she tugged at her shirt and looked toward the hall, where another cat strutted. The white-haired feline, wearing an elf costume, swayed forward and gracefully leaped into the chair with the other costumed cat.

"Okay, this is strange," Chase said and studied the woman.

She didn't answer. Then a voice boomed from the adjoining room, "Eat the tuna and pick up a gallon of milk."

Chase swung around, instinctively pointing his gun. He darted to the entrance of the kitchen, his gaze zipping between the woman and the direction of the voice.

She squirmed on the sofa. "Are you going to shoot my refrigerator?"

Holding his aim, he stared at her. "The fridge talks?"

She nodded and tucked her shirt between her bare thighs.

His impression of her took on a new dimension. Oh, she still rated a ten on the gorgeous scale. He'd bet his wet socks her lying skills hadn't improved, but his definition of her being slightly nuts no longer fit the bill. This woman, with her Christmas-costumed pets, vibrating recliners, and a talking refrigerator, took crazy to a whole new level.

He leaned forward and spotted the appliance in question. All silver, it looked like something out of a sci-fi movie. He glanced back at her. "Any other appliances talk?"

"The microwave and litter box," she answered, as if the question hadn't been strange. "And the fish on the wall. It sings."

He blinked, mentally digesting the absurdity of it all. "What's your name?" Maybe he had died on the bottom of the river and this was Hell . . . or Purgatory, he decided, finding her too pleasant to look at for it to be Hell.

"Lacy." She hesitated. "And yours?" she added, as if in afterthought.

He stared at the television. "They haven't said it?"

"It's on mute. I only saw your picture."

At least she hadn't tried to lie about that. He shuffled a few steps to the old chair and sat down before he fell. "Chase Kelly," he answered. Feeling something in the chair, he reached behind him and pulled out a wet towel and bright purple phone.

"What did you do?" She stroked the fidgeting dog, her gaze on the phone. "If . . . you don't mind me asking."

He heard the hesitancy in her voice, as if she was unsure she really wanted to know. Fear still shadowed her eyes, but now they also simmered with indignation.

"I'm a narcotics officer," Chase said. "My partner set me up to look like a dirty cop. I didn't do anything." He set the towel and phone on the hardwood floor, stifling a moan as he leaned back.

The dog wriggled in her lap. She didn't move. "What . . . are you accused of?"

He could lie, but he didn't see any reason. "I think they're accusing me of stealing cocaine and maybe of killing a fellow officer. I'm being framed."

"Oh."

"You don't believe me?"

She sucked her bottom lip into her mouth, then it popped out, moist, and a shade redder than the top lip. "Of course I do." She brushed the left side of her chin against her shoulder.

"No, you don't," he said. Her eyes widened and he held out his hand. "Don't worry. I don't blame you. If I were you, I wouldn't believe me either." He dropped his head into the palm of his hand and squeezed his temples. Why had Zeke done this? Why?

"You should leave before my husband gets home," she said.

He looked around the room. On the mantel, above the fireplace, sat a row of framed pictures. Most of the frames held photos of cats and her strange dog, but one displayed an elderly woman. Another held a black and white wedding photograph. The woman in it had black hair, but she wasn't Lacy.

He focused on her again. "You're lying."

"I am not. He must have gone to the store . . . for milk." She nodded toward the kitchen. "Didn't you hear my fridge? We're out of milk." Her face paled and she blinked repeatedly.

He believed the fridge but not her. Standing, he crossed the room toward her. Each step unfurled a new pain. "Show me your left hand."

She glanced down to where her fingers lay hidden beneath the dog's white curly fur. "I . . . I don't wear a ring."

"And the T-shirt?"

She looked down at her shirt and her cheeks regained their color. "It's old. I was divorced and I got married again. People get divorced and remarried.

20

My parents got divorced and my mom remarried—lots of times."

"So are you no longer desperate or delicious either?" He regretted the flirtatious remark as soon as the panic hit her eyes. "Sorry. I didn't mean . . . I'm not going to hurt you."

He glanced around the room, noting the holiday-scented candles burning. "Look. I need a place to lie low for a while. As soon as I'm strong enough, I'll be out of your hair. Until then, however, it's best if you just come clean with me. Does anyone besides you live here?"

She stared at the two costumed felines basking in the vibrating recliner. Slowly, she faced him. "I live alone, but people drop by all the time." This time she didn't blink.

"Are you expecting anyone soon—today or tonight?" He recognized the tune now playing as "Here Comes Santa Claus."

She blinked. "Yes."

"Don't lie." He sat beside her, and the sofa sighed with his weight. "I'm not going to hurt you or your Christmas munchkins."

"I'm not the stuffy type whose friends feel as if they need to make an appointment to visit."

"I'd never call you stuffy." *Weird, maybe.* He leaned back against the butter-soft leather sofa and closed his eyes, fighting the aches pulsing though his body. Forcing his muscles to go slack, he listened as the song changed to "Rudolph the Red Nose Reindeer," and held the gun in his lap. The home's heater took the chill out of his air and the grandfather clock ticked, and yet a different song began to play. The woman shifted. The sofa dipped. Chase opened one eye.

"Where you going?"

"To the bathroom." She lost her color again and resettled.

"Where's the bathroom?" he asked. When she pointed toward the kitchen, he stood. "Let's go."

"Never mind." She fell deeper into the sofa.

"I won't watch, if that's what you're thinking." He palmed the back of the couch to steady himself. The movement brought a jingle from the handcuffs that hung around his belt loop. Sticking his hand in his back pocket, he felt around for his key. Relief sighed through him when he touched it. No doubt she would balk, but until he could get her to believe him, he didn't see a choice. He unlocked the cuffs from his belt loop.

She stared at the cuffs. "I don't have to go that bad."

"Come on." He motioned for her to rise.

She nudged the dog from her lap and hurried to the kitchen.

"Not so fast." He caught her arm.

She paled and stared at his shoulder. "You're bleeding."

Glancing down, he saw bright red blood spotting his shirt. "Use the bathroom, Lacy. I don't have time for games."

The ring of the phone punctuated his words. Hope brightened her blue eyes. "If I don't answer, they might call the police."

"Yeah, and if you do get it, you'll say something to tip them off. Go to the bathroom."

Suddenly the recorder answered. *"Hi, you've reached Lacy Maguire Photography. I'm probably in my studio with my eye to the lens, so leave a message and I'll get right back to you."*

22

"Lace!" a female voice practically screamed across the line. "I'm very disappointed in you. You know how I feel about people hanging up on me. Now, I realize your sex life is none of my business, but I'm your mother. If you can't talk to me about this, then who can you talk to?"

Chase's eyes widened at the expression on Lacy Maguire's face. The voice on the recorder continued: "Because I know how difficult today is for you, I'm going to forgive you. But don't let it happen again! And don't let today get to you. Bye, love. Kiss-kiss."

The machine clicked off. His captive turned on him, the fire in her eyes more intense. "Don't look so amused."

"This look isn't amusement. It's pain. I'm hurting like hell. Go on to the bathroom."

"Not with you, I won't." Her shoulders stiffened, her defiant posture telling him more about her character. Not a wimp, this girl.

"Then I'll just check it out," he said.

"You think I've got a gun hidden under the toilet?"

"No. But you might have an escape hatch or high-speed Internet connected to the john." His gaze shifted to the talking fridge.

He pushed past her to glance inside the small half bath. It did, for all general purposes, appear normal. Then again, the toilet seat had fish painted on it.

Stepping away, he motioned for her to enter, then he turned his back. "Don't close the door."

Chase leaned against the washer and dryer lining the wall and waited.

Hearing the flush, he turned around. When she appeared, she had a glint in her eyes that he didn't like. He needed to get her handcuffed to something so he could raid her medicine cabinet for antibiotics and some painkillers. He wasn't hungry, but realizing he hadn't eaten in more than thirty-six hours, he decided to see what the talking refrigerator held. He wondered if the appliance would tell him if he asked.

"You got something I can eat?" He nudged her forward. "Bread, milk?"

"Didn't you hear? I'm out of milk." She pointed at the loaf of bread on the counter. "I wasn't expecting company. But help yourself to the bread."

"You want anything?" he asked.

"My appetite fails me for some reason." Her sarcasm hung thick.

He pulled a chair to the center of the room. "Sit here and try real hard to believe me." He spotted some knives on the counter and eased the chair a little farther from them.

Keeping an eye on her as she sat, he searched the fridge. He found several bowls of leftovers, but opted for jam. Pulling a spoon from the open dishwasher, he spread strawberry preserves haphazardly on one slice of bread. Folding the bread over, he buried his teeth into the soft sandwich. "Thanks."

"Eat the tuna and pick up a gallon of milk," the appliance repeated, and Chase shook his head.

The phone rang again. The answering machine played its message and another female voice came on the line. "Hey, girl. I thought by now you'd have flipped at Kathy's chosen topic for tomorrow night. Have you read your e-mail? If you haven't, do so *now*. I swear that woman is a few fries short of a Happy Meal. But I have to say, our discussions are never dull when she chooses the topic. And yes, I still say your topic of World War II last week was a bore."

Chase pushed the last bite into his mouth.

The voice continued. "Anyway. Call me. You didn't seem like yourself yesterday. Something going on? Besides being horny?" The caller chuckled. "I can't wait to see what you pull up on this one. Kathy was blown away by your research on multiple orgasms."

The jam sandwich caught in Chase's throat and it took three tries to get it down. He gazed at Lacy and smiled. Her face held three different shades of red. So, his gorgeous yet nutty hostage was horny, huh? And she knew a thing or two about multiple orgasms. If things were different, he would have been happy to help her out of her . . . predicament, and to further her research.

"You think it's funny?" Her blue eyes squinted. "You threaten to shoot me and my dog. You come into my house, invade my privacy, and eat my food. And now you're laughing at me."

"Sorry." His smile fell flat because he knew any discussion on the multiple orgasm would probably lead her to believe he intended to do some things he didn't. "I didn't threaten to shoot you. Let's go."

"Where?" She stood, pulling the hem of her shirt down.

"To the bedroom."

"I don't think so!"

"I've already told you I don't intend to hurt you. I know you don't believe me. But when I walk out of here, you're going to be saying to yourself, 'Damn, he was telling the truth.' Now come on." He pushed his gun into the waist of his pants and took her by the elbow.

She tried to jerk away but he held on and pretended he didn't hurt. He headed back through the living room and down the hall as the song, "Grandma Got Run Over by a Reindeer," piped through the stereo system. "You're a real Christmas fan, huh?"

Each step brought a new pain to his body. He wondered why Lacy lived in the boonies, away from neighbors.

He wondered, too, why any woman who looked like her would be horny. Even with her talking appliances and obvious Christmas fetish, men should be lined up outside her door.

The man's hand wrapped around Lacy's forearm. Not tight enough to cause pain, but tight enough to trigger alarm. *Fight him!* her inner voice screamed. But she'd heard never to fight until it could count. She needed a weapon. *The lamp in the bedroom. The bat in the garage.* Desperate, her gaze darted to the singing fish hanging on the hallway wall.

He stopped outside her studio and glanced inside. The Christmas tree twinkled in the corner and her camera perched on top of the tripod. The man looked back at her as if she needed a straitjacket. Fabio, horns now hanging sideways, darted between their legs and took his position in front of the tree.

"I think I get it. You're a photographer," he said. "You were taking pictures of the animals. Like Christmas calendars or something."

She nodded, her eyes searching for weapons. Fabio ran past them and hotfooted it into her bedroom. The bedroom . . . where this man, with a gun and handcuffs, was taking her?

Fear curled inside her stomach. Exactly what did

he have in mind? His handcuffs clinked as he shifted.

"What is today?" He nudged her farther down the hall. When she didn't answer, he squeezed her arm lightly. "Look at me. I'm not going to hurt you. I need your help. Relax. Talk to me and you'll figure out that I'm not a bad guy. What is today?"

She glanced up, a thousand thoughts swirling in her head. "What do you mean?"

He pushed open her office door, peered in, and prodded her to step forward. "Your mother implied that you were depressed because of today's date. I figured maybe it was your—"

"It's none of your business!" No way would she talk to him about her life. No way would she let him kill her—leave her to be found stiff, wearing a *Divorced, Desperate and Delicious* shirt.

He shrugged. "Is it your birthday? You turn thirty today?"

*Thirty?* Lacy's head jerked up. "Do I *look* thirty?"

"No. I . . . I . . ." He glanced down the hall.

The urge to fight and fight dirty washed over her. Reaching back, she snatched her talking-fish from the hall wall and swung hard. Catching him unaware, she managed to wallop him a good one on his head.

He dropped to his knees as the fish started singing, "Take me down to the river . . ."

Piscine weapon tight in hand, she tore down the hall. She passed the grandfather clock, cleared the recliner, almost had the doorknob when he snatched a handful of her T-shirt. She took two more steps, then flew back into him like a stretched rubber band. Refusing to go down easy, she swerved and gave him everything she had.

# FOUR

"Where to now?" Bruno asked.

Zeke stared out the Chevy windshield and pressed a fist into his thigh until he felt it bruise. Twenty years he'd given to the force. He'd been shot twice, knifed once, lost his wife and kids because he gave so much of himself to the damn job. Now they wanted to hand him a gold watch and a joke of a pension.

"Take me back to my car." For five years, Zeke had been subsidizing his retirement fund. Two months ago, when his last partner retired with a little cushion of his own, Zeke had been worried about taking on a new partner. But rumor had it Kelly was a suicidal maniac, a man who ghost-walked through life, waiting to join the ranks of the dead. Zeke had thought he'd be an easy mark. If he couldn't pull it off behind Kelly's back, he could always bribe him.

"What we gonna do if he turns us in?" Bruno asked, his tone more whining than afraid.

"I've fixed that. They already think he's dirty." Zeke pounded his fist on the dashboard. The rumors were wrong about Kelly. Sure, the man seemed to have a death wish, but he had some kind of black mojo keeping him alive. Every stupid risk the man took, he came out strutting high. And whenever Zeke would hint at maybe making a little extra income on the side, Kelly would blow it off as if he'd meant it as a joke. The man didn't have what it took to go on the take. Zeke knew that, but was counting on the others not knowing it.

"Damn it!" Zeke spat out the words. "I didn't want this to go down like this. He's supposed to be dead. I'm supposed to know he's dead! He could be holed up somewhere, biding his time. He's shot, damn it! There can't be more than fifteen homes he could have gotten to. I'm going to talk to every freaking homeowner in the area." He cracked his knuckles to relieve tension. "You're going to come back and drive this area until—"

"He's probably dead." Bruno started his car and put it into gear. "Besides, I gotta go dancing at six. Promised my girl—"

Zeke jerked his gun out of his holster and pointed it right between Big Bruno's eyes. "You're going to do what I tell you. And if you screw up, you'll die regretting it."

Bruno stomped his foot on the brake. The car jerked. Zeke's finger slipped.

The gun went off.

Lacy swung the fish left, swung right. The intruder dodged her blows but never struck back. Somewhere in the recesses of her brain, it occurred to her that he had a gun and all she had was a fish. The thought brought on an overwhelming desire to run.

Swinging around, she started for the door, but her bare foot landed on a towel. With no traction, her feet flew up, and she landed headfirst against the chest she used as a coffee table. The impact loosened her death grip on her weapon and it skidded across the floor.

"Jeez! Are you okay?" His words rang in her ears.

He rolled her over, carefully. Her head throbbed. The fish started its song again. "Take me down to the river . . ." The words, "You better not cry. You better not pout. . . ." also pumped through the house. She closed her eyes as the lyrics merged together. She wasn't going to cry. She wasn't going to the river. But she could do some serious pouting right now!

Masculine fingers moved over her head. A soft purr sounded in her ear and cat whiskers tickled her cheek.

"Lacy? You okay?" He sounded winded and concerned.

She opened her eyes and tugged her shirt down. Leonardo hovered on one side of her, while her abductor leaned over the other. His face came so close that his warm breath brushed her cheek and some delusional section of her addled brain registered that his eyes were the same vivid green as Leonardo's—a vivid green that seemed to draw her in and soothe her as gently as the fingers that parted her hair.

"It didn't break the skin, but you're going to have a hell of a goose egg. I'll get some ice." He moved away.

Closing her eyes again, she tried to gather her thoughts. The man had an injured shoulder, and she'd clobbered him over the head with a talking fish, but he was getting *her* ice. Her head did hurt, but his injury had to be worse.

Sitting up, she leaned against the pine chest. She heard the refrigerator dispense ice: clunk, clank. Then the recorder on the fridge played its message. "Eat the tuna and . . ."

She had never seen eyes so green. They really were almost the same color as Leonardo's. Her gaze suddenly caught on the back door. Reality hit. Why in the dickens was she sitting here waiting for ice, contemplating his eye color, when she should be escaping?

Prepared to lunge up, she heard him step back into the room. Carrying one of her dish towels in his hand, he moved closer, groaned as he knelt, then held the clothbound ice to her head.

"I'm fine." She pushed his hand away.

"Hold the ice to it," he insisted.

Glaring at him, she grabbed the ice and flung it to the floor. Fabio barked. The man glanced down the hall at the dog, then slowly he rose.

"Damn it!" He started down the hall, away from her.

No lollygagging this time! She leapt up and almost got to the door when she heard him say, "Don't do it. Please. I need your help. I really, really need your help."

She imagined him with the gun aimed at her back. Her breath caught on her tonsils and her knees locked. Reflexes from watching reruns of *Charlie's Angels* almost brought her hands up in the air. Then she remembered her lack of clothes beneath the shirt. "Don't shoot me." She faced him.

He stood there, legs slightly apart, and stared. Instead of the gun, he held Fabio. Her dog leaned his head back and licked the intruder's chin. While Fabio's pink tongue lapped across his jaw, the man's gaze never left her face.

"I stepped on your dog when I came after you. You may want to check his leg. I don't think it's broken." He slumped against the doorframe as if dizzy. "And I'm not going to shoot you."

First the ice, and now his concern about Fabio. She edged closer, her heart racing, and took the dog from his arms. Fabio, appearing unharmed, started licking her neck. Ignoring the canine kisses, she moved her hand over the dog's legs. When he didn't whimper, she set him down. He limped on his right hind leg, but after two or three steps he started putting his weight on it.

"He's fine." She glanced up at the man.

"I'm sorry." He pressed his hand against his temple. "I don't intend to hurt you, your dog, your cats, or your talking refrigerator. I just need some time, then I'll leave."

She studied him. Tall, dark, and . . . His straight brown hair, a couple of weeks past needing a haircut, brushed against his neck. He had the body of a well-built baseball player, not too bulky, but far from wiry. Bright red blood stained his shirt.

"I'm not the bad guy here." His voice echoed honesty and weariness. But echoes could lie.

She looked at his face, assessing: square jawline, a nondescript nose that fit with his face, full, shapely lips. Not the face of a murderer. Then again, how would she know? She'd never met a murderer.

Her heart pumped fear, her palms grew sweaty,

but somewhere deep inside her the smallest amount of doubt started to flicker. Could he be telling the truth? "Prove it. Call the police."

"I will . . . eventually. But first I need to try to make sense of this." He leaned his head against the doorjamb.

"Make sense of what?"

"Everything. I'm too tired to think." He stood straighter. "Grab the ice and come on."

She noted his gun sticking out of his pants and the handcuffs hung again from the belt loop of his jeans. Her heart pounded to a higher speed. She picked up the ice. Fabio darted beside him and he backed up as if not wanting to step on the animal again. Would a cold-blooded killer watch his step so as not to hurt a dog?

"Come on and hold the ice to your head," he insisted.

She placed the ice-filled towel to her bump. As they moved down the hall, the phone rang again. Her machine answered it.

They got to the bedroom, and her sound system put the song "Santa Claus Is Coming to Town" on hold while it piped in Sue's voice. "Call me on my cell. Bye," her friend said.

The intruder glanced around her bedroom. Walking over to her unmade bed, he picked up her gray sweats that lay on top and tossed them at her. "Here. Put these on." Her red silk panties, with the words *Hot Stuff* splashed over the front, fluttered to his feet.

She caught the sweat pants, set the ice on the dresser, then, careful not to expose herself any more than she already had, slipped her legs into the sweats. When she gazed up, he still studied her discarded panties. Her heart stopped when he raised his eyes.

"I'm not going to hurt you. Believe that and you'll feel better. And so will I." He touched his head. "You swing a mean fish." He grinned, but pain etched lines into his face.

His gaze shifted toward the LCD television mounted from the ceiling. "Turn it on, would you? And can we axe the Christmas music? I think I've heard this song three times."

She leaned against the wall and hit a switch. The music stopped. Then she picked up the remote control. A tampon commercial blared across the screen. Sweetie Pie, red elf suit hanging crooked, strolled into the room, and jumped up on the bed to claim his space beside Fabio.

Staring at the animals, the man inched closer. As his shoes squeaked against the floor, fear squeaked inside her head.

"Give me your hands," he said.

"Why?"

"Because I'm going to handcuff you."

"And you expect me to believe that you don't intend to hurt me?" Her gaze shot from him to the lamp as she thought about weapons.

"Have I hurt you yet? That fall wasn't my fault."

In a blink, he had her right wrist cuffed, then he connected the other end to the bed. She gave it a yank. The metal ring clanked against the brass pole of her headboard and panic swelled inside her. He had her now. Caught, trapped. Oh, God!

"I'm *not* going to do anything. Sit down." He picked up the lamp and set it out of her reach as if he'd read her mind, then he took the phone and set

it away. "Relax, Lacy. Soon all this will be over. Sit."
He pointed to the bed.

She sat. Her phone rang. Sue . . . again. "I know
you're working, but I don't have a husband, I'm too
emotionally weak to take a lover, and you and Kathy
are all I have. Call me! You're not going to believe
who I got a letter from. Yes! Yes! Yes!"

Lacy attempted to ignore Sue, which took concen-
tration. Just her friend's voice could make one dizzy.
A perfect candidate for Ritalin, Sue didn't breathe
when she talked. And Sue always talked. "So, I was
thinking . . ." Sue continued.

Tuning out her friend's chatter long enough to
worry about the fact that she was handcuffed to her
own bed by a gun-toting stranger, Lacy watched her
kidnapper step into her bathroom.

"Nice," she heard him say, knowing he referred to
her Jacuzzi with the attached television. Then she
heard him rummaging through her drawers, followed by the creak of her mirrored medicine cabinet
being opened.

He walked back inside her bedroom carrying several bottles of pills. "Is this an antibiotic?"

He tossed a bottle in her lap. She let go of the remote control and picked up the pills. The handcuffs
clinked. "Why do you need an antibiotic?"

"They usually give you one after you've been shot."

"Shot?" Her gaze darted to his shoulder. "I mean,
I saw you were bleeding but I thought . . . How bad
is it?"

"I'm not dead yet," he said. "What was the antibiotic for?"

She glanced at the bottle. "I don't think this will
help. And it expired six months ago."

"What was it for?" He ambled closer.

"A female infection." Her face grew warm.

"It's better than nothing." He took the bottle, opening it with a little difficulty, and swallowed the last two pills. Then he held out another bottle. "What are these for?"

She bit down on her lip and hesitated before answering. "Menstrual cramps and bloating."

"Good, I hate to feel bloated." His eyes crinkled into a grin as he opened the bottle and popped two tablets into his mouth. "You got any rubbing alcohol and bandages?"

"Under the cabinet in the bathroom." She shifted and the cuffs jingled against the bed again, making her cringe.

"Thanks. I'll replace everything I use."

"Don't you think you should go to the hospital?"

"If I go to the hospital, they'll have the cops there within ten minutes. I'm not going in until I've thought this through."

"But you're shot! You're not Arnold Schwarzenegger or James Bond. You could die. And I could be stuck here, handcuffed to the bed, with your body. You'd start stinking and I—"

"The bullet only grazed me." He walked back to the bathroom.

She heard him moving around, then he hissed and let out a few choice words.

A few minutes later, he came back into the room, shirtless. The smell of rubbing alcohol scented the air. Her gaze moved over him, and her heart, having played fear's beat for the last half hour, now thumped to a different drum. God help her but the man was a near-perfect specimen of the male sex.

And it had been a long time since she'd had the pleasure of looking at one.

His thick arms had biceps that seemed to say, "Let me hold you," without screaming "Look at me." Between those biceps, she found a flat stomach and torso, with just a hint of a six-pack that made her believe he'd come by it naturally. Just enough hair dusted his chest to make him look masculine without appearing Neanderthal. Her gaze followed a thin treasure trail of dark hair that whispered down his abdomen, swirled around his navel and tiptoed into his jeans. Wet jeans molded to every dip and contour of his . . . maleness.

Aware that she ogled, she looked away. "You're still shot. You should see a doctor. It looks red around your shoulder." She hoped he'd think she'd been staring at the bandage.

If he'd noticed her bold-faced lie, he managed not to gloat. He moved to the opposite side of the bed and dropped his gun on the bedside table. "You wouldn't happen to have a shirt I could wear, would you?"

"In the hall closet there are a few promotional T-shirts in a box." She wouldn't have been so accommodating, but getting him dressed seemed important—getting him out of the room crucial.

He disappeared into the hall. She heard the closet door open. Her gaze targeted the gun. If she could just . . . She rolled over onto her stomach, scooted as far as the cuffs allowed her and stretched out her arm. Close. She could almost feel the steel, but her fingers didn't quite . . .

"Hey." The sound of his voice stopped her cold.

# FIVE

It took her one very long second to realize his voice had come from the hall and not the doorway. She hadn't recovered when he continued talking. "There are some sweats in here, too." His voice rang out, closer.

She jerked her arm back, her breath caught. He still wasn't at the doorway.

"Do you mind if I slip them on while my jeans dry?"

She dropped her face on a pillow and squeezed a little air into her throat. "If you'll uncuff me and . . . leave, I'll even have your pants sent to the dry cleaners and delivered to you."

Arm stretched out, she tried again. The handcuffs clanked against the metal head post. If only she had longer fingernails.

"Thanks." His voice startled her again.

The sound of a zipper sent panic ripping through her. Then came his footsteps. She flung herself over, and sat straight up. The handcuffs jingled. He walked in, looking at her, then shifted his gaze to the gun. His left eyebrow twitched.

She blinked and stared at him, hoping to appear innocent. He wore a white T-shirt with *Maytag* printed across the front and a pair of gray sweats that matched her own. Carrying his wet jeans, he walked to the bedside table, moved the gun to the floor, then limped into the bathroom. Seconds later, he returned and stood on the other side of the bed.

"It's like this," he said. "I haven't slept in forty-eight hours. I need a nap in the worst way right now. When I wake up, I hope I'll be able to think straight and I'll leave. Until then"—he pointed to the bed—"that half of the bed is yours. This half is mine. I won't cross the line and neither will you."

She jangled her handcuffs. "I think I'll stay right here."

"Yeah, that's what they all say." He grinned, but the smile faded. He pointed at Fabio and Sweetie Pie taking up part of his half of the bed. "Would you explain the rules to them?"

"They don't follow rules. As far as they're concerned, this is their bed. They just let me sleep in it."

He glanced down. "Okay, guys. Do you mind?" He picked up her white down comforter and crawled in between the sheets, nudging both Sweetie Pie and Fabio until they moved over. Fabio rose on all fours, shook his head until the reindeer horns fell off, then he cuddled up beside the man, resting his head on the stranger's stomach.

"Lie back and relax," the intruder told her.

Oh, sure she was going to relax! "Fabio, come here. He's not your friend." She grabbed the horns, before they got too wrinkled, and set them on the bedside table. If she lived through this, she had to finish the dad-burned photo shoot. The magazine was expecting to see proofs in two weeks. "Come here." She patted her lap.

Her dog's bulging eyes focused on her, but he didn't move.

Chase—if the man had told her his real name—patted the little traitor on his side and smiled. "See, your dog trusts me. I'm not a bad guy. Lie back, I'm not crossing the line."

He fluffed the pillow behind his head and looked up at the television. A close-up of Oprah appeared on the screen. "We are women, hear us roar!" Oprah's crowd cheered.

Lacy rolled her eyes. Handcuffed and held hostage in her own home, she felt a bit low on feminine power.

Letting out a deep breath, Chase turned his head, and his vivid green eyes met hers. "I'll wrestle you for the remote."

His words brought forth an image of them frolicking around on the bed. She squelched the image. Was she so sex-deprived that she had put aside her fear? And here she'd just blamed Fabio for trusting the man.

She threw the remote at her unwanted bed partner. "Thought you were going to nap and leave."

He picked up the remote and frowned. "I am, but I wanted to see if there is any news on about me."

He flipped through the channels, then stopped when he came across a news reporter talking into a microphone. "Police are searching the lake and combing area neighborhoods. While Detective Kelly is only a suspect, police say he could be armed and dangerous."

Lacy watched him clench his hands and the lines in his face deepened. He cast his gaze at her and seemed to plead for her trust. "I'm not going to hurt you."

"What if the police come here?" she asked, giving herself another shot at convincing him to leave.

"I don't think they'll look this far up from the lake."

Fabio launched off the bed and started barking. A second later the doorbell chimed. Chase jumped up, snatched the gun, and moved to the window. Pulling back the blinds, he stared outside. "It's not the police."

The doorbell rang again. Fabio dashed out of the room, two barks to every step. Lacy's heart thumped in her throat.

The front door opened. "Lacy?" Sue's voice echoed. "Down, Fabio. Where's your mama?"

Chase Kelly swung around, his green eyes desperate.

"It's my friend," Lacy whispered, a knot in her throat.

"Shit!" he said.

"Lacy?" Sue's footsteps clicked down the hall.

"Get rid of her. Please." He backed into the bathroom, closing the door behind him. "Please," he added again.

"But she'll see—" Lacy jerked at the handcuffs, then clasped her free hand over her mouth. Sue's footsteps drew closer. Lacy heard her studio door being opened.

"Lacy, I stopped—" Sue's words halted. "Where are you?"

Options buzzed in Lacy's head. Scream for Sue to

run and hope Chase didn't catch her, or just get rid of her before she got caught up in this mess, too. Lacy slung her legs up on the bed, jerked a pillow over her wrist to cover the handcuffs and leaned her head down. "In here," she called, knowing Sue wouldn't stop until she found her.

"You okay?" Sue walked into the room. Concern puckered her forehead. "I thought you'd be taking Christmas card photos."

"Well, I'm just . . . I got a migraine."

"Migraine?" Sue eased down on the edge of the bed. "I didn't know you got migraines."

"I don't get them often," Lacy said, careful not to move her wrist, so the handcuffs wouldn't clank against the bed.

Sue touched her brow. "You don't feel feverish."

"I'm fine," Lacy insisted. "Just need rest. Bad headache."

Sue sat still, worry tightening her lips. "I don't want to scare you, but migraines could be symptoms of something serious."

"Sue, I'm fine. Really. It's nothing."

Her friend shook her head and her blond hair bobbed around her shoulders. "You should see a doctor."

Lacy closed her eyes, wishing she'd not claimed to be sick. As well-meaning as Sue was, she was a well-meaning hypochondriac. Sue went to the doctor monthly. The woman even had regular podiatrist checkups.

"Who's your doctor? I'll call and tell them we're on the way." Sue's gaze moved to the bedside table that had been cleared of the lamp and the phone. "Where's—"

"Okay, I'm lying." Lacy bit down on her lip, knowing she'd better think fast.

"Lying?" Sue glanced over at Fabio, who scratched and barked at the bathroom door.

"I'm not sick. I'm . . . I'm depressed," Lacy said.

"Depressed?" One of Sue's eyebrows arched upward. "About what? Oh, Jiminy Cricket, you haven't slept with Peter again?"

"No!" Lacy refocused on the barking dog. "Fabio, stop that!" She glanced back at Sue. "I swear I didn't sleep with Peter."

"I hope he was better in the sack this time. If I recall correctly, he was guilty of early withdrawal."

"I haven't slept with Peter." Lacy's gaze flickered to the bathroom, wondering if Chase had his ear pressed against the door.

"Then what's wrong?" Sue brought her feet up to sit Indian style on the bed. "You didn't sleep with the FedEx man, did you?"

"I haven't slept with *anyone*." Lacy clutched the handcuffs so they wouldn't jingle. Then she remembered the real reason for her depression. "It's . . . remember what today is?"

"Oh goodness. I forgot." Sue's five-foot-two frame bounced up from the bed. "You're coming to my house and we'll eat Rocky Road ice cream until we're sick. Come on!"

Lacy held up her free hand. "No! I just want to hide under the covers. *Alone!*" Lacy darted a look at the bathroom door.

Sue plopped back onto the bed. Lacy's heart plopped with it. Fabio continued to whimper at the bathroom door.

"Lacy, I hate to say this, but maybe your mother is

right. It's been a year now. Almost two when you consider you didn't come the last time. Maybe"—she held one finger in the air—"and keep an open mind here, but if you brought that FedEx man inside and screwed his living brains out in every room of this house, you'd be over Peter."

"Sue!" Lacy snapped. "Being my friend means you never agree with anything my mom says! Now leave and let me lick my wounds."

"What about the vet? Bet he'd lick your wounds."

"Sue, please."

"Okay, this calls for desperate measures. We'll break out the red wine and discuss the possibilities of becoming lesbians." Sue grinned at her own joke. "Not that you'd be my type. If I'm switching sides, I'm going after someone like Anne Heche, Ellen's old girlfriend. But I think she went straight, didn't she?"

Lacy imagined Chase Kelly hearing every word. "I don't want to become a lesbian." Her voice came out squeaky.

"Nah, me either." Sue glanced at Sweetie Pie. "Now, aren't you cute." She petted the cat. "Did Kathy's e-mail set you off?"

Lacy moaned. Normally Sue's perkiness didn't bother her. But normally, Lacy didn't have a murderer hiding in her bathroom.

*Suspected* murderer, a voice echoed in her head.

"I haven't read the e-mail," Lacy said. "Now please—"

"Let me save you the trouble," Sue explained. "Friday night we'll be contemplating if it's the length or girth that really makes a man. Or should I say, makes a man good! I'd say it's length." Sue chuckled. "Of course, girth does count."

44

Certain she would die from embarrassment, Lacy darted her gaze to the bathroom door and then back to Sue. They could both die. Chase Kelly, great biceps and abs aside, might step out and shoot them. Oddly, the thought didn't instill any real fear.

*"I'm not going to hurt you."* His words echoed in her mind.

Sue continued talking. "I do say it will be an interesting discussion, more so than your World War II topic."

"It was educational," Lacy said, hoping to keep the discussion from sex, girth, or lesbianism.

"It was boring. Length or girth will be educational." Sue finally took a breath, and the TV interrupted the second of silence. Sue glanced up. "Did you hear about the dead cop?"

"Dead?" Lacy swallowed.

"Well, they're searching the lake behind my place. I spent all morning peeping through my fence. Then a Detective Dodd came to my door. Jason Dodd. What kind of name is Dodd, anyway? He left his card with me and said to call him if I spotted anything. I almost told him I'd spotted something all right—his cute tush." She hesitated as if visualizing. "Face wasn't bad, either. Blue eyes, nice kissable lips. And blond hair. I seriously thought about calling him."

Dropping back across the foot of the bed, Sue started pedaling her feet up in the air. "But then the warning bells went off." Sue's feet stopped in midair. "You know, the warning that says, 'men are all jerks,' and I decided I couldn't do it." Her hips fell back to the bed and she pressed a hand over her forehead in mock anguish. "Besides, cheating isn't my style. I couldn't be unfaithful to my vibrator." She sat upright again. "Which has both length *and* girth, I should add."

A naughty smile appeared on Sue's lips. Fabio barked. Lacy moaned. "Go home, Sue."

Sue bounced up and off the bed. "I'll put the key back under the fake dog poop." She took a step, then danced back around. "I forgot to tell you. Guess who I got a letter from? The editor." Sue started swishing her hips. "She said she loved my book and it's on the senior editor's desk with her recommendations to buy."

"That's great," Lacy said. "We'll celebrate later, okay?"

"Killjoy." Sue skipped down the hall. The woman couldn't do anything slowly, not walk, not talk, not think.

As Sue disappeared, Lacy collapsed against the pillow. She closed her eyes, listening as the front door shut, and waited for the man in the bathroom to come out. He probably had a busted gut by now from trying not to laugh. Lacy heard Sue's car drive away. The bathroom door squeaked open.

"Is it safe?" He wore a nonchalant expression.

Furious at him for invading her privacy, she wished she had something at arm's reach to throw at him. Then it hit her—anger was *all* she felt. She really wasn't afraid of him. "Don't you say a word!"

"What?" His eyes seemed serious but a light grin danced at his lips. Then it disappeared.

"Nothing." She dropped her head back on her pillow. Maybe he hadn't heard Sue through all of Fabio's whimpering. Maybe she would live through this and one day laugh about it. Length and girth, talk of lesbians—just what you wanted some strange man to overhear while he had you handcuffed to the bed.

His weight shifted the mattress. She stared at the ceiling, trying to understand her lack of fear. What was the name of the syndrome when one started trusting her kidnapper?

The comforter billowed upward as he crawled into bed beside her. "Thanks for getting rid of her."

"I didn't do it for you," she snapped. And yet if not motivated by fear, then why had she done it? Why hadn't she attempted to send Sue some silent message to go straight home and call the police? Why hadn't she screamed out, "Sue, get the fish and finish off the man hiding in my bathroom?"

Cutting her gaze toward him, she frowned. She really didn't want to remain handcuffed to the bed with him resting beside her.

Did she?

Their eyes met. He clicked the mute button on the remote.

Drawing in a deep breath, he settled his forearm over his eyes. Silence hummed through the room. Golden silence and then, "Just for the record," he said, half his face hidden from her, "you're much better looking than Anne Heche."

He laughed, then jerked his hand over his side as if it hurt. Lacy buried herself deeper into the pillow.

Zeke pulled his Mustang into the drive of the brick house as Bruno's Chevy eased down the street ahead of him. Bruno had gotten lucky; other than a hole in his windshield and probably a blown eardrum, the man had escaped injury. At least now Bruno knew he meant business.

They'd walked every inch of that lake again, for nothing. Kelly's body wasn't to be found. Maybe Bruno was right. Maybe Kelly's corpse had gotten lodged somehow at the bottom of the lake. Maybe the fish were nibbling at his flesh right now. God, Zeke hoped so. But he couldn't just sit by and hope. Kelly could have survived and made it to someone's home. Zeke wouldn't rest. He wouldn't let up until he personally laid a hand on the man's dead body. And if he found the man alive . . .

He got out of his car and walked to the front porch. The last three homeowners he'd visited had been more than willing to show him in, let him look around. Of course, his badge always gave people a sense of security. People were idiots!

# SIX

Lacy twisted in her sleep, only to have the clinking of metal against metal startle her awake. She lay there staring at the ceiling while her brain registered several thoughts at once: handcuffs, sexy man, length or girth?

Turning her head to the side, she saw that her free hand rested low on Chase Kelly's abdomen. Right beside his "length and girth!" She blinked, swallowed, and offered up a quick Hail Mary that he still slept.

Raising her gaze to his face, she swallowed again. The prayer might have worked if she'd been Catholic. As it was, he stared right into her eyes—directly into her Presbyterian soul.

"You crossed over to my half of the bed." His devilish eyebrows quirked up and his green eyes, filled with sin and heat, glittered with humor.

She jerked her hand away. "You've napped. Now leave." She knew he'd slept because she'd spent at least an hour watching his chest move up and down before she'd succumbed to sleep herself. During those slow sixty minutes, she'd mentally gone over her entire conversation with Sue. She didn't know which of Sue's statements caused her more mortification—the vet licking her wounds, screwing the FedEx man's brains out, or becoming a lesbian. Embarrassment flared inside her and she considered going after Sue with the fish next. But guilt bit her, too. Had she even congratulated Sue on her letter about her book?

The clock on the bedside table caught her attention. It was almost five and she'd wasted all day in bed—with a sexy man, but that was beside the point.

He rose up on his elbows. His biceps tightened. The sight of his T-shirt, soft white cotton pressing against hard muscles, made her mouth go dry. She frowned.

"Are you always grumpy when you first wake up? How about I fix us some coffee?" His gaze moved around the bed, studying Sweetie Pie, Leonardo and Fabio.

Then he caught sight of the newest addition. Samantha, the shy gray tabby, stared at him as if she hadn't realized he'd been there. She meowed, dashed off, then scurried under the bed.

"How many cats do you have?" he asked.

Lacy frowned, remembering what her mother had said about a woman with more than three cats. "Just three. And I'd rather you leave, as opposed to fixing coffee."

He sat up, scowling as if still in pain. "Do you take cream and sugar or drink it black?"

She dropped back on her pillow and studied the ceiling without answering. When he didn't continue moving, she turned her cheek to rest on the pillow and looked at him. He remained sitting up, staring at Leonardo sleeping between his knees.

He glanced up from the cat to her. "You know, we should get a bigger bed."

Rolling her eyes, she turned away. He chuckled and the mattress shifted as he rose.

"Do you need to go to the restroom?" he asked.

"No." She needed him to uncuff her and get the heck away.

"Okay, I'll be right back." He groaned as he moved. "Damn, it hurts."

"You were shot. What do you expect?"

"I don't think that's what's hurting," he said. "It was the fall."

"You fell, too? What did you fall off of?"

He ignored her question and asked his own. "Your coffeemaker doesn't talk, does it?"

Without waiting for an answer, Chase shuffled down the hall. Every muscle in his body cried for mercy, but thankfully the few hours of sleep had taken the edge off his exhaustion.

"If I were coffee, where would I be?" He scanned the kitchen until he spotted a red canister sitting beside the coffeemaker. Moving slowly, he started the pot and then went to the fridge.

"Eat the tuna and pick up a gallon of milk."

Chase stared at the appliance. "Okay, we'll eat the tuna. Does that make you happy?"

The fridge didn't answer. Not that he really expected it to, but then again, who'd have guessed he'd be listening to an appliance to begin with? He opened a few Tupperware bowls until he found the suggested menu. Just to be safe, he gave it the sniff test and the important once-over for any unnatural green substance. Deeming it safe, he found mayonnaise and pickle relish. Grabbing a utensil from the dishwasher, he added a spoonful of both.

Waiting for the coffee to brew, he raked a hand though his hair, flinching when he came to the knot on his head where his captive had bashed him with the singing fish. "It could have been worse," he mumbled, and an image of Zeke holding a gun to his temple flashed through his mind. He looked at the phone on the counter, wondering who he should call, or if he could trust anyone. He remembered that Lacy's friend had said they were at the lake looking for his body. She had also mentioned Detective Dodd. Detective Jason Dodd.

Chase couldn't help but wonder what his ex-partner was thinking. Would he believe Chase was guilty? Chase tried to think of what he'd feel if the tables were turned—if Jason were suspected of stealing coke, of taking the life of a fellow officer, of being dead at the bottom of some river. The scenario brought a gutful of regrets into Chase's stomach.

He'd met Jason upon entering the force eleven years ago. Jason had stood as best man at Chase's wedding and had spent almost every Sunday at Chase's house eating barbeque and drinking beer. Sarah had welcomed Jason as part of the family. Then Sarah got sick and everything in Chase's life changed. Everything.

A different ache attacked his heart.

Chase scrubbed a hand over his face. He needed to concentrate on his problems with Zeke, not sit around taking trips down memory lane. Looking around the kitchen, he knew he shouldn't wear out his welcome here either. Lacy Maguire had been more than hospitable, considering she was handcuffed to the bed. Well, she wouldn't go hungry with him around. And according to her fridge, she liked tuna.

Chase remembered waking up to the feel of her hand low on his belly. A smile pulled at his lips as he recalled the conversation he'd overheard between her and her friend. Running a hand over his mouth, his mind flashed to the look on her face when he'd stepped out of the bathroom without a shirt. Lacy's eyes had held more than fear; some genuine female interest had flickered in those vivid baby blues.

"Don't go there," he said to himself. When this mess ended, he'd visit Jessie and work off his sexual frustrations. Maybe he'd even bring the handcuffs.

With Jessie, his neighbor, he found gratifying, no-strings-attached sex. It was a bodily function that brought release and pleasure, like taking a hot shower, or getting a massage after a workout. It had taken him over a year after burying Sarah to realize the difference between sex and what he'd shared with his wife. Basic sex was a function, a release. What he'd shared with Sarah had been intimacy and love.

Closing his eyes to the past, he squared his shoulders and locked the emotion back in the black box he stored away deep inside himself. A second later he found dishes in the cabinet, chips in the pantry. Then, with two plates balanced on one arm and two cups of coffee held in the other hand, he started down the hall.

"Dinner is served," he said, entering the bedroom. He found her sitting up in bed, her legs stretched out in front of her and crossed at the ankles. She looked . . . divorced, desperate and delicious, surrounded by the two cats, now lacking their costumes. Her hair appeared a little mussed, like a woman should look in bed. She wore no makeup, which pleased him. Chase had always preferred his women au naturel. What she didn't look, he realized with a great amount of relief, was afraid.

She shifted.

His gaze went to the slight sway of breasts beneath the pink cotton shirt. Why couldn't she have been ugly?

"Hungry?" he asked, trying to shake the attraction. The two cats jumped off the mattress and darted around his ankles. He glanced down at the prancing felines, then up at her. Careful not to step on the cats, he edged closer, placed a plate in her lap and the coffee on the table closest to her. She turned her legs and slid her feet over the side of the bed.

The white feline jumped on the bed and Lacy nudged the cat aside. She looked down at her plate, picked up the sandwich, studied it, then set it back down beside the chips.

"What is it?" she asked.

Chase sat at the foot of the bed. "Tuna salad sandwich. Your refrigerator said you liked it." He grinned. "I didn't take the time to boil an egg, but I found some mayo and pickle relish."

She blinked, stared at the plate, and then her eyes grew round.

"What? You think I'm trying to poison you?" He scooted over and swapped plates with her. She stared wide-eyed as he took his first bite of the sandwich.

Her lips twitched as if she wanted to smile, but she

seemed determined to keep the emotion in check. She might not be afraid of him, but she appeared unwilling to share something as lighthearted as a smile. And that made it a challenge. Before he left here, he'd win a smile. One smile.

"You didn't think I could cook, did you?" he asked. "I'm not helpless in the kitchen. My father ran a restaurant." He blocked the orange feline from his plate. "You're not eating. Still don't trust me? You want to swap plates again?"

"It's not that. It's . . ." She bit down on her lip.

He picked up his other half of the sandwich and continued to eat. "It's what?" The words formed around the bite in his mouth.

"It's just . . ." She watched him take another bite. Her lips twitched again, but she still held back. "I've never been fond of . . ." Her eyes met his. "I didn't have tuna in my refrigerator. I accidentally opened one too many cans and . . . well, that's Fancy Feast."

"But your fridge said—"

"I ate the tuna yesterday."

"You're joking." He stared, hoping she'd blink repeatedly, give him some sign that she lied. She didn't. His gaze darted to the last bite of the sandwich he held between his thumb and forefinger. The bite in his mouth grew bigger, and he couldn't bring himself to swallow.

"I think this is flaky white fish and tuna. It's Leonardo's favorite." She pointed to the cat moving toward him.

The red tabby nibbled at the sandwich. The lump of bread and Fancy Feast lay heavy on Chase's tongue.

He dropped his plate on the bed and spat the half-chewed lump of sandwich into his hand. Jumping up, he moved to the bathroom. He could swear he heard laughter over his shoulder. But if she'd smiled he'd missed it and *that* didn't count.

Zeke cracked his knuckles and pulled up to the security gate at Chase Kelly's condominium. He'd paid visits to all fifteen houses within a two-mile radius of the lake. No one had seen or heard anything, and Zeke's gut told him no one had lied. Which meant one of two things: either Chase Kelly was fish bait right now, or he had superhuman strength and had managed to pull himself out of the water, shot and beaten. While impressed a time or two with Kelly's abilities, Zeke didn't think he could have done that. He hoped not anyway.

"Raise the gate?" Zeke called out the window to the punk manning the entrance.

"You have to punch in your code or call someone to let you in," the man said, and continued eating his hot dog.

Zeke threw his car into park and jumped out. He banged on the glass window, making the slob with ketchup on his chin jump two inches off his chair. "Open the damn gate!"

"Why?" the man snapped, wiping dribble from his face.

"I'm the freaking police, that's why!" Zeke slammed his badge against the glass. He'd searched the place three times, but desperation drove him back. He had to find the book and destroy it, just in case Kelly survived.

The man hit a button and the gate rose. Zeke got back into his car, sorry the man had relented; right now, he was aching for a fight, real fist-to-fist combat.

Driving through the gate, he parked his car and sat there for a good five minutes, white-knuckling the steering wheel, trying to get his blood pressure down. Finally, he walked into the first floor of the condo building and headed for the office to get a key. He cracked his knuckles again as he waited for the redheaded old woman inside to notice him pacing the length of the counter. "Need the key to 215." He flashed his badge.

The old woman squinted at him. "Fine, but you're signing my clipboard like the rest of them. I don't want somebody to come back and say that I've been letting every Tom, Dick, and Harry walk into the unit without permission." She handed him a clipboard. "Like I told all the others, that Kelly man was as good as gold around here."

"Someone else been here today?" Zeke asked. It had been two days since the anonymous tip brought the force to search Kelly's place. And they'd found just what they were looking for, too, so they really didn't have a reason to be here today.

"Yeah." She pointed a red-painted fingernail at the clipboard.

Zeke read the name and suspicion bit into his backbone and hit a raw nerve. Jason Dodd—Chase Kelly's old partner. They had had some falling-out, and rumor said Dodd had finally requested to get the hell away from Kelly. Why was Dodd checking Kelly's place? Scribbling his name down, Zeke snatched the keys from the old biddy's hand.

The thought hit Zeke that being here could be a waste of time. He needed to be searching for Kelly, maybe extend his search, check the houses a few miles farther out.

He'd made it to the elevator when his cell phone rang. "Yeah?"

"Duncan? You'd better come into the station." The captain's dead-serious tone made Zeke's gut burn with indigestion. What did the man know? But damn, he didn't have time to go in. He had to find Kelly.

"Why?" Zeke asked. "What's going on?"

Chase walked out of Lacy's bathroom a few moments later. "That wasn't nice." The fishy taste on his tongue was now mingled with the minty flavor of toothpaste.

"I didn't do anything!" She bit into her lip.

He met her eyes and found himself thinking a smile wouldn't do it. He wanted to hear her laugh and see that laughter light up her eyes. "You let me eat a cat-food sandwich."

"I . . . I was still trying to figure out what it was."

"Funny how I'd almost eaten the whole thing by the time you finally figured it out." He walked closer, picked up one of the coffees, and sat beside her.

"Well, how was it?" she asked, and picked up the other cup.

"Actually"—he ran his tongue over his lips—"it could have used a little more relish."

She lost it then: The sweetest laugh came from her lips.

His half-drawn breath caught in his throat. Damn, but she was pretty. He sat there enjoying the view and debated if seeing her like this wasn't worth eating cat food. Heck, when he was six, he'd eaten a worm to get a girl's attention. And Lacy was much better looking.

Her laugh continued and her hand shook, sloshing coffee over the cup's edge. Chase leaned over and took the coffee from her hand.

"Laugh all you want. But I used your toothbrush to get the taste out!"

"Ugh!" she said, and then, "You should have seen your face when . . ." Her laughter bubbled up again and she couldn't talk. Leaning forward, her head almost made contact with his shoulder.

He sat there with his nose an inch from her hair, enjoying the smell of her fruit-scented shampoo. Then she shifted slightly and several silky strands, the color of dark chocolate, caught in the stubble of his two-day-old beard. Chase brushed it back. His fingers lingered at the spot right behind her ear and he wanted to touch more, to move his fingers down to the sweet curve of her neck, over her shoulder and . . .

She pulled back, and he stared at her smile, at the laughter still lingering in her eyes. Taking in another scented breath of air, emotion pulled deep inside him.

Attraction.

Desire.

He'd felt it since he'd first laid eyes on her. But this moment, the way her smile touched his heart and her laughter tickled his soul, it seemed like more—so much more that he got the eerie sensation one gets when someone stands too close, or when someone stares directly into your eyes for a second too long. He leaned back, wanting space and yet wanting to get closer at the same time.

Wrong time. Wrong place. Wrong situation. The last thing he needed after climbing his way out of the mess that Zeke had laid out for him was to have to answer to a sexual harassment accusation from a civilian. Hell, already if she complained he'd be up to his ears in trouble trying to explain why he'd handcuffed her to the bed. It probably hadn't been a wise move, but at the time he hadn't been thinking too clearly.

He reached over her legs to set her coffee down on the bedside table. The movement brought his face close to hers. In spite of his internal warning, he noted how thick and long her eyelashes were, how they swept upward, and how sweet her mouth looked.

She glanced up. Their gazes met . . . and held. Her pink tongue dipped out. He watched it glide across her bottom lip, then she sucked that same bottom lip back into her mouth. The need to taste her mouth overpowered the warnings. He leaned a breath closer.

# SEVEN

His lips almost brushed against hers. Lacy pulled back. The clank of her handcuffs broke the silence. She blinked.

"Can I . . . can I go to the bathroom now?"

Chase drew back, feeling almost dizzy, and nodded. Drawing in a breath, he dug the key from his back pocket. "Sure."

When the cuff fell open, she rubbed her wrist. He found himself wanting to take her hand in his, to soothe away any of the pain that he'd caused.

"Sorry."

She walked into the bathroom without acknowledging his apology, leaving Chase feeling emotionally baffled. Something flashed across the TV screen, drawing his attention. He looked up and saw the reporter was back on; the scene showed her standing in front of the lake.

He dug around in the blankets on the bed until he found the remote and turned up the volume. "Officers still aren't saying exactly what Kelly has done to raise their suspicions, but we do know that a rather large amount of drugs was found at his home. And we're told that Kelly worked undercover in several known drug busts. One case is still being reviewed by Internal Affairs due to some missing drugs."

The reporter turned her head away from the camera. "Detective Dodd?" She hurried from one spot to another just in time to catch Jason, who was attempting to get into his car. "Can you tell us any more about this case? Were you not partners with Kelly for a while?" She shoved the mike in front of Jason's face. Chase leaned closer to the screen. "Can you tell us about it?"

"There's nothing to tell. Nothing has been proven yet. I believe the rule is that a person is innocent until proven guilty," Jason said, his tone accusing. Then he left the woman stupidly holding up the microphone.

Something warm stirred inside Chase's gut, something he hadn't felt in a long time. Jason wasn't buying Zeke's lies. Even after everything Chase had put the man through this last year, Jason still believed in him. It occurred to Chase that this was the first time that he'd taken any blame for the fallout between them. And something told him that if he gave the issue more thought, he'd find that *all* the blame lay on his side of the fence.

He cupped his hands over his knees, fighting the emotional upheaval that made him weak. At least now he knew who he would be contacting.

As Lacy walked out of the bathroom, Chase glanced up and then back at the television. She stepped closer and watched the screen. The reporter was saying:

"Well, there you have it. Right now all we know is

that Detective Chase Kelly is suspected to be dead, shot we're told by a longtime member of the force, Zeke Duncun. According to Sergeant Brown, Duncun is having a hard time dealing with the fact that he was forced to shoot his partner and fellow officer."

"Heartbroken, I bet," Chase bit out. From the corner of his vision, he saw Lacy watching him. A second later, she sat down on the other side of the bed.

"Meanwhile, Officer Brian Stokes is still in critical condition, but doctors are hopeful that he will pull through." The screen flashed back to the originally scheduled program.

Chase jumped up as the words replayed in his head. "He's alive!" He grabbed Lacy by the shoulders, pulled her off the bed and kissed her on the lips. When he realized what he was doing, he jerked away.

"Stokes is alive," he said, still grinning in spite of the fact that he knew kissing her had been a mistake. A big mistake, because he could see the shock in her eyes. A mistake because he wanted to do it again in spite of that shock—in spite of the crazy warning buzzing inside his head.

"That's good," she said, her face flushed.

"Damn right it is!" Chase moved across the room. "He's a good man. Two young sons. And"—Chase gripped his hands—"that son of a bitch, Zeke, was trying to hang me out to dry for shooting him. He can't do that now." He ran a finger along the elastic of his sweat pants. "Thank God he's alive."

"I'm . . . I'm glad he's okay." Lacy sucked on her bottom lip. Her eyes still held surprise from the kiss.

Chase stopped pacing. His gaze focused on her lips, while thoughts of how her mouth tasted swirled in his head. Then the realization struck.

"Damn! Stokes isn't out of danger. Zeke doesn't want him to make it. I need to get in touch with Jason." He moved to the bedside table. "Where's the phone?" he snapped.

"You . . . you took it," she answered.

"Oh. Sorry." Moving to the other side of the bed, he grabbed the phone from the under the mattress. He glanced back to see the clock on the bedside table. "It's almost six. Knowing Jason, he'll probably be at the hospital."

It took him a second to remember Jason's cell number. He hadn't dialed it in over six months. Regret tugged at his gut. How could he have just pulled away from Jason? Chase closed his eyes, thinking of everyone else whom he'd pulled away from these past years. He'd barely answered his sister's calls from California, and when he did, he resisted the idea of them getting together. "Too busy," he'd told her.

His mind turned to his late wife's family, whom he hadn't seen since the funeral. He gritted his teeth, realizing he had a lot of wrongs to right when he got back to his life.

He had started to punch in the number when it occurred to him that Zeke could be at the hospital, too. While he trusted Jason with all his heart, he didn't want to catch him off guard. He stared at the phone, then back at Lacy.

"You talk to him. Find out where he is and who is with him and, if Zeke isn't there, hand me the phone."

Her eyes grew wide. "Me? He doesn't know me."

Chase shook his head. "Yeah, but Jason knows so many women, it'll take him a while to figure out he doesn't know who he's talking to. Just start talking to him like you know him. Ask him where he is, and when he answers you, ask who else is there."

She frowned, but then she nodded. "Dial the number."

He did and handed her the phone. He waited. She shook her head. "It's going to his voice mail."

"Hang up," he said, and she did.

He took the phone and dialed Jason's home line. It rang seven times. Chase hung up. "Damn!" He paced across the room. "I've got to stop Zeke from getting to Stokes."

Her touch on his arm brought him to a stop. She moved her hand as if touching him hadn't been a good idea. And he had to agree; that quick touch had sent an emotional jolt straight to his gut.

"They said he was still in critical condition. That means he only gets short visits from close relatives. That man—whatever his name was—probably can't get to him now."

"You're right." Chase paced back across the room and then dialed Jason's cell phone again. Chase handed it to her. She shook her head and clicked the off button again.

She held the phone back to him. "I'm hungry," she said. "I'm going to fix myself something to eat. You want anything?"

Remembering his sandwich, he smiled. "Had my dinner. Thanks," he said. "I'm purrfect."

She grinned, and he had to stop himself from leaning closer and kissing her again, only deeper. The kind of kiss that led to other things. As if she could read his mind, she turned and hurried down the hall. Chase changed the channels on the TV to see if he could pick up any other news, then went to sit down at the foot of the bed. Rubbing his aching shoulder, he thought of Stokes and the pain he must be feeling. He couldn't let Zeke get to Stokes again. He'd give himself up if he had to.

How could he have messed up this bad? Zeke paced the cold halls of the hospital, hating the antiseptic smells, hating being here pretending he cared when . . . "Damn it to hell and back!" he muttered. He could have sworn Stokes had died. And now—

Someone placed a firm hand on his shoulder and Zeke turned to find Officer Powell, who had partnered with Stokes a few years back. "Hard to believe, isn't it?" Powell said. "I mean, it's bad enough he takes a bullet, but to take one from one of our own. Kelly's going to eat shit for this. I swear, I'll shove it down his throat with my own hands." Powell's eyes began to water.

"Yeah." Zeke brushed off Powell's touch. "He's a bastard. I should have seen it. I should have stopped him."

Powell curled his hands into fist. "You know Stokes has two boys, don't you?" He raised his fist in front of him, then, taking a deep breath, lowered it again. "Captain said you got a shot at him. I hope it was in the gut. I hope like hell he's lying somewhere suffering right now."

"I just don't get it," someone said behind Powell.

Zeke turned to see several officers from the precinct grouped behind him. Damn it, he had already escaped from them once. He needed to be alone, to think, to plan.

Officer Candace started talking. "I mean, I knew Kelly had his head screwed on backwards lately, but . . . but he wasn't like that before."

Knots formed in the pit of Zeke's stomach. "He told me he did it," Zeke said. "He bragged about it. That's when I lost it. I fought him, got his gun . . . Damn it, if only I'd gotten there sooner, I could have . . ." Zeke looked away, scared his acting skills weren't up to the task. Powell's hand landed on his shoulder again, as if to offer condolence. Candace, however, didn't appear convinced. Zeke had never cared too much for the man.

"You can't blame yourself," Powell said.

"Hey." Another officer walked up, one who looked too happy. "Good news! The doctors say Stokes might just pull through this."

Cheers and some backslapping filled the hall. Zeke snatched a pack of antacids from his pocket and chewed them into sweet chalk.

He spotted some more people moving toward the group. He recognized Stokes's wife. A young, teary-eyed boy clutched her hand. Jolts of unnamed and unwanted emotion rippled through Zeke's chest.

"I need some fresh air." Zeke took off down the opposite hall. Yet even as the guilt tore him apart, he knew that he couldn't let Stokes live. He *couldn't*.

Chase sat on the bed for ten or fifteen more minutes, trying to find the missing piece of the puzzle. Zeke had to have reasons for setting this whole thing up, but what? Chase looked up at the doorway and suddenly realized that Lacy could be getting in her car trying to run or perhaps dialing the police right this minute. But she believed him now, didn't she? Or was he fooling himself? Just because they'd shared a laugh together didn't mean . . .

Glancing at the phone he still held in his hand, he clicked the on button and prayed he'd hear the hum of a dial tone. He brought the phone to his ear. No dial tone. Then he heard her voice on the line.

"You've got to believe me." Lacy's voice carried through the line, sending waves of disappointment into Chase's chest.

# EIGHT

Chase gripped the phone. Betrayal tightened his chest. He had no reason to expect her loyalty, yet for some reason he had expected it. Hell, he'd more than just expected it, he'd needed to have someone believe in him right now.

Her voice sounded over the line again. "Please believe me. I'm fine, Sue. I just wanted you to know that I'm excited about the editor's letter."

*Sue?* She'd called her friend. She hadn't called 911 to report that a lunatic had invaded her home. So she *did* believe him. The heaviness in his chest evaporated and his thoughts flipped to their shared kiss. Although brief, it had left him hungry for more. Much more.

"I know how much this means to you," Lacy's voice came again. "Now I've got to go. I'll see you later. Bye."

Before he could hang up, the connection went silent. Had she heard him pick up the line? He stood, then walked down the hall. If she asked him to go, he would do it. He hadn't a clue where he'd go, but he'd do it.

He stopped short when he spotted her in the kitchen. With her head poked inside the freezer, her shapely backside encased in gray sweats protruded outward. His next thought curled around the fact that she wasn't wearing any panties. The image of the silky slip of material that had fluttered at his feet whisked through his mind and hung there like a piece of forbidden fruit.

"Are you sure you're not hungry?" She glanced back and over her shoulder, obviously having heard his steps. "I've got potatoes that I could bake, and some steaks."

He stared at her, his sexual hunger growing. And with only thin gray sweats covering his growing part, she would know all too soon about his appetite if he didn't get himself under control.

"What?" she asked, as if noting his gaze.

"Nothing," he said, and tried to shake the sexual pull he felt from just being near her. "You believe me now, don't you?" He almost mentioned picking up the phone line, but decided to let her bring it up if she wanted to.

She hesitated for a second. "Yes. I believe you."

"Thanks," he said. "And I'm sorry about hand-cuffing you. I didn't know what else to do. But . . . it wasn't a smart thing to do. Your wrists okay?"

"Fine." She buried her head back in the freezer. "You want a steak or not? Because I'm starving and if I only cook one, I'm not sharing. I'm an only child. Never learned that sharing thing."

Her words, the lightness in her voice, told him she didn't hold a grudge.

"I was willing to share *my* dinner," he teased.

"Yeah, well . . ." Her bottom wiggled. "Could I tempt you with some milk bones or kitty chow?" She glanced over her shoulder, a smile on her lips.

She could tempt him all right. Her smile could win awards, and that perky backside . . . "Steaks sound good. Thanks."

Grabbing a couple of packages, she stuck them into the microwave. "Steaks, defrost. Five minutes," she said to the box.

"It not only speaks, but it takes orders, huh?" he asked.

She looked up, the teasing look reflected in her eyes. "Yeah."

He watched her, his curiosity growing, and questions about her formed on the tip of his tongue. The phone rang. He looked at the portable phone he had carried from the bedroom.

"Does Jason have caller ID?" she asked. "Would he know to call back?"

"I don't think so." He held out the phone. "Do you want to answer it?"

"Nah. Let the machine get it," she said.

"Answer if you want. I don't care." If she trusted him, he owed her his trust in return.

"Thanks, but I'd just as soon not chance talking to my mother. She might disown me for hanging up on her earlier."

"She's a handful, huh?" he asked as the phone continued to ring.

"More like an armload." She looked back at the

recorder while her message played. "My mother claims she's missing the thingamabob in her brain that catches dialogue before it spills out of her mouth. She thinks it, she says it. And she thinks very blunt and tacky things—makes Rush Limbaugh sound like a pansy. So yeah, she's an armload."

The caller came onto the line. "Hey, Lacy. It's Kathy. Sue said you were down and out. Listen, girl. It's *my* week to be depressed. My jerk of an ex-husband didn't pay his child support this week, and my plumber is hinting that if I cleaned out his pipes, he wouldn't need to bill me. The scary thing is, I'm considering it. So I'm winning the Most Depressed award this week, and probably the Horniest, too. The plumber is kind of hot. Besides, you won Horniest last week."

Chase leaned against the counter and smiled as Lacy's face turned an attractive shade of pink. He said, "I'd say everyone you know is missing that thingamabob. Between that Sue girl and now Kathy, you've got some pretty . . . outspoken friends."

Lacy frowned. "They're not outspoken. What you heard are just conversations that aren't meant for a man." Her tone left no doubt as to her loyalty to her friends.

Chase shrugged, feeling a little chastised. "I was . . . just teasing."

She cleared her throat. The conversation on the phone continued: "And his butt . . ."

"How do you like your steak?" she asked, perhaps to get his attention away from her friend's wacky message.

"Medium is fine." Still grinning, he pulled out a chair and sank into it.

She turned around, and a flicker of concern passed her gaze when he reached up to massage his side. "Are you okay?"

"Fine. More sore than anything." The phone machine clicked off. Palming the phone in his hand, he dialed Jason's number again, and on the fifth unanswered ring he hung up.

"Where did you fall from?" she asked, holding two potatoes in her hands and leaning into the sink.

"Some bridge about four miles north of here." He leaned back in his chair. "By the old railroad tracks."

"Oh, my. If it's the one I'm thinking about, it's a wonder you didn't break your neck." She turned on the water in the sink then scrubbed the potatoes with a brush.

"I was lucky," he said, his eyes on the way her pantiless backside shifted with the scrubbing action.

"Steaks, five minutes," the microwave spoke.

Chase pointed at the appliance. "I wouldn't trust it. The last time I listened to an appliance I ended up eating a cat-food sandwich."

She chuckled. The sound came out purely feminine and somehow seductive.

He'd been determined to get one smile and a laugh, and already he'd exceeded his expectations. In a purely male part of his brain—the one that women insist resides between a man's legs—he couldn't help wondering what else he might exceed at.

Chase watched her step around the kitchen. She moved like an ice skater, with slow, fluid strokes, or like music that flowed effortlessly from one stanza to another. The woman had grace, a character trait he hadn't noticed in a long time. Would that grace be revealed when she made love? Would her moves be slow, rhythmic, beautiful?

She turned, knelt, and pulled a pan from beneath a cabinet. He watched her breasts sway slightly. The room's temperature seemed to rise, and he remembered the kiss back in the bedroom. He licked his lips, expecting to find a taste of her lingering there.

He shook his head, hoping the movement would send his thoughts scattering. But his gaze went right back to her. Barefoot, wearing sweats and a large shirt—somehow the woman made casual-sloppy appear totally sexy. He continued to watch her, his curiosity and desires growing again.

"What is today? Why is everyone worried about you?" he asked, thinking conversation would help distract him.

She turned from the sink. "If you tell me I look thirty again, I might come after you with a steak this time."

"You don't look thirty," he said, and chuckled. "I just remember . . ." My wife. He stumbled over the memory. "I know how women can react to their thirtieth birthday."

Her eyes seemed to widen as she digested what he'd said. She bit down on her lip, hesitated and then spoke. "Are you married?"

"No," he answered calmly, but the question set him back to that awkward feeling of needing space, of wanting to pull away. He dialed Jason's number again, gazing down at Lacy's dog that bounced into the room carrying a chew bone for a beast at least three times bigger. Chase listened to the ringing phone.

No one answered, so he hung up and stroked the dog with his bare foot. "So, you're not going to tell me what today is," he said, wanting to find level ground with his hostess again.

"It's nothing, really." She didn't look back.

"Okay." He knew all about not wanting to talk about things. Hell, he'd just half lied to her so he wouldn't have to talk. No, he didn't have a wife. But he hadn't bothered telling her that the reason was because less than a year after her thirtieth birthday, an inoperable brain tumor had ripped her out of his world. And before he'd lost her, he'd stayed by her bedside for six months, held her hand, feeling impotent, and watched her die a little each day.

"Can I help?" he asked, needing a distraction from the direction of his thoughts. "I'm really good in the kitchen."

She turned around. "I've got it, but thanks."

He nodded and dialed Jason's number again. This time he heard a click as if someone answered. Hurrying to Lacy's side, he handed her the phone. "I think he's answered this time."

Lacy dropped the aluminum foil and took the phone. The receiver still possessed warmth where Chase had held it. She met his green eyes and almost forgot about talking. Why had she asked if he was married? It made her sound interested in him. She wasn't interested. She wasn't. Uh-uh.

"Detective Dodds." The voice on the other end of the phone line sounded stern, serious.

"Uhh, Jason?" She curled a handful of loose sweat pants in her hand.

"Yeah," came the hesitant answer, as if he were trying to figure out the voice.

"Where are you?" she asked, remembering what Chase had wanted her to find out.

"On my way to the hospital. Who—"

"Who's with you?" she asked in a casual tone, and bit down on her lip. He didn't answer. "Jason?"

"Who is this?" he asked.

She froze, searching her mind for something to say. "Please, don't tell me you're with another woman." She chuckled, hoping the lightness in her voice would put him at ease.

"I'm alone." He grew quiet again. "An officer was shot this morning. I'm going to see about his family at the hospital."

"You sure you're alone?" She bumped against the counter.

"Kay? Is this you?"

"No. Uh, I'm not Kay. But just a minute." Lacy placed her hand over the bottom of the phone. "I think he's alone. He thinks I'm Kay."

Chase took the phone and his smile said thanks. Lacy stood there studying him and wondered how she could have ever been afraid. Even with a two-day five-o'clock shadow going on, the man didn't look dangerous. Then her gaze swooped down his body and she had to amend that thought. Oh, he looked dangerous, but not in a life-threatening sort of way.

"Jason, it's me." Chase pulled the phone away from his ear, as if Jason was yelling. Actually, Lacy could hear Jason's voice clear across the kitchen. The man sounded furious.

"I know. I'm sorry," Chase said. "I got with you as soon as I could." He paused between sentences. "No. Yes, but I'm fine. Yeah. The whole freaking thing is a setup." He paced the area between the kitchen table and the bar. "It's Zeke. No, I'm serious. I'll be damned if I know. No, I swear."

As Lacy marinated the steaks, she pretended not to listen. But of course, she listened.

"I don't know. He said something about a book." Chase raked a hand over his face. "Hell, I don't know what he's talking about. Yeah, but you have to watch out for Stokes. I'm telling you. No, I didn't see him do it, but he confessed to me." He paused long enough to scowl. "Because he was about to do to me what he did to Stokes." Chase's voice rose with anger, then he closed his eyes as if to calm himself. "Sorry, it's been a freaking bad day! Yeah, but I'm telling you, Zeke's going to try something."

He moved back to the table, the phone held tightly to his ear. "The book is the piece of the puzzle that's missing. All I've got to do is to figure what the hell *book* he's talking about." He sank into a chair and reached up to rub his shoulder.

Lacy wondered about his physical condition. The man had been shot. Maybe she should insist he go to a doctor. Then again, he didn't really look that worn down. He looked rather . . . good. Too good.

Fabio pranced into the kitchen again and, wanting to play, he dropped his chew bone at the man's feet. Chase knelt, grimacing as he lowered himself, picked up the bone, and tossed it into the living room for Fabio to fetch.

"Well, I'd like to know that, too," Chase said into the phone.

The dog went careening to get the bone, and Leonardo came slinking into the room and brushed up against Chase's leg. Lacy added another sprinkle of salt to the steaks as Chase continued talking to Jason, moving his hand downward to stoke the feline's back. The cat purred and glanced at her as if to say, "This man has good hands."

Biting into her lip, Lacy realized that Chase Kelly had a weakness for animals. A tough cop with a soft spot for animals. A tough, sexy cop with good hands. Realizing her wayward thoughts, she turned back to the meat on the counter and tried not to focus on the prime cut of man sitting at her table.

As she salt-and-peppered the steaks, her attention stayed trained on the conversation. Part of her felt rude for listening in, another part said he'd forced his way into her life and she had a right to listen.

She sprinkled the steaks with garlic powder. Fabio came bumping into her with his bone. Reaching down, she tossed it for him. Then, piercing the T-bones with a fork, she continued eavesdropping.

"I don't know. I've . . . uh, kind of told her I'd be leaving soon. Scared her to death at first." He stood and stepped closer as if he didn't want to be talking about her without her listening in. "Clobbered me in the head with a singing fish." He laughed. "No, now she's fine." He paused. "Must be my charm."

Lacy could feel him standing a few feet behind her, and breathing became difficult.

"I'll ask," he said. "No, she's definitely not hard to look at. Yeah, I just bet you would."

Lacy felt him staring, and her heart jumped around like a Mexican jumping bean. He was going to ask to stay for a while. Her pulse raced alongside her thoughts. She didn't want him to stay, did she? But if his leaving meant he could be hurt . . . well, she didn't want to be responsible for that.

She took a deep breath. For two years she'd attempted to ignore the fact that her body had needs . . . that she wanted intimacy, sex! She'd been celibate, except for that one night with Peter. And hadn't that been a joke? Early withdrawal, Sue had called it, but in truth the man didn't even have much to deposit.

Everyone and their pet gerbils assumed that her anti-man campaign came from an everlasting love she held for Peter. Wrong. Okay, maybe there were a few residual feelings lingering after two years. Feelings like hurt, disappointment, and a nauseating disgust. But it wasn't those feelings that kept her celibate. She had her own reasons.

She washed her hands and then went into the living room to retrieve a beer from the recliner's cooler. Standing up, she twisted the top, took a long drink, then glanced at the photos on the mantel. Oh yeah, she had reasons. She was, after all, Karina Callahan's daughter, and granddaughter to Sabrina Gomez. Between the two, they'd acquired twelve divorces. Add Lacy's to the equation and the number went up to thirteen. And her mother already had claws in a man she'd met on her last cruise; Lacy gave her a month before she tied the knot again.

"Why, isn't love grand?" Lacy mumbled beneath her breath and stared at the picture of her mom and dad on their wedding day. They both looked so happy. At least for a while, until they'd decided to take a ride to Divorceville.

Lacy's gaze moved to the photo of her grandmother. *"We're just fools for love,"* her grandmother had told her one day. Well, Lacy may have been a one-time fool. Okay, a two-time fool if you counted Brian

Bankhead. She hadn't made it all the way to the altar with him, but rings and promises had been given. More importantly, her heart had been broken. Twice.

The third time *wouldn't* be a charm. There would be no third time. Not when one engagement and one marriage had nearly taken her under.

Somehow, some way, she would *not* follow in her mother's and grandmother's footsteps. And if it meant denying herself sex and men to avoid the path down Divorced Lane, then so be it. So what if she never had sex again! Who needed it?

Zeke had burned rubber straight from the hospital and gone back to Kelly's condo. He couldn't get to Stokes yet, but he had to do something constructive. He couldn't slow up or his whole freaking world could come falling down on top of him. Time. He didn't have much left. And neither did Stokes.

Hospital policy wouldn't let anyone in ICU except immediate family. Well, screw hospital policy. Zeke had screwed and been screwed by every other policy in his life. What was one more? That was why he didn't care, why it didn't matter how bloodshot that kid's eyes had been, or how much pain he'd spotted in Stokes's wife's expression. As his English father would say, he'd been shagged by every damn thing in life. Time had come for the tables to turn. If someone got hurt, they wouldn't be the first. They could join Zeke's own world of hurt.

He'd find a way to get to Stokes. But first things first. He wanted to do one more search of Kelly's place. If Kelly had the book, Zeke had to find it.

Letting himself into Kelly's apartment, he stood in the middle of the mess and tried to think where he might have hidden the book. Feeling his blood start to boil, he darted down the hall to the bedroom. He jerked out dresser drawers and emptied the contents on the floor; he slung over the mattress. Back in the living room, he took off the sofa cushions. Nothing. Nothing. Nothing.

He'd only seen the book once. Pablo Martinez had pulled it out to show Zeke his undercover work. Like a scrapbook, the man had journals, photographs, and plastic pockets that he claimed held recorded conversations from a long list of criminals. The lowlife punk thought of himself as a cop. He swore his plans included taking classes so he could enter the police academy. But right now the only academy Martinez belonged to was Hell. Zeke had made sure of it. He hadn't messed up with him: the bullet to the man's head had done him in.

"Think, think!" Zeke grumbled, roaming around the living room, kicking anything that got in his way. "What did Martinez say that last night?"

Zeke closed his eyes as the words replayed. *"If you lay one hand on me, Kelly will collar your ass. He knows, he knows everything and we're partners. Give us your sources and we'll let you off easy."*

As if Zeke would really give details to that piece of shit. Zeke cracked his knuckles and the popping sound vibrated through the silent apartment.

Kelly had already used Martinez on numerous occasions when the snitch first approached Zeke, hinting he knew things. Zeke hadn't believed him, but that night he'd had Martinez followed. Bruno had followed him straight to here, to Kelly's place.

Bruno said the man had stayed for over two hours. Two hours? They'd had to be up to something! That's when Kelly had gotten called to go undercover. In truth, Zeke had arranged the assignment. He'd needed Kelly out of the way for a few days while he figured out how to deal with the situation. The beginning of Kelly's end, and he'd had it all planned out. So why was it all falling apart? Why did he have to kill Stokes twice? Wasn't once enough? Zeke's head filled with the image of Stokes's wife holding her son's hand.

Zeke grimaced. At least the man had family who would mourn him. Lucky bastard! If Zeke went down today, who would grieve for him? Would his children, Lindsey and Phillip, even care? They sure as hell hadn't wanted to see him in almost a year. And when Zeke had tried to force visits upon his teenage son and daughter, he'd been told by the lawyer that he couldn't push. To give them time. Just keep making the support payments and they'd realize their mistakes later. So every month he sent money, hoping the five hundred dollars would buy him a little compassion. It bought him shit! Yeah, Stokes was lucky that someone cared about him. Zeke couldn't and wouldn't let him live.

Slamming the door on his way out of Kelly's place, Zeke hurried to his car. He had a man to kill, and he couldn't let teary-eyed kids or a mourning woman get in his way.

But even as he hurried to his car, Zeke saw their faces in his mind and acid churned in his gut. He cracked his knuckles again.

Lacy took another sip of cold beer and stared at the pictures on the mantel. Sex was bad for her. It messed her up. Like an allergy. People who were allergic to peanuts didn't go around wanting Reese's, they simply gave them up. They didn't talk about it, or hold group discussions about it with their friends. Maybe that's where she'd gone wrong. Maybe she should tell Kathy and Sue that she couldn't talk sex anymore.

"I'll give you five bucks for your thoughts?" Chase's voice caused Lacy to jump.

# NINE

"Only five bucks?" Lacy turned and stared at him. "You'll have to do better than that."

"You okay?" His breath whispered across the back of her neck and she flinched.

She hadn't noticed that he'd finished his conversation. His hand pressed against her shoulder; it felt warm, strong, and . . . masculine. She swallowed, and tried to remember where her brain had been before he touched her. Oh yeah, she'd been thinking about how she didn't need sex.

"I'm fine. Not a need in the world." Every nerve in her body slow-danced to a song of passion. She pressed the chilled bottle to her forehead, amazed that between her body heat and the cold beer, a puff of steam didn't float up to the ceiling.

"Just getting a beer to marinate the steaks." She looked at the half-emptied bottle in front of her nose. "But I think I've drunk my marinade." Bending over, she hit the button that ejected the cooler from the side of the chair and grabbed another beer.

"Wow!" Chase said.

"Every man's dream chair," she said. "It massages, cools, heats, can lift you up when you don't feel like lifting yourself, and you have your own minibar within arm's reach."

"Pretty neat." He looked from the chair to her as if he wasn't altogether convinced.

"I hate it," she confessed, running her hand over the blue leather. She'd used more than two cans of Lysol on the piece of furniture, yet to her, the chair still smelled like Peter's aftershave.

"Then why do you have it?" he asked.

"Because I'm *not* a selfish person. There are others to consider," she said. "Others who love this chair."

He arched an eyebrow. "Really? Who do you keep it for?"

"Watch this." She hit the button on the chair's side. The recliner started vibrating and immediately, Samantha, Leonardo and Sweetie Pie came running down the hall. Samantha, of course, spotted Chase and hightailed it back into the bedroom.

"They love it," Lacy said, and waved her arm as the two other cats piled into the seat.

"You bought an electronic chair for your cats?" he asked, clearly disbelieving.

"Bought it? Are you kidding? This thing runs about ten thousand dollars. No, it was given to me. I work a clause into most of my contracts. I get free or amazingly discounted merchandise when I do product shoots."

His laugh was deep. "That explains all the high-tech appliances. And here I thought you were just some kind of weird electronic gadget collector. The

TVs, the fridge, the microwave." He touched his head. "The fish."

She smiled. "I just take pictures. And the fish was a gift from my friend Kathy's little boy." She took another sip of beer. "But if you ask my mother, nothing is weirder than a photographer. She'd rather I work at Wal-Mart." Lacy gave the wedding photo of her mother one last glance, hoping it would give her strength to resist the temptation standing in front of her. "You want a beer?"

"Don't mind if I do." Retrieving one from the opened cooler, he pushed the door closed as if to see how it worked. "Pretty neat." Standing up, he followed her into the kitchen.

"Thanks for talking to Jason," he said into the silence.

"It was nothing." She doused the steaks with beer, then pushed them into the broiler and turned around. Their eyes met—blue to green, green to blue.

"Listen, uhh, Jason thinks it's best if I lie low for a few days and let him do some digging on the inside while I try to figure out why Zeke's going after me." More green to blue. "And I thought . . ."

She stopped listening and watched his mouth move. The memory of their brief kiss in the bedroom made her lips tingle, and the tingling spread. She grabbed her beer and held it up to her cheek, even though more southern regions of her body needed cooling off.

"And I was wondering . . ." His voice became a whisper.

She bit her lip, feeling his heat all the way across the room. Oh, Lord. This man had trouble stamped all over him. He took a step forward. She held out a hand.

"Stop!" Her voice sounded an inch from desperate. "You can stay, but you sleep on the couch. And lose the handcuffs." *And no sex. No sex!*

He smiled, his eyes never leaving hers. "Fair enough."

No, it wasn't fair. It ranked right up there with locking a hunger victim in Baskin-Robbins in hundred-degree weather and not letting her indulge. Oh, right now, she could really use a triple dip of sex. But was she capable of devouring this man's body without giving him her heart and soul, without wanting to throw herself on the altar?

She shook her head, trying to clear it. Hadn't she been against matrimony since her mother's fourth marriage ended after only three weeks? Hadn't she sworn to never be pulled into the idea of white gowns, tiered cakes, and wedded bliss? As she grabbed a dish towel and started cleaning counters she admitted: She'd sworn all right. But then came Brian in the twelfth grade. He had hardly popped her cherry in the back of his Falcon before she'd started humming, "Here Comes the Bride" and believing in forever-type love. Sex had caused a huge brain malfunction.

She moved to the next counter. With Peter, she'd promised herself it wasn't serious, just sex— uncommitted sex and not even good sex. And she hadn't even experienced her first big O with him when she started thumbing through the bride magazines.

"Can I do anything?" Chase's question jarred her out of her counter-swiping reverie.

*Can you grow a paunch and a wart on your nose real quick, so I won't think you're attractive?* "No." The dish-towel she tossed landed in the sink with a wet pop.

The phone rang. On tiptoes, she snatched two water glasses from the cabinet and faced the counter so she wouldn't have to look at him. Maybe if she never looked at him, she would be okay. But how long could she simply not look? Her answering machine picked up the call again.

She bumped up against the stove, expecting to hear Sue's voice, and prayed it wouldn't be her mother.

"Lace," a male voice said. It sent her into a panic.

One of the glasses slipped in her hand, but she caught it. Placing both glasses on the stove, she swung around and stared at the phone as if the machine might look up at her, wink and say, "Just joking." It couldn't be. Surely it . . . No, she hadn't spoken with him in . . . a year. A year today.

"Listen, I'm on my way over." Peter's voice piped through her sound system. "I was going to just send roses, but I wasn't sure what kind of card to put on them. 'Happy fifth anniversary' didn't seem to fit. Anyway, I picked up a bottle of wine, and I thought I'd just drop by . . ." The phone line crackled. "Are you screening your calls so you don't have to talk to your mother? Or are you out with those girlfriends of yours?"

A growling echoed in her ears and it took a minute for Lacy to realize it had been her doing it and not Fabio. Why didn't Peter think she would be out with a man? Why didn't he think she would be here, fixing dinner for some hot, sexy man? Her head snapped up and she stared at Chase. She *was* here with a hot, sexy man.

Peter kept talking. "I was hoping we could get together tonight. You know, for old times' sake, like we did last year. Do you still have that red negligee?"

Lacy clenched her jaw. He expected her to go to bed with him? *Again?* And after last year's flop performance? And, ohh, she hated that red teddy!

Needing to wrap her hands around something, preferably Peter's neck, she found her victim in the dish towel. After wringing it out until it gave up its last drop of moisture, the counters received another vicious wiping. Only men would think women enjoyed wearing something that flossed crevices never intended to be flossed.

"Put it on, will you?" Peter said, lowering his voice to a husky tone, as if that would turn her on. "Be ready when I get there. You like it fast and hard, don't you? Damn, I'm getting hard just thinking about you."

Fast? She liked it fast? Hell, no! Fast was his way, because he couldn't last. She liked it slow. Shaking with anger, she looked at Chase, who frowned at the phone machine.

"Excuse me," she said, and slapped the dish towel back into the sink. "But I'm going to have to get this call. And ignore everything I say in the next few minutes."

She cleared her throat, trying to decide how to play it. One more deep breath, and she had a plan. "Hello? Hang on a minute," she said sweetly into the receiver. She held the phone away from her mouth a few inches. "Hey, Chase sweetie, would you grab me a beer? You know where they are." Chase started moving to the living room but she grabbed him by the arm, shook her head and pointed to the phone.

"Come on, I've shown you a dozen times which button it is." She glanced back at the phone, trying to think fast. "Not the vibrate button." She laughed, hoping it sounded flirty, and then cut her eyes at Chase to see if he'd caught on to her plan.

The pinched expression on his face softened and he smiled. She focused on the conversation again.

"Stop it. You are a bad boy. I need to get the phone," she purred. Then she brought the receiver back to her lips. "I'm sorry. Who is this?"

Chase crossed his arms over his chest and almost laughed at Lacy's charade. She sounded like she was reading a bad script from a B movie. The woman really sucked at acting and lying.

"Oh, Peter? I never dreamed I'd be hearing from you. Just a second, sweetheart."

She moved the phone away from her lips again. "Chase, stop that. It's my ex-husband. I need to talk to him." She put the phone back to her ear. "What's up, Peter?" she asked.

Chase leaned against the wall and listened.

"What? Yes. I do have company." Lacy's grip on the phone tightened. "Why would I lie?" She stared at the ceiling and her foot started tapping on the white tile floor. "For your information, I'm over you. Been over you. And there *is* someone here."

The woman needed help. Feeling quite helpful, Chase moved closer and wrapped his arms around her waist. She jerked and a little squeal slipped from her lips. When her wide eyes met his, he pointed back at the phone. She blinked, but seemed to understand. "Stop it . . . Chase." This time her voice came out wispy.

He pressed his mouth to the curve of her neck. Another squeal left her lips. "Please. I need to . . . get . . . this call." Her head leaned back, offering him all the neck he could want. And he wanted. He moved his hands over her abdomen, upward, until the backs of the thumbs brushed the outer curves of her breasts.

"Ohh!" Her breath came out in a whoosh. "Peter, I think . . . I think this is a bad time." Her voice sounded winded, honest—and sexy as hell.

He bathed her ear with his tongue.

"Oh, heavens," she said. "I've got to stop this."

If that jerk didn't believe her now, he was as hard of hearing as Chase was hard. Taking full advantage of the situation, he pulled Lacy closer. Her soft bottom pressed against the growing heat between his legs.

"Why would you say . . . that?" She frowned into the phone. "I am not pretending . . . anymore."

That did it. Ready for her to get off the phone, Chase leaned closer, sliding his fingers up under her shirt. Her skin felt like silk, soft, moist. He dipped a finger beneath the elastic waistband of her sweats and circled her navel.

"Lacy, hang up. Would you, babe?" he said, close to the receiver and loud enough for the jerk on the other end of the line to get the message. "You can talk to your ex later." He let his tone drop an octave. "I need you right now." And he did. Oh, yeah.

Her sharp intake of breath brought a smile to his lips. He pulled his hand upward, glided his palm around her flat abdomen and higher, until the swell of her breasts brushed the sides of his thumbs. She melted into his touch, then leaned against him as if her knees might fold. He ached to explore higher, to hold the weight of her breasts in his hands, to know the feel of her nipples hardening between his thumb and forefinger.

Good sense told him not to go into high gear. Before he took it further, he needed to know how much of what happened here was for the phone call's sake and how much was . . . real. But damn it, this felt real. Did she feel it, too?

His sex throbbed with need, her backside brushing against him, and he inhaled with the pleasure. He glanced down over her shoulder and could see her nipples pressing against the cotton shirt. Oh, she felt it all right. And so he glided his hand across her abdomen again, her head rolling back against his chest as she moaned. He smiled when he realized she held the phone out in front of her as if she'd forgotten Peter entirely.

Chase pressed a moist kiss to the line of her jaw, moving slowly to her ear. "Don't forget the phone," he whispered, and dipped his fingers into the waistband of her sweats again.

She snapped the phone back to her ear and cut her gaze to him. In those blue eyes he saw a mixture of emotions: passion, gratefulness, and . . .

Fear?

Wrapping her fist around his wrist, she jerked his hand from the waist of her pants and took a step back. That one little in-reverse motion said so much. Had he read her all wrong? Had she not . . . not been a part of that? The panic in her eyes slammed into him with accusation. But damn, he'd never attempted to park his car in an no-parking zone. And until this moment, he hadn't seen the will-be-towed sign.

She slumped against the counter then brought

the phone back to her mouth. "I've got to go." No pretense, no innuendos, just sheer panic sounded in her voice.

Damn!

# TEN

"I hate telephones." Lacy blurted out the first thought that sped through her fogged brain. She dropped the receiver and leaned on the counter for support. She didn't dare look at Chase; if she did, she might throw him down on her kitchen floor, crawl on top of him and treat herself to that triple scoop of sex she'd imagined earlier.

Triple? Who was she kidding? She'd never had a *double* dip of sex. Either multiple orgasms were a myth or she'd had two of the worst lovers in Texas. Kathy and Sue swore they weren't a myth, the Internet swore they weren't a myth, *Redbook* and *Cosmo* swore they weren't a myth. Why hadn't she ever had a multiple orgasm?

"They come in handy sometimes," Chase said hesitantly.

Lacy jerked her gaze up. He looked as if he'd just suffered a terrible blow. "What comes in handy?" *Multiple orgasms?*

"Telephones," he answered, his tone unsure.

"They cause trouble," she said. "Prank calls, mothers . . ." Blinking, she stared at the square tiles at her feet. Her red painted toenails stood out against the white ceramic. The next thought zipping through her turned-on brain was that she had never had sex on the floor before. She wasn't certain how the image of red toenails against white tile led to floor sex, but that was where it took her. "Unwanted calls come in all the time. Phones are bad."

"Like horny ex-husbands?" His tone brought her gaze up.

"Alexander Bell should be shot." She glanced back at her toenails and her thoughts careened back to sex. She'd had sex in only two places: a car and a bed.

Think about something else, an inner voice screamed. Think about anything else but Chase Kelly, sex, and . . . telephones.

Her mind searched for a topic and landed on one easily enough—chocolate mint ice cream. Sweet. Creamy. Temptation at its best. Then she stared at Chase. Temptation at its better-than-best. She couldn't accept what he offered. Ice cream, her inner voice screamed, think ice cream!

She could turn down ice cream. Oh, she loved ice cream, especially chocolate mint, but she could walk away from it without shaking. Okay, maybe she shook a little, but nothing like she shook now.

"Lacy?" His voice sounded closer.

She looked at him, her gaze going straight to his mouth. His beautiful sexy mouth. He took another step closer. If he touched her again, she'd melt like ice cream. Her heart ping-ponged around in her chest. "Turn the steaks in fifteen minutes," she said, then zipped away before she caved.

"Lacy?" His footsteps sounded next to her, but she didn't look at him. Looking at him created major problems. He could stay here, because she didn't want him to wind up dead, but she was going to have to walk around with blinders on.

"We need to talk," he said.

"Nothing to talk about." *We almost had sex, but we didn't.* Okay, they hadn't really almost had sex. They'd touched a little, and not even where it counted. And she'd been on the phone the whole time. She hated phones.

Then she wondered if this qualified as phone sex, ménage à trois phone sex? Probably not. Which meant she'd never had phone sex. *Just call me the no-sex queen.*

She kept walking. When she passed the fireplace, she spotted the photos of her mother and grandmother on the mantel. She refused to be like them. Refused, refused, refused.

"Please, Lacy," Chase said.

Samantha, her gray tabby, stood outside the bedroom door. The feline heard Chase's voice, saw them heading down the hall, and in a snap she darted back inside, probably to hide under the bed.

Hide? Lacy shared the cat's plan. A good plan, blast it. Why did people look down on the art of avoidance? A lot could be said about spending days under the bed. Just ask Samantha. Sometimes, confronting the issues hurt more than bumping your head on the bottom of box springs.

"Can't we talk?" His question hung in the air.

Sure they could talk. She *could* confront Chase Kelly instead of hiding. Something told her that if she turned around and said, "Look, Buster Brown,

I'm not going to have sex with you," he'd nod and give up the teasing and flirting. Let's face it, she wasn't the type of woman who drove men crazy. She was like a plain vanilla wafer: good on occasion, but boring on a regular basis. Brian had proved that with that cute little professor in their first year of college, and then Peter with his secretary.

Sure, men looked at her. Eric, the vet, and Hunky, the FedEx man, enjoyed looking. But men were like dogs. Whenever only one bitch graced their presence, dogs went after her, even if that bitch was just a vanilla wafer. Dogs would eat anything.

Ice cream. She needed to think about ice cream. She could walk away from ice cream.

"Lacy. Talk to me."

She ignored him and kept moving. Oh yeah, she could tell Chase to stop and he would. But she wasn't going to tell him to stop. Not because she wanted to be persuaded. She *wasn't* going to be persuaded. But because . . . Let's face it. Even vanilla wafers needed their egos stroked. So for the next day or so—surely this couldn't go on for more than that—she would let herself feel wanted. But she couldn't look at him, and he definitely couldn't touch her anymore. So he wouldn't actually be stroking her ego, only boosting it up without touching it, of course.

"Where are you going?" His voice came from somewhere over her shoulder. The voice of temptation. A mental image of her and Samantha huddled under the bed, both trembling, came to mind.

"To take a shower," she answered. A very cold shower. She'd never experienced sex in the shower. The image of steam and moist male body parts fitting up against damp female parts filled her mind.

"I wish you would talk to me." He sounded way too close.

"And I wish you were ice cream." She stepped into her room and slammed the door.

Zeke left the condo and hightailed it back to the hospital. His hands shook when he took the keys from the ignition. He shook with rage, he shook with remorse that he fought to deny. He hadn't wanted to kill Stokes the first time.

He'd involved the man so there would be a witness to Kelly paying off the drug dealer. But Stokes hadn't wanted to buy Kelly's guilt. The whole time they were together, the man just kept praising Kelly, insisting Zeke had read him wrong.

All that praise for a freaking suicidal maniac. Zeke had blown a gasket, and he knew that no matter how well he'd set it up, Stokes would give Kelly the benefit of the doubt.

So, Stokes had done this to himself. And if the man had just died the first time, Zeke wouldn't have had to see the hope in his wife's and sons' eyes. Grief he could handle, but hope got to him. Maybe because Zeke knew all about hope. He'd hoped his wife would have given him a second chance, he'd hoped his kids would understand when she didn't, he'd hoped to make sergeant seven years ago.

A lot of hope, and now here he was, feeling something akin to hopelessness. He walked down the hall of the ICU. Somehow Zeke had to make sure that when Stokes left ICU, the place he'd be going was the morgue.

He would have hired someone to do it for him, but

he didn't have time. So he lingered around the waiting room to hear a few of the precinct guys say that Stokes still hadn't come to. Zeke stopped outside the ICU's double doors. From the small glass window he could see the nurses manning the station. He wondered how in the hell he was going to take Stokes out before Stokes came to and brought the whole freaking police force down on him.

Closing his eyes, he tried to think. When he opened them again, he noted that the nurses' station faced away from the small room where Stokes lay. If he just went in, maybe he could—

"They're not allowing visitors," a deep voice said from behind him.

Zeke turned and faced Jason Dodd. The man looked at him as if he were something disgusting stuck on the bottom of a shoe. Suspicion burned Zeke's gut. What did Dodd know? Could Kelly have told Dodd something before he'd gone undercover? Or could Kelly still be alive and was he now communicating with his ex-partner?

"Somebody needs to get to Stokes and get his statement so we can collar the bastard who did this," Zeke said.

"They can get it after he recovers," Dodd replied, his stare dark with accusation.

"*If* he recovers," Zeke said. "We need a statement before—"

Dodd's eyes grew colder. "Stokes is going to make it. Believe me. I know that *in here*." He thumped his chest.

"Didn't take you for a man of faith," Zeke said.

"I'm not really. I just know people usually get what's coming to them. Stokes doesn't deserve this."

Zeke raised an eyebrow. "What about Kelly? Should he get what he's got coming?"

"I think whoever shot Stokes should rot in hell, and I'll be happy to help him get there."

The weight of Dodd's words landed on Zeke's chest. Dodd knew something. Damn it to hell, he knew something. But for some reason the man wasn't acting on it. Why? Something didn't make sense.

As soon as Zeke cut the corner of the hall, he jerked out his cell phone and punched in Bruno's number. "Meet me in thirty minutes in the alley behind Westwood Apartments," he said. "I got another job for you."

Chase stared at the stove and listened to the popping and hissing of the broiling steaks. The hearty aroma filled the kitchen but his thoughts didn't play on food. At least not steaks.

She wished he was ice cream. What the hell did that mean? Did it hold some sexual connotation? Or was she wishing he'd melt into a puddle so she could mop him up or feed him to her animals?

Why had she run out like that? Had he taken her game too far? Had his being here messed up her screw-the-ex-husband night? He had a long list of questions and felt certain of only one thing: Lacy Maguire was sexually frustrated. And instead of him helping her out, she'd managed to get him into the same condition.

A few minutes later, Chase cut off the steaks and turned up the potatoes; then he found some salad makings in the vegetable bin. "Eat the tuna and buy a gallon of milk," the fridge said.

"Like I'm going to listen to you." He slammed the

fridge door and took a knife to the carrots. Then he diced celery and tore the lettuce into shreds, taking his sexual frustration out on the vegetables. He could have sworn she'd been enjoying herself, that his touch had been welcomed.

Stepping back, he scowled at the minced salad. He should be trying to get a handle on what Zeke wanted instead of thinking about Lacy, her ex-husband, and that red nighty.

Fabio pranced into the kitchen. He dropped his chew toy and his triangle-shaped ears stood at attention.

Chase frowned down at the beast. "At least I'm not taking it out on you," he told the dog. "But just for the record, I shouldn't even like you. You're god-awful ugly, you got me in this mess, and you growled at me this morning."

Fabio's ears dropped. Chase shook his head. Now he was talking to refrigerators and dogs.

The shower had stopped ten minutes ago and she hadn't come out. He glanced at the clock. Five more minutes and he was going in. She had every right to feel any way she wanted, but he deserved to know what he'd done wrong. Didn't he?

Okay, maybe he didn't have any rights. He'd forced himself into her house, managed to scare her half to death, handcuffed her to her bed, and . . . and . . . He had no rights.

The dog whimpered. Chase knelt down and looked the animal in the eyes. "She still loves him, doesn't she? Peter treated her like dirt, and she still loves him."

Fabio flopped down and rested his pugged face on his paws. His bug eyes glanced up as if offering condolences.

"Hey, it's no skin off my nose," Chase said. "I'm not in this for the long haul. Believe me, I'm a short timer."

The dog sat up, cocked his head at a strange angle and studied Chase. Like Yoda in the movie *Star Wars*, the dog seemed to possess infinite wisdom.

"It's not as if I don't like her," he explained. "She's gorgeous, sexy as hell, and when she smiles and laughs, she makes everything around feel brighter . . . better. It's just—"

He heard the bedroom door open. Standing, he leaned against the fridge. The nervous tickle in the pit of his stomach brought about a sense of déjà vu that he didn't understand.

"Steaks done?" She scooted around him without meeting his gaze. Tension hung in the air like dense fog.

"Yeah," he answered and studied her. She wore a pair of jeans that hung low on her hips. Her shirt, a fitted white blouse, came just below the waist and clung to her breasts.

With the top two buttons left open, he got a glimpse of her bra strap. So she'd armed herself with underwear. Good. Then he remembered the red panties he'd seen in the bedroom. His gaze lowered to her hips and full-color images started appearing in his head.

"Potatoes?" She poked her head into the oven.

"Done. I think." He tried not to stare at her backside and attempted to understand the odd feeling making his gut tight. He understood what made things below the belt feel tight, but the other, vaguely familiar and unwanted, emotion concerned him.

She turned to the counter, eyeing the lettuce he'd

neglected to put back in the fridge. "You made a salad?"

He half expected her to nag him for not cleaning up after himself. "Yeah." He pointed to the bowl of beat-up vegetables beside the stove top. The uncomfortable emotion stirred his gut again.

"Good." She reached for the glasses on the counter and went to the fridge. The refrigerator gave up ice and the clanking noise of it falling into the glasses sounded somehow angry.

"I'm sorry, okay?" The apology fell out of him unexpectedly. As soon as the words left his lips, the meaning of that déjà vu and the emotion came raining down on him.

They were arguing—well, not out-and-out arguing, but having a male/female spat. The one where the woman was mad about something and the man remained clueless to the reasons. And although he wanted to ask what he'd done, he knew that asking would make matters worse, because women just expected men to know things. Didn't women know that men didn't know shit?

He hadn't had a spat with a woman since . . . since Sarah. He never argued with Jessie. He went into her apartment, they talked about sports, the weather, her cat's kidney problems. He cooked dinner. They ate, had sex, and he left. Twice a week like clockwork. It was easy and uncomplicated, even if he did occasionally worry about the cat.

He looked at Lacy Maguire. Lacy was complicated. She had an ex-husband, talking appliances, pets, and a red nighty tucked away somewhere in her bedroom.

In the back of his mind he realized that Jessie had

those things, too—with the exception of talking appliances, of course. He just hadn't seen Jessie or her baggage as complicated.

"You want me to go?" He let out a breath. "Let me make a call, and I'll be out of your hair." He reached for the phone.

# ELEVEN

She finally looked at him and Chase waited for her to speak. Her gaze appeared panicked. "I didn't say you had to leave."

The words, "What did I do?" lay on the tip of his tongue, but he bit them back and decided to take a wild guess on what this was about. And it was about something. Something more than his touching her. Being wrong about the problem usually brought about less fury than admitting to being clueless.

"Look," he said. "If you want, I'll call the guy back and explain. If he did half of what I think he did, you're a nutcase to still care, but who the hell am I to judge?"

"Call whom back?" she asked.

"Your ex. I can call him, tell him I was just messing with his head, and then I'll leave. You can put on the red nighty and wait for him." He raked a hand though his hair. "I didn't mean to mess things up for you. I . . . I thought that was what you wanted."

"You think I'm upset because Peter isn't coming?" She sounded baffled.

"Hell, I don't know what to think." He flinched. That wasn't exactly "I don't know what we're arguing about," but it came close, and he waited to see her explode. When she didn't, he continued cautiously. "One minute you seemed to be . . . enjoying things, then you looked as if you thought I was about to rape you. Next you started on a rampage about the perils of telephones. Then you ran off, telling me you wished I was ice cream. I haven't figured that one out at all."

She darted around him to the cabinet and took down two plates. Moving to the table, she set down the dishes. When she raised her face, she had her bottom lip sucked into her mouth again. It popped out all moist. "I did *not* want Peter to come over, and I appreciate you . . . convincing him that I wasn't alone."

Chase set the phone down. "And?"

"And what?" she asked, glancing back at the table, apparently still reluctant to look at him.

"You seemed afraid of me. You care to explain that one? Because I thought . . . I thought we'd gotten past that."

She moved the plates around on the table. "I didn't think you were going to rape me. I'm not afraid of you. I said I believe you and I do. I just . . . Can we eat? I'm starved." She glanced up and shot him a smile.

Although it was obviously forced, that smile did it to him again: made all the wrongs in his life seem a little less wrong. Made him forget that his partner had tried to kill him, that IA had him down as a drug dealer. It even made him want to forget that the one true love in his life had been unjustly taken from him.

"*You* at least had Fancy Feast," she added. Her smiled teased, and the expression seemed genuine this time.

He studied her and realized Lacy didn't argue like a woman. The smile, the attempt at humor—all were male tactics. He knew, because he'd used them a hundred times on Sarah. "Okay, let's eat, but first I'm dying to know about the ice cream comment."

"And I'm dying of hunger." She whirled around, showing him her back.

"For ice cream?" he asked, deciding that if she planned to argue like a man, he could argue like a woman. Meaning, he could beat a subject to death until she gave in and told him what he wanted to know. Or at least what he wanted to hear. Wasn't that what women did?

"I'm hungry for steak." She hotfooted it to the fridge and stuck her nose inside. "What kind of dressing do you like?"

"What kind of ice cream do you like?" he countered.

He got Italian dressing and absolutely no answer about the ice cream comment. But he could live with it, because they were back to where they had been before the phone rang.

They chatted their way through dinner. He found one subject Lacy could and would talk about with gusto: her animals. Two of her cats had been shelter kittens, and one, the skittish gray one, had climbed up in her car motor to stay warm. After nearly

killing it when she drove off, Lacy had her vet save
the little feline and she took it in. Fabio, as she told it,
had been a three-time shelter returnee.

She looked at the animal in question, who was sitting patiently at her feet. "They said he was too hyper, too noisy, and—"

"Too ugly," Chase finished. He cut a piece of steak, popped it in his mouth and chewed.

"He's not ugly. He's unique and has personality."

Chase swallowed. "That sounds like a description of the two blind dates I let Jason's girlfriends set me up with." He pointed his fork at her. "And believe me, they were ugly."

Lacy laughed and went on to tell another animal story. He supposed that for most guys, it would have been torturous, but his mother had been a bleeding-heart animal lover who had belonged to every animal protection society in Houston. He had grown up with a houseful of pets of all species. Some they'd fostered until they found appropriate homes. The really desperate ones they'd kept, from the cat and dog varieties with obvious deformities—a missing ear, a missing limb—to raccoons. Then there had been Mel.

He told her about Mel, the de-fumed skunk who'd been handed over to a shelter. "What could Mom do? It was adopt the poor creature or let him go to the gas chamber. You should have seen my dad's face when she walked in, plunked the skunk in his lap and said, 'At least now you'll have someone to blame when you eat my turnip greens.'"

Lacy laughed so hard she dropped her fork. Chase continued, "And when door-to-door salesmen showed up, Mom would open the door with Mel in her arms, tailside pointing out. They always left really quick."

Lacy's new mood, her laughter, filled the airy kitchen with warmth. Sitting across from her, Chase knew he'd never seen or heard anything quite so lovely.

"Are your parents still alive?" she asked, when they were finishing up dinner.

"No. They died when I was seventeen." He stacked the plates. "Plane crash," he said, realizing he hadn't talked or even thought about his parents in a long time.

"I'm sorry," she said. "That must have been hard."

"It was, but I had my sister, Leigh. She was nine years older, and she did okay by me. I moved in with her until I finished high school, and then I joined the Army for four years and then signed on with the HPD. Life goes on."

*Life goes on.* Understanding slammed into his sore ribs. That was what he'd been doing these last two years. He'd been fighting it—fighting the fact that life would go on. Hating the fact that he would reach a place and a time when he would accept Sarah's death, accept it as he had ultimately accepted the death of his parents.

His soul shook a little, but when he looked up into Lacy's soft blue eyes, there came a calm. Maybe it was the calm that appeared before the storm. He didn't know, but he wasn't going to question it. "What about your parents?" he asked.

Lacy picked up her fork and twirled the utensil in her fingers. Her sudden change in posture and expression seemed to say, "Pets are one thing, parents another." But he let the silence and the question hang between them until she finally spoke.

"My dad was in the Navy. He died when I was a baby. I don't even remember him. My mom, she . . . well, you heard her on the phone. It's the thingamabob thing." Guilt entered her eyes and she seemed to need to explain. "She was a good mother. She's just . . . A little of her goes a long way."

Chase took the plates to the sink and chewed on the information she'd given him. "It's just a mother/daughter thing," he said, thinking he offered her comfort.

She rolled her eyes. "Just a mother/daughter thing? When I ask her, 'How's my hair look?' and she answers, 'Like you ran it down the disposal . . . twice,' that's more than a mother/daughter thing."

He laughed. "Leigh felt the same way about our mom. Leigh used to say our house was like a cross between a Dr. Seuss book and the song 'Old Mac-Donald.'" He walked back to the table. "Growing up she used to swear she would never have indoor animals. She was even embarrassed at Mom's . . . way of life. However, the last I heard she has two cats, one dog, four hamsters and a pot-bellied pig. What is it they say? The apple doesn't fall too far from the tree. Like mother, like daughter."

Lacy's expression flickered from friendly to something far darker. She dropped the fork onto the table. "I don't believe that. People make their own destinies. They just have to choose to be different. Make different decisions. Who we are is our own making. Not our parents'." Her tone came out defiant, almost angry.

Instantly, Chase knew they weren't talking about Leigh and his mother. "So what is it about your mom that you can't be? Besides tactless."

His question caused her frown to deepen. "Nothing." She took her glass to the sink, putting an end to the subject and the easy camaraderie.

He almost pressed, but then he remembered that he had his own secrets. "Dinner was great. Thanks," he said, wanting to turn things around.

"Thanks for helping," she answered, the anger gone but the edge still there.

Chase carried his glass to the sink. Lacy took one small step to the side to avoid his hip brushing up against hers. And that was a mistake. Until then, he hadn't been thinking about touching her. Okay, he had thought about it, but it wasn't the foremost thought in his mind. He glanced over at her, appreciating the package. Her hair, her lips, chin, neck and . . . lower.

Yep, now he wanted to touch her. To wrap his arms around her waist, let his hands move under that shirt, all the way up. Up, until he felt her nipples harden against his palm.

And down. He wanted to move his hands down, under, and into. He thought about unzipping her jeans just an inch and dipping his hand in the tight space between denim and firm belly, between silky panties and moist woman. Moving deeper into the petal softness of the folds of her sex. Exploring her slick tightness with one, maybe two fingers.

She spoke to him, but he didn't hear her words; all he could do was watch her move around the kitchen as she filled animal bowls with food and water. The woman even fed animals with grace and looked sexy doing it.

He couldn't remember ever wanting to touch a woman so bad. He couldn't ever remember thinking a woman needed touching this bad. Lacy needed to be touched. She needed to be driven to the brink of passion and back again. She needed to be tasted, licked, and suckled until she screamed. She needed to have her ex-husband throughly and permanently screwed out of her brain and heart.

And if she was taking applications for the man to do it, he'd be the first in line. Hell, he'd go ahead and shoot the competition, just to make sure he got the job. But therein lay the problem.

Not in shooting anyone. That would be justifiable homicide. But in the fact that she wasn't taking applications. Her one little sidestep couldn't have screamed it any louder. Lacy Maguire was off-limits.

The silence seemed to draw out, and he desperately searched for something to say.

"Look at the time," she said. "It's almost ten. I'll get you some bedding for the couch."

She turned around and walked away. A few coy remarks tickled his tongue like, *Don't worry, I'll just share yours,* or *Wouldn't we be more comfortable in the bed?* But by the way she held her shoulders as she moved down the hall, square and straight, he knew she'd turn him down. He could live with it. He'd give her tonight. Tomorrow brought new possibilities. Some sleep and he would be up to the challenge of changing her mind and driving her wild. His gaze moved down to the front of his sweats and he realized that he stood up for the challenge right now. No doubt about it, it was going to be a long, hard night.

"You're going to follow him." Zeke slapped a piece of paper with all of Dodd's information into Bruno's meaty palm. The dark alley reeked of piss; no doubt some bums hung out close by. Lowering his voice, he spoke again: "Everything is on the paper. Home address, license plate, car and make. He was still at the hospital when I left. Don't let him out of your sight."

"But what does he have to do with Kelly?"

"Lower your freaking voice," Zeke hissed. Raking a hand over his face, he took in a desperate breath. "He was Kelly's old partner. They had some falling out, but now he seems . . . I think he knows something. Either Kelly got to him earlier and told him about Martinez's suspicions or . . . or Kelly's in contact with him now."

"Now?"

"Yes, now," Zeke repeated, and balled his hands into fists. Even standing out under the dark sky, Zeke could feel the walls closing in on him. His time had almost run out. Before he'd left the hospital, he'd managed to grab one of the ICU nurses. She'd told him that Stokes probably wouldn't come to for several hours, and possibly for days because he'd lost a lot of blood. If only Zeke had waited a little longer before leading the police to the warehouse, maybe Stokes would have died.

If only . . . if only . . . He didn't have time for those games. If he didn't get to Stokes before the man told the truth about who had shot him, if he didn't find Kelly, all Zeke's doings for the last five years would come bubbling to the surface.

"Find Dodd and keep him in your sight. I don't want that guy taking a piss that you don't know about."

Bruno shook his head. "And what are you gonna do?"

"I am going back to the hospital and will wait for

113

my chance to make sure Stokes doesn't come to and say something that would take us down."

"Us?" Bruno's brown eyes grew round. "All I did was pick up Martinez, and I may have punched that Kelly guy once or twice, but—"

"You shot a cop, idiot," Zeke said.

Bruno flinched. "I'm not sure if my bullet even hit him. And he wasn't dead or we'd have found his body. I didn't kill him."

Zeke shook his head. "If you'd have killed him we wouldn't be in this mess. And listen to me and listen good. If I go down for any of this, you're going to go down harder, I'll make sure of it."

Chase indulged in a cold shower in the bathroom that connected Lacy's study and her studio. She'd given him clean towels and linens for the couch; then, after a curt goodnight, she'd disappeared into her bedroom.

Grabbing a beer from the chair cooler, Chase went into the kitchen and snatched up the phone to call Jason. He wanted news on Stokes. Sometime between his shampoo and cutting his chin with the dull razor he'd found in one of Lacy's bathroom drawers, he'd decided he couldn't just sit back and do nothing; his patience had worn thin. Being here felt too much like hiding, and hiding just wasn't his style.

He tried figuring out what book Zeke could have been talking about, but Chase didn't have a clue. He needed to go back to his place and search the apartment inch by inch. But with his face plastered on the news, he needed to make a few changes to his appearance before he could go out in public.

"It's me," he said when Jason answered. "Can you talk?"

"Yeah, I'm on my way home from the hospital," Jason said, and Chase heard him turn down his Led Zeppelin tape.

"How's Stokes?" Chase asked, feeling fidgety.

"He's going to make it. I've talked a few guys into taking shifts sitting at the hospital. Zeke's not going to get him."

"How did you manage to pull that off?" Chase asked, sipping his beer.

"I told them I suspected you were set up, and the only one who could have pulled this off was Zeke."

"And they believed you?" Chase propped his feet up on Lacy's coffee table. Zeke had been on the force so long, Chase would have suspected his fellow officers of being loyal to him.

"It seems that Zeke has made a few enemies along the way. Lots of guys have harbored suspicions about him."

"Really?" Restless, Chase rose and started pacing. "I've partnered with the guy for two months. How could I have missed that?"

Silence met Chase's question, then Jason finally answered, "Face it. You haven't been your usual observant self lately."

"That's an understatement. Why don't you just tell me that I've been a real bastard?"

"I think I did, right about the time I put in for a request to change partners."

"You should have just kicked my ass."

"I thought about it," Jason said, then chuckled. "Actually, I was giving you about two more weeks and then I planned on meeting you in a dark alley and doing just that."

"You never could have taken me," Chase teased back.

Another silence filled the line before Jason said, "I've been worried about you." Jason wasn't one to show his emotions, but his tone gave him away.

"I'm sorry." Chase took a long sip of cold beer. "I'm working on getting things right in my life now."

"Damn red lights!" Jason said, an obvious attempt to change the tone of the conversation. "Listen, before I went to the hospital, I stopped by the precinct. I managed to grab some of your and Zeke's old files. I'm going to comb through everything, especially the drug bust you and Zeke took down when you two first hooked up. The drugs they found at your place had to be from that bust. I'm thinking maybe I'll find something to explain why he's doing this. Have you figured out what book he wanted?"

"No. The only books I have at the apartment are Sarah's old romances." He paused, realizing that while saying his wife's name still brought a pain to his gut, the pain had lessened. The silent phone line made him speak. "Are they still dragging the lake?" Chase sat down in the blue recliner, one leg folded over the other. He pushed a button, wanting to experience the massage. Instead, the damn chair raised up and tossed him out. He dropped the phone in an effort to catch himself. "Sorry," he said, picking it up and glaring at the recliner.

"Zeke seems to be losing hope that you'll show up dead. At the hospital tonight the captain mentioned setting up a search party outside the general lake area."

"How far outside?" Chase frowned. If they extended their search, someone could knock on Lacy's door. He'd already pulled her into this too deep.

"Captain said he was giving it another day, that maybe your body would just float up somewhere."

"The captain always did like me." Chase walked to the couch.

"Not even the captain wanted to think you were dead . . . or guilty. But with the coke at your place, it didn't look good."

"What did you think?" Chase smeared dewy prints over the cool beer bottle.

"What do you mean, what did I think? I never believed it. But it was hell trying not to believe you were dead while I stood by the lake this morning."

"Really." Chase remembered Sue's dialogue from this morning and smiled. "You weren't so upset you weren't trolling for chicks."

"Chicks?" Jason said.

"The woman you gave your card to and told her to call you."

Jason grew quiet. "The petite blonde? I wasn't—"

"She knew your 'Call me' meant something."

"Is that where you are? Is the blond chick Lacy?"

"No," Chase said. "I'm a few miles up from there. The last house off Langly Road."

"Then how do you know about the blonde?"

"A good cop always knows." Chase chuckled. "She thinks you have a cute ass."

"Really?" Jason said. "Maybe I'll have to stop by again."

"She's committed." Chase grinned. "To her vibrator."

It took Jason a second, then he laughed.

"And she might possibly have a little bit of the lesbian thing going," Chase added.

"Jeez! Now I know I'm going to run by."

They laughed a few minutes, then Chase said, "Look, there's something I need. Can you go by my place and pick up . . ."

Lacy had tossed and turned for three hours, trying to sleep. Then she heard the front door open and close. She threw her covers off and ran to the window, getting there just in time to see Chase Kelly walking down the alcove of pine trees to her side yard.

"Ungrateful nitwit," she mumbled.

She'd agreed to help him, and he'd left without even a crummy good-bye. Probably left the door unlocked so any other man could step in, take her hostage, and handcuff her to her bed. Well, she'd had enough excitement for at least a week. Besides, the next guy might not be so darn good-looking.

Going to her closet, she slipped on her Donald Duck slippers and went to lock the front door. But once she got there she wondered if maybe he'd just gone out for fresh air. She opened the door, intending only to stick her head out. When she didn't see anything, she stepped out into the cold night and cut across the yard to the tree-lined trail.

Inky darkness surrounded her as she made her way down the meandering path. She kept going, knowing it would end at the two picnic tables her grandmother had placed there years earlier.

Unable to see the tips of her shoes, she stumbled when Donald's beak caught on a rock. Righting herself, she continued on. If she didn't find him stargazing at the picnic tables, she was going back in and locking the door. A cool breeze raised the hem of her black silk nightshirt. She shivered and added some speed to her steps.

Another moment and she could swear she heard someone talking. She stopped, listened, hearing only night sounds: an owl, a small animal scurrying in the brush. Then even those noises stopped and silence hung heavy. The darkness suddenly felt thicker, shadows grew suspicious, the wind became colder, and Lacy tasted fear on her tongue. Should have brought my fish, she thought.

*Turn around. Go back.* The thought jumped into her brain at the same time someone jumped out from the shadows and knocked her to the ground.

# TWELVE

Both Chase and Jason had heard the footsteps at the same time.

"Someone followed you," Chase whispered. They drew their guns together and melted into the trees.

Chase kept his gaze on the path. The concern gripping his gut wasn't for himself or even Jason, but for the woman sleeping in the house. Would Zeke and his cronies go after her now?

"No one followed me," Jason whispered, his gun aimed into the darkness beyond the trees. Another sound came.

A figured appeared, and both Jason and Chase lunged toward it. Jason made contact first. The figure went down.

"Police. Hands out by your sides!" Jason said. "Move and I'll shoot."

Chase's heart pounded as he noted the size of their captive. He kept his gun aimed toward the path, waiting for Big Bruno or Zeke, and wanting to take off to the house to check on Lacy.

"He's clean," Jason said, his voice still edgy. "I mean . . . damn! *She's* clean," he said, his tone low and unsure.

Chase swung around. The darkness prevented him from seeing much, but the bright yellow Donald Duck slippers attached to the feet beneath Jason could only belong to one person. "Jeez! Get off of her!" Chase knelt as Jason rolled away.

Lacy had her mouth open as if she were about to scream. He leaned closer. "It's me, Chase. You okay?" he asked.

She clamped a hand over her mouth. He slipped his arm behind her back and helped her sit up. Swearing under his breath, he checked her elbows and knees for blood and breathed easier when she appeared unharmed. Unharmed but . . . even in the darkness, he could see the anger in her eyes.

"Did you hit your head again?"

She pulled away. "I'm fine." She moved her gaze from him to Jason, who stood a few feet away. "Aren't you supposed to say, 'Police. Stop right there,' and not jump the suspect and fondle her breasts?"

"Sorry. I didn't mean . . ." Jason tucked his gun in his side holster. "You must be Lacy. We spoke earlier."

"So that gave you a right to grope me?" She got to her feet and dusted herself off.

"I'm really sorry," Jason said. "I didn't hurt you, did I?"

"No," Lacy mumbled, and Chase heard the edge of her anger slip away.

Then Chase noticed her giving Jason a second glance. It was the kind of visual rundown Jason always got from females aged two to sixty. Make that ninety. Even Mim, Sarah's great-grandma, had fallen for the man three Christmases ago. Jason, with his linebacker build, blond hair and blue eyes, was a chick magnet. Even Sarah used to tease Chase that he should be lucky she'd fallen in love with him before she met his best friend.

"I'll be right in," Chase said, suddenly wanting her away from Jason. She cut him a look and then took off at a marching pace.

Jason reared back on his heels and tucked his hands into the pockets of his jeans. A smile curved his lips. "A bit uptight, but really nice breasts."

"Give it a rest," Chase snapped. Let Jason meet a girl, and within ten seconds the man knew how her breasts felt.

"What's she uptight about?" Jason asked.

"Sexually frustrated," Chase answered, the truth slipping out before he thought.

"Mmmm," Jason whispered, and looked toward the path down which Lacy had disappeared. "If I can help . . ."

Chase grabbed the bag that Jason had dropped beside the tree. "This one is mine. I've already decided to kill off all the competition, so save your life and go after her girlfriend instead."

Jason chuckled, then pointed to the bag, a seriousness entering his expression. "Don't do something stupid. You might be able to dupe some crackpots on the street with that disguise, but Zeke's no fool, and as you said, he's not working alone on this."

"I just want to check my place and find whatever damn book Zeke's looking for," Chase said.

"Whatever Zeke wants isn't at your apartment. When we went to search for the drugs, your place had been ransacked. Somebody already searched there. I went back and did another myself. And I'll do another one, but—"

"I can't just hang out here and do nothing!" Chase snapped, slapping the bag against his leg.

"Yeah, it must be hell. Having to stay with a nice-breasted, beautiful, sexually frustrated woman . . ."

"You know what I mean," Chase said, kicking at a pinecone and wincing when his bruised body protested the sudden movement. "I feel as if I'm hiding. The guilty hide out. I'm not freaking guilty!"

"Give me a couple days," Jason said. "I'm just getting started going over the files. I know I'll find something. And Stokes is doing well. He'll wake up in a day or two and then he'll set everything straight."

Chase ran a hand over his face. "Zeke is going to do everything possible to make sure he doesn't wake up."

Jason nodded. "Well, he's going have to go through a cop to get to him. I mean it, we've got someone watching ICU twenty-four–seven."

"How's Stokes's wife doing?" Chase asked, and right then came a noise from the bushes. They both swung around . . . and it was a rabbit hopping through the brush.

After the second of tension faded, Jason spoke. "It's been hard. She brought the boys up to the hospital with her. Talk about heartbreak—seeing her with those two boys gets you deep. Real deep."

Chase drew a breath. "Zeke's a bastard, Jason. If he could shoot Stokes, you know he's capable of anything. Watch your back. If something—"

"Don't worry," Jason said as they came to the edge

of the wooded trail. "I'll be fine. You just keep trying to put the puzzle together. Figure out why Zeke's doing this so we can prove what he's doing."

At one in the morning, the hospital halls were quieter, dimmer. On top of the antiseptic smells came the scent of blood. The coppery scent seemed piped through the air ducts.

Zeke tried to keep his footfalls from making noise as he drew closer to the ICU. In the pocket of the janitor's uniform he'd stolen from the laundry room he had a syringe with enough heroin to promise Stokes the trip of a lifetime. His last trip.

When he had called earlier to check on his "good buddy," Zeke had spoken to the nurse on duty. Tonight only two nurses manned the station, and in about five minutes one of them would be heading out for a break. If he had to, he could take the other nurse. The knife he carried would cut a throat easily enough, but he hoped to slide in and slide out undetected. He didn't enjoy killing.

The smell woke Lacy up—coffee mixed with hints of cinnamon and vanilla. She pulled herself up and gave the four obligatory pats to everyone in bed with her.

Samantha, who always seemed to sleep the closest yet stayed farthest away during the daytime, purred ever so lightly. Only in the mornings would the cat accept affection. So Lacy didn't hurry; she stretched back out and gave the animal what she deserved, a few minutes of her time. But even as she stroked the gray fur, Lacy's thoughts went to the man who had

124

obviously cooked in her kitchen. She couldn't allow him to stay much longer.

As she lay there, she practiced her send-off speech. *"Well, it's been nice. Hope you don't wander off and get killed. But you can't stay here because I really want to have sex with you. And if I have sex with you then I'll want to marry you."* Yeah, that would send him out the door. Didn't most men prefer death to marriage anyway? So she was doing the guy a favor.

Crawling out of bed, she dressed in jeans and a pink T-shirt and went to face the music.

"Perfect timing." Chase started talking as soon as she entered the kitchen. "I hope you like French toast. It's my specialty. Sit down." He pulled out a chair and placed a cup of coffee on the table.

She sank into the chair, hesitantly, and tried to remember how the beginning of her speech went. The back of his hand brushed against her neck and she stared at the steam coming off the cup, wondering if he could see the steam coming from her ears. It was way too early to start feeling this sexual pull.

He leaned over her shoulder. "My dad used to say the way to a woman's heart was through her stomach."

Lacy sat up straighter to escape the warm feel of his breath against her neck. "I thought it was the other way around—the way to a *man's* heart is through his stomach."

"It works both ways," he said, his smile apparent in his voice. "You can cook lunch."

His hand glided across her back, leaving a trail of goose bumps. Why, she wondered, had she been so adamant that he had to leave right now? She had to work today; she would be in her studio and he would be in here. She wouldn't have to look at him. And she wouldn't have to worry about him getting killed yet.

"Sorry about last night," he said as he stepped to the stove. "I asked Jason to bring over a few things I needed."

Lacy sipped her coffee, and a plate of hot French toast magically appeared in front of her. Her mouth watered as the smell of melted butter, maple, and cinnamon drifted up to her nose. She heard him take the seat across from her and she raised her gaze. Sucking on her bottom lip, she took in his wide shoulders, sexy grin and hands. Hands that had touched her last night and made her feel things. Wonderful things.

"Eat before it gets cold." He winked at her, then picked up his fork and sliced into a piece of his own thick French toast.

She wished she could have pushed the calorie-laden plate away, but she loved French toast almost as much as she did chocolate mint ice cream. Picking up her fork, she gave in to the temptation to eat. The man offered her French toast and sex. She'd resigned herself to saying no to sex, but the French toast was hers! *Come to Mama,* she thought, forking a piece of crusty fried bread into her open mouth. "Mmm," she said, and closed her eyes as the warm sizzle of flavor moved across her tongue.

When she opened her eyes, she found him staring.

"You like?" he asked.

"No. I love," she answered, and continued to eat.

While she devoured the best breakfast known to mankind, Chase talked about his friend Jason.

"I could make more." He smiled as she swirled the last bite around her plate to collect the remaining maple syrup.

"Don't tempt me. I'm full." She hesitated, not wanting to think about temptation. "You look like you're feeling better," she said, noting the ease with which he moved.

"My entire body hurts less, my shoulder hurts more. Or maybe my shoulder hurts the same, and I know it because my entire body hurts less."

"You should probably clean the wound again." She lowered her fork and spotted a drip of syrup on the edge of her plate. Running her fingertip over it, she brought the syrup to her lips.

His eyes widened with interest as she licked her finger. She was just a vanilla wafer, but he didn't look at her like she was a wafer. He looked at her like he would look at one of those bakery cookies that had nuts and marshmallows in it. And right now she felt like a cookie with marshmallow and nuts. With her finger still in her mouth and him studying her with heat in his eyes, she felt *sexy*, like a seductress who had the power to make men go weak.

She withdrew her finger. "Thanks for breakfast."

"You're more than welcome." His gaze lingered on her face.

A voice came out of the dining room. "Good kitty, now cover it up!" It was an electronic voice.

Chase smiled. "I nearly shot your kitty box last night."

"I told you it talked."

"I forgot." He set down his fork.

Lacy wished she could forget last night—forget what it had felt like to have Chase's hand running over her bare stomach. How he'd seductively dipped his finger into her navel, a unique ploy to make a woman think of . . .

She downed her coffee in one gulp and got up from the table. "I'll clean up later." And she'd tell him later he had to leave. Like a girl on the lam, she darted out of the room.

As she walked away, she felt like Ally McBeal in the old sitcom. In her mind's eye her conscience had split into two halves, and she imagined one sat on each of her shoulders. One, a saintly presence dressed in white linen, said: "Turn back around and give him his walking papers." The other wore a really hot little red dress, and after telling Miss Perfect to go sing a hymn, she suggested a few things that Lacy could do with her leftover syrup. Lacy ignored both of them and went into her studio.

Zeke chewed another handful of aspirin and washed it down with hospital coffee from the cafeteria. His head pounded with each thud of his heart. No sleep. He couldn't remember the last time he'd closed his eyes, but he couldn't and wouldn't rest.

Last night, Lady Luck had been on his side. Right before he'd crossed the path of the waiting room, he'd heard someone talking to a nurse. Backing off down the hall, he'd waited and listened until he recognized the voice.

Officer Candace. When the nurse suggested he could go home, that she'd make sure to call with any changes in Stokes's condition, Candace had been blunt in telling her that he planned on staying the night. The question that bit Zeke and made his head hurt worst was why Candace felt the need to sit outside the ICU.

He knew everyone at the precinct cared. Hell, they all would go out on a limb for another officer, but staying all night went beyond the call of duty. Zeke had stopped by the precinct this morning to find out if a guard had been assigned to Stokes. No paperwork led him to believe it, but something in Zeke's gut told him that someone had unofficially set this up. Who? Only one person came to mind: Dodd.

Last night Zeke had practically run back to his car. Sitting in the dark, he'd considered taking his nest egg and heading to Mexico. Then it hit him: that damn gold watch he had coming in two months, the one he'd scoffed at. Suddenly he wanted it. Someday he'd make sure his son got it.

If Zeke got caught, if he didn't pull this off, his ex-wife and his kids would feel justified for cutting him out of their lives. Right now he didn't care if his wife rotted in Hell, but he still had hope about his two kids. Hope that, after he retired, when the children were away from the clutches of his ex-wife, he could find a way back into their lives. And he'd have enough money to give them things, things he hadn't been able to give them earlier. That made taking out Stokes easier. Because if Stokes lived to turn him in, Zeke's own kids would pay a price. What father wouldn't kill to protect his own flesh and blood?

Zeke's cell phone rang and he jerked it out of his pocket. He'd tried to get Bruno at least a dozen times, but the man hadn't answered. "Duncun!" Zeke said, hoping to hear Bruno's deep voice.

"Hey." It was the man he was hoping for.

"Where the fuck have you been? I tried to get you all night. You're on him, right?"

"Yeah, but he didn't come home until two this morning," Bruno said.

"I told you he was at the hospital." Zeke squeezed the words out through clenched teeth.

"By the time I got there he was gone. I wound up parking at his apartment and waiting. He still hasn't gone anywhere this morning. Do I have to tail him all day?"

"Only if you want to live."

Bruno cleared his throat. "I'll let you know when he's on the move."

"You do that. And answer your cell phone when it rings. I'm going to head back to the lake and snoop around the neighborhoods a little farther out. If I find him I might need your help."

"I'm not killing anyone," Bruno snapped; then the line went dead.

The Christmas music started as Chase loaded the dishwasher. He had the kitchen almost cleaned, all to the tune of "Silent Night," when the doorbell rang. He took off for the living room just as Lacy stepped out of her studio and into the hall. Panic filled her face.

"Go to my bedroom," she said. "I'll get rid of them."

Feeling a little of the same panic rumble in his chest, Chase grabbed his gun from where he'd stowed it under the couch.

# THIRTEEN

Chase sent Lacy one more glance, then started past her. Fabio, wearing horns again, came barreling out of the studio barking. As Lacy sidestepped the dog, her shoulder brushed up against Chase's.

"Thanks," Chase said, offering her a smile, and he came within a breath of pressing a quick kiss on her cheek. Jason was right; he was a fool to want to leave here.

Stepping into Lacy's room, Chase backed against the wall beside the window where he could listen and possibly peer out without being noticed. He heard the front door open.

"Hi, Hunky." Lacy's voice carried, and Fabio barked in the background.

*Hunky?* Chase pushed open the blinds a half inch to see who stood on Lacy's porch.

The blond guy standing outside Lacy's door wore a FedEx outfit and a smile—a big outfit and a big come-on smile. He looked more like a weight lifter than a deliveryman. And he stared at Lacy as if he'd

131

love to lift her a time or two. So, this was the guy Lacy was supposed to bring inside and screw his brains out in every room of the house? Not! Chase thought.

"Have lunch with me today?" the man said, passing an envelope and clipboard to Lacy.

"Wish I could, but can't," Lacy said, matter-of-factly.

"Okay, then have sex with me," the man said.

"Real smooth talker," Chase muttered.

"Wish I could, but can't," Lacy said in the same nonchalant tone. She signed the clipboard. "But thanks for the offer."

The man laughed. "Am I wasting my time?"

"Yes," Lacy answered, and returned the clipboard with a bright, flirtatious smile. "But don't stop asking."

"You're *killing* me, Lacy," the man said.

*No*, Chase thought. *I'm going to do that.*

"Bye," Lacy said and closed the door.

"I won't give up," the man called out.

*Yes, you will!* Chase walked out of the bedroom and met Lacy in the entranceway. Fabio danced at her feet. "You know, you could call and report him for harassment."

Lacy glanced at Chase and then opened her envelope. "He's not harassing me." She pulled out what looked to be a check and then went and tucked it into a basket on the antique sewing machine beside the front door.

"He asked you to have sex with him," Chase snapped. "Or did you miss that part? I think it came right after he asked you out for lunch."

"He was joking," she answered. "Besides, he asked nicely."

"Right," Chase said. "Maybe if you stopped calling him a hunk, he might ease up on the invitations for sex."

Lacy looked up. "I called him Hunky . . . which is his name."

Chase shook his head, angry at her, angrier at himself for sounding jealous. No, not just for sounding jealous, but for being jealous. Jealousy didn't belong in the type of relationships he intended to have for the rest of his life, and it certainly didn't belong here and now.

Sifting through his feelings, he decided it was his cop instincts making him overreact. "You don't know him. He could be a rapist or a serial killer. You're out here in the boonies and he could push his way inside and attack you."

"Yeah, I never know when someone might take me by gunpoint and handcuff me to the bed. Or throw me down on the ground and grope me! But wait, that's just the police who do that, not FedEx guys." She shook her head and walked past him.

Fabio, sitting at Chase's feet, barked to get his attention. Chase looked at the dog. The animal cocked his head and stared up, his reindeer horns sagging. Chase scowled and pointed to the closed door. "Next time bite him, got it?"

Lacy high-stepped it into her studio. Warm emotions stirred in her chest, and she smiled in spite of herself. She might just be a wafer to him, but Chase Kelly was jealous. And that did a lot for her vanilla ego. Then her insides turned to marshmallow again, and she knew she'd better send Chase Kelly packing soon. At lunch, she promised herself. She'd tell him to leave at lunch.

\* \* \*

"Come on. Don't be shy. Give me your sexy pose."
Lacy whistled, trying to get Leonardo to look toward
the camera. Suddenly Fabio's horns dropped forward, and Lacy groaned. "No."

"Let me help."

Lacy turned to the door, unaware that Chase had
been watching. "It's okay. I can do it," she said.

"I got it," he argued, and he sat down on the floor
in front of the tree. He patted his lap so Fabio would
come closer. "Do you always listen to Christmas music when you shoot, or is it just when you shoot
Christmas photos?"

"Just when I shoot Christmas photos." She glanced
through her lens, thinking the man wouldn't look as
good through her 50 millimeter as he did face-to-face.
Nope. He looked darn good through the lens, too.

"And when you shoot Easter pictures?"

With her eye still on the camera, she sang. " 'Here
comes Peter Cottontail, hopping . . .' "

He grinned and fixed Fabio's horns. "How's that?"
He glanced up at her, then tilted his head back to the
dog.

Lacy saw the shot and clicked the camera. When
the flash went off, Chase turned. "Hey!"

Leonardo, hat askew, stepped up on Chase's leg.
Fabio, a bit jealous, scooted closer. Chase glanced at
the cat, tilted his eyebrow, and Lacy clicked again.

She moved her eye from the lens and smiled.
"Sorry, when I see a shot I click. It's habit. You have
to be fast when you shoot animals."

Chase grinned and reached over beside the tree
where Lacy had piled Christmas items. He picked
up a piece of fake mistletoe and dangled it front of

# GET UP TO
# 4 FREE BOOKS!

You can have the best romance delivered to your door for less than what you'd pay in a bookstore or online. Sign up for one of our book clubs today, and we'll send you **FREE\* BOOKS** just for trying it out...with no obligation to buy, ever!

## HISTORICAL ROMANCE BOOK CLUB

Travel from the Scottish Highlands to the American West, the decadent ballrooms of Regency England to Viking ships. Your shipments will include authors such as CONNIE MASON, CASSIE EDWARDS, LYNSAY SANDS, LEIGH GREENWOOD, and many, many more.

## LOVE SPELL BOOK CLUB

Bring a little magic into your life with the romances of Love Spell—fun contemporaries, paranormals, time-travels, futuristics, and more. Your shipments will include authors such as KATIE MacALISTER, SUSAN GRANT, NINA BANGS, SANDRA HILL, and more.

As a book club member you also receive the following special benefits:

- **30% OFF all orders through our website & telecenter!**
  (Plus, you still get 1 book FREE for every 5 books you buy!)
- **Exclusive access to special discounts!**
- **Convenient home delivery and 10 days to return any books you don't want to keep.**

There is **no minimum number of books to buy**, and you may cancel membership at any time. See back to sign up!

\*Please include $2.00 for shipping and handling.

# YES! ☐

Sign me up for the **Historical Romance Book Club** and send my TWO FREE BOOKS! If I choose to stay in the club, I will pay only $8.50\* each month, a savings of $5.48!

# YES! ☐

Sign me up for the **Love Spell Book Club** and send my TWO FREE BOOKS! If I choose to stay in the club, I will pay only $8.50\* each month, a savings of $5.48!

**NAME:** _____

**ADDRESS:** _____

_____

**TELEPHONE:** _____

**E-MAIL:** _____

☐ **I WANT TO PAY BY CREDIT CARD.**

☐ VISA    ☐ MasterCard    ☐ DISCOVER

**ACCOUNT #:** _____

**EXPIRATION DATE:** _____

**SIGNATURE:** _____

Send this card along with $2.00 shipping & handling for each club you wish to join, to:

**Romance Book Clubs**
**1 Mechanic Street**
**Norwalk, CT 06850-3431**

Or fax (must include credit card information!) to: 610.995.9274. You can also sign up online at www.dorchesterpub.com.

\*Plus $2.00 for shipping. Offer open to residents of the U.S. and Canada only. Canadian residents please call 1.800.481.9191 for pricing information.

If under 18, a parent or guardian must sign. Terms, prices and conditions subject to change. Subscription subject to acceptance. Dorchester Publishing reserves the right to reject any order or cancel any subscription.

JOIN NOW!

his face. "So, what type of compensation does a fellow get for being exploited?"

Both Leonardo and Fabio moved to sniff the plastic mistletoe in his hands. Lacy snapped another picture. "Hold it a little higher," she suggested.

Chase rolled his eyes, but he followed instructions. "I don't work for free, you know."

Fabio put his front paws on Chase's leg and, leaning forward, gave his cheek a lick. The camera flashed.

Lacy laughed, the thrill of the shoot igniting her artistic side. "Now that was priceless. Do it again." She moved her eye back to the camera.

Chase glanced at the dog. "You want me to kiss a dog?"

Lacy chuckled. "I'm sure you've kissed a few."

"Yeah, but I was drunk at the time." He held the mistletoe over the dog's horns and made a kissing sound. The dog leaned forward and obliged him.

The flash went off. "Perfect," Lacy said, grinning as she moved from behind the camera. "Every female pet lover in America will buy these Christmas cards. I don't know why I didn't think to use a male model."

"Yeah, next you'll ask me to take off my shirt," he said.

Lacy considered it for about two seconds. "Nah. You got that bullet wound; it wouldn't look good."

Chase laughed again. "You really don't plan on using those, do you?"

"Not if you don't want me to," she said. "But I would like to. Seriously."

"Well, if the pay is good." He twisted the mistletoe, leaving no doubt as to his meaning.

Lacy grinned in spite of the heat filling her belly. "I could make you another cat-food sandwich."

"I had something else in mind." Sex appeal and humor filled his eyes, and Lacy clicked again.

This one she wouldn't send off. This one she would keep. And on desperate lonely nights she'd stare at his face and think about what she'd missed out on. *Missed*. The word hung in her thoughts, and she realized she would miss more than just the sex that she wouldn't allow herself. Chase's sense of humor, his easy company and . . . when would she find another man who would actually kiss her dog?

"I could make you a famous model," she said, and looked again through the lens.

"Is that a turn-on for women?" he asked, looking directly at the camera. "Women like models?" One eyebrow arched seductively.

She snapped another pic. "Oh, yeah. You'd never have to kiss another dog," she teased, pulling away from the camera.

"Speaking of kissing . . . maybe we can negotiate." He stood up and inched toward her like a big cat about to pounce on its prey.

She stared at the mistletoe still in his hands and realized *she* was that prey. Feeling the heat of the moment, she took a step back as the words to "Jingle Bells" began to play in the background. But the bells she heard were warning bells, and the things jingling were her nerves.

"One kiss, Lacy. For my modeling services," Chase said seductively, now standing in front of her. "Then you can have the shots blown up on a billboard for all I care."

"I'd rather just offer you a cat-food sandwich. Or money. I could really pay. I'll have to figure out what—"

"I don't want your money." He grinned, and she couldn't help but let her gaze focus on his lips. She had noticed them before, how sexy his mouth looked, but now . . .

"One kiss." He brushed the mistletoe down one side of her face.

"No tongue," she said without thinking.

The same surprise she felt at her words filled his eyes. He leaned back his head and laughed. "But Lacy, what's a kiss without tongue?"

"No tongue or no deal," she said, realizing the wisdom of her words. Because she should be able to handle one quick chaste kiss, as long as . . .

"Okay, I won't use *my* tongue, but you have to use yours."

She considered it. The photographer part of her heart pounded as the quick images she'd just snapped flashed around in her head. The female part of her heart drummed for different reasons altogether.

"You'll sign a release?" she asked. "That will give me the right to use them."

"I'll sign a release." His whisper caressed her cheek.

"Okay," she said, but she wasn't thinking about Christmas cards—she thought about his lips and about the quick kiss they'd shared yesterday.

He dropped the mistletoe and brushed his hands down her forearms, then he leaned forward to claim payment. "Let me see your tongue," he said against her lips.

It was just a tongue, but Lacy felt as if he'd just asked to see her breasts. Blood rushed to her face.

"Come on, Lacy." He touched her cheek as if he noticed her blush. He grinned and his fingertips moved across her lips.

Oh, jeepers! She'd made a very big mistake. Kissing him could prove fatal. But what a way to go. Her tongue emerged, wetted her top lip.

The green of his eyes grew brighter. "Sexy," he said, his voice husky. "Do it again."

His hands drifted up to cup each side of her face. His nose touched hers and she felt his breath on her lips.

"A little tongue, Lacy. Give me just a little . . ."

Her tongue, against her better judgment, slid from one corner of her lip to the other.

He took her tongue into his mouth, suckling ever so lightly. His lips nibbled against her mouth, tasting her as if she were something to be sampled and savored slowly. Time stood still as he kissed and kissed. His fingers moved over her cheeks, behind her ears. She dipped her tongue into his mouth— only because she'd promised to do so. He moaned.

His hands left her face and she felt them moving beneath her T-shirt, around her waist, over her bare stomach, and up. She went to catch his hands, but hesitated.

"Tell me to stop and I will," he whispered into her mouth, never breaking the kiss.

She didn't tell him to stop. Not one darn good reason popped into her head, even though she knew there had to be a thousand floating around in her brain. His hands continued upward, until he had her silk-covered breasts in his hands. Her nipples tightened instantly, and he pinched the hardened peaks between his fingers. She moaned with pleasure. Heat pooled between her legs, and she moved her hips closer to him.

His response came immediately. He shifted against her, moving her against the wall. His thigh pressed between her legs, right where she ached, where she needed to be touched. And she needed it so badly.

She grabbed two handfuls of his shirt and pulled him into her, lost to everything but the heat and the sweet, painful ache burning between her thighs. Before she knew what was happening, he had her in his arms, carrying her toward her bedroom, toward her bed. He never stopped kissing her and she never wanted him to.

He placed her on the mattress and then lowered himself beside her. His touch moved over her with a swiftness and gentleness that made her insides melt. His hand came between her legs, cupping her sex, pressing and squeezing her through her jeans. She pushed against him. Once, twice.

He pulled away, and she cried out in protest. "Please."

"I'm not going anywhere," he said against her neck.

Somewhere deep down she realized she should tell him to stop, he'd had his one kiss and she had a release form for him to sign, but then his hand was on the zipper of her jeans.

The good-girl side of her conscience whispered in her ear to tell him no, but the hot-looking chick wearing red on her other shoulder promptly cold-cocked the idiot in white. Lacy pressed her head deeper into the pillow. Then his mouth was on her breasts, suckling her nipples through the cotton shirt and silk of her bra.

His hand slipped inside her jeans, moving beneath her panties, and his finger parted her sex.

When she felt it, felt him there, her hips rose off the bed with the pleasure.

"You're so wet," he said. "So ready." He kissed her chin and she remembered how he'd kissed her neck last night.

Lost in a world of want, Lacy gave up all pretense of fighting. She needed Chase, she needed this. Just this. Sex, it was just sex. She wouldn't fall in love with him—wouldn't marry him. Her hips shifted up and down and she moved her hands beneath his shirt to touch him, to know him. But she kept her eyes closed, as if in doing that, she'd make it less real.

His finger moved deeper until it slid inside her and she moaned again. He raised her shirt with his free hand and his mouth moved over her stomach, breathing butterfly kisses down, down, down.

"Can I use my tongue now, Lacy?" he asked. "I need permission. Tell me yes."

"Yes," she sighed.

Dipping his tongue into her navel, he used the same slow, easy pace that his finger dipped inside the opening between her legs. She wriggled beneath him, so hot, so ready for more. She felt her jeans slip down over her hips, and she rose up to help him, not wanting him to stop any of the things he was doing to her. But definitely not wanting it to happen too fast.

Her jeans came off and landed with a whoosh against the wood floor. His mouth lowered from her navel to the edge of her panties.

"What do you want, Lacy? What do you like?" he asked.

"More," she said. He pulled away and it all stopped—the touching, the kissing. She moaned.

Then the silky feel of her panties being whisked down her thighs made her breath catch.

"Patience is a virtue." He chuckled and she heard him unzip his own jeans. "I promise I'll make it worth the wait."

The sound of his voice brought her back to some awareness, not enough to stop, but at least enough to make her think about things she should. Like protection.

She opened her eyes. Sitting up on his knees, he leaned his head back as he pulled his shirt over his head. The muscles in his arms bulged. Her gaze riveted to his chest, to the ripple of hard flesh and muscles down his abdomen. Nothing existed on this man that wasn't positively male. And she wanted that positive male on top of her, inside of her.

But first, she wanted to touch him again, to be touched again. His green gaze moved over her, filled with heat, emotion. He tossed the shirt away, but never moved his gaze from her face. "Your shirt has to go, too."

"Touch me some more," she begged, wanting this to last longer, not wanting him to climb on top, to find his piece of Heaven and leave her in Purgatory. Oh, how many times had she wished she could be faster? But quickies had never been her specialty and it seemed Peter had only had one speed. "Touch me more. Touch me a long time."

"As long as you like." He ran a hand down her belly, between her legs. "I just need to be naked beside you." His hands went back to his jeans and he pushed them down on his hips.

"Protection." She managed that one word. She kept her eyes on his face, embarrassed to glance down where she knew she'd find further temptation.

His expression changed. He stopped tugging at his pants. "You don't . . . have any protection?" he asked.

"No." She paused, bit into her lips. "You don't keep them in your wallet? All men keep them in their wallets."

"No," he said and inhaled sharply. "You're not on the pill?"

She shook her head and closed her eyes. The bed shifted. Heavy footsteps sounded on the wood floor, and then the bathroom door closed with a whack— not a completely I'm-pissed-off slam, but almost. Even while cringing deeper into the mattress, Lacy didn't get upset at his show of anger. She knew exactly how he felt.

# FOURTEEN

Lacy stared at the tip of her nose and decided to count to ten and then she'd get up, slip on something soft and cottony, and give herself a hard swift kick on her cotton-covered butt. No, she'd give herself two. One for not having condoms, and another lick for letting herself get this close to having sex in the first place. Then, after she'd given herself a good talking-to, she'd hand Chase Kelly his walking papers. No, *running* papers. He'd have to move really fast or she'd go after him and drag him back.

She hadn't counted to three when the bathroom door opened again. Naked from the waist down, she reached for the edge of her comforter and pulled it over her. Chase's footsteps approached, then the mattress shifted in the familiar two-in-the-bed way that wasn't so familiar to her anymore. The subtle give of her Serta just reminded Lacy of how long she'd been alone. She closed her eyes and felt the whisper of his breath across her chin.

"I'm sorry," he said. "I should have asked about

protection before I started this, and slamming the door was stupid." His lips brushed over her cheek.

"We can't do this." She put her hand on his naked chest to push him back, but she didn't push. Instead, she just felt him: chest hair soft against her palm, firm flesh over firmer muscle. His heart thumped against her hand. Her heart thumped against her rib cage and the empty ache doubled between her legs.

"I can't let this happen," she said. "It would be stupid, and I'm a lot of things but stupid isn't one of them."

"I know," he said. "But I can still . . . make you happy."

His hand slipped under the comforter. She caught it around her belly button. "No," she said.

"Lacy," he whispered in her ear. "Let me pleasure you. Let me do this for you." He dipped his finger into her navel.

She shook her head, wondering why she'd never known before how sensitive that little dimple in her tummy was. "No. I'm fine. Let's just call this one big mistake and—"

"You're not fine," he said. "And the only mistake here is we don't have protection. It's been too long for you. You're shaking. I can do this. I can give you what you need without ever—"

"But I don't think I can," she said, still holding his wrist tight against her lower stomach.

"I'm not asking you to return the favor," he whispered, and kissed the edge of her lips. "This is all for you. Just you."

"You don't understand. I don't think I can come without . . . Just stop." She draped her free hand over her face and wished her Serta would swallow her up, or all those Serta sheep would show up and take Chase Kelly to dreamland.

"Oh, I see. Well, then, you'll just have to let me try." He nudged her palm from her eyes. "I'm really good at it." He kissed her again. "Of course, I'll have to use my tongue . . . and my fingers." His wiggled his hand against her belly. The soft tap of his five fingers caused the ache between her legs to grow more intense.

"No." She bit down on her lip. "It won't work." His lips brushed against her temple, and her hips shifted and her grip on his hand loosened.

"Don't you remember how it was when you were a teenager and didn't want to go all the way? Didn't you . . . experiment? I'll keep on my jeans, but I can make you feel like a million bucks. Sex without sex."

*Sex without sex.* The words echoed inside her head. She'd never had sex without sex. Sure she'd learned to take the edge off her celibate frustration, but solo orgasms were like cooking for one: With no one to help stir the sauce or taste the spices, it hardly seemed worth it. And while the food might curb the hunger, eating alone made one feel . . . lonely.

"A million bucks, Lacy. It's like a home run without actually going to bat."

Lacy considered all the ways he might help her knock the ball out of the stadium. Her two previous partners hadn't exactly won awards in the art of foreplay. Peter considered undressing a woman all the stimulation a female needed—and most of the time he'd wanted her to come to bed naked. Why, five times out of ten, sex with Peter brought to mind the country western song, "I Shaved My Legs for This?" While Brian had been a better lover, even he'd struck out more times than not. Well, he hadn't struck out; she had. She simply wasn't good at it.

"Sex without sex," Chase whispered against her throat.

No, she'd never had an opportunity to have sex without sex. No double orgasms, no sex on the floor, no phone sex, no shower sex—she truly was the no-sex queen. So maybe sex with no sex was right up her alley.

He kissed her again, softly, seductively, and she loosened her hold on his hand a little more. If it wasn't really sex, then she wasn't really in danger of throwing herself on the altar, was she?

"I won't take off my pants, I promise."

She let go of his hand. She expected him to go directly to work, because it might take a lot of work. Instead, he pushed back the covers and reached for the hem of her shirt.

"You get to come. I get to look." He winked and slipped the pink T-shirt over her head. Sliding his hands beneath her back, her white bra fell loose.

The man knew his way around women's underwear. Probably knew his way around a woman's body as well. She had a feeling sex without sex was going to be a wonderful thing.

*If I can do it.*

Insecurities bubbled to the surface, giving her a hive-raising case of stage fright. What was it Peter had said to her in defense of his elevator fiasco? *"You're not frigid, but you're barely lukewarm."*

The silky feel of her bra whispering over her breasts sent old doubts scattering.

"Mmm," Chase said, and cupped her breasts in his hands as his thumbs brushed back and forth over her tightening nipples. "You're beautiful." He sounded breathless. Stretching out beside her again, he kissed one breast and then the other. "How do you like it? Soft?" He took her nipple in his mouth and suckled. She moaned and arched upward.

He raised his face. "Or like this?" His teeth grazed her nipple, nipping at the tender skin. Her breath caught.

"And the verdict is . . . ?" he asked, and turned her face to look at him. "Hard or soft?"

"Both," she said, and her eyelids fluttered shut.

"Look at me," he said, running a finger down her neck.

She opened her eyes.

Chase studied Lacy, lying on the bed before him. Her baby blues were so readable, so honest, and desire burned in the irises. He wanted her to see him, not to go somewhere off in her head and pretend he was her ex-husband. "I want to see the passion in your eyes, Lacy. Keep those baby blues open for me, okay?"

She nodded and he kissed her again. He moved his hand to the waiting dampness and, parting her with two fingers, he watched her face as he searched for just the right spot. When her eyes widened, he knew he'd found it. But he'd no more than touched the tiny nub when she tightened her legs together.

"Have you really never come like this?" he asked, hoping she was telling the truth. The idea of being a first for her thrilled him. He rubbed his finger over her again.

"Never." The word barely left her lips and she pulled away from his hand as if embarrassed or concerned. "And I . . . don't think . . . I can. Look, I'm just a vanilla wafer, a lukewarm wafer at that."

"And I'm ice cream. Isn't that what you said?" he asked, and kissed her—one of those open-mouthed kisses that came hard, wet, and was given to changing a woman's mind. "Don't fight it," he whispered against her lips, and his hand found her under the covers again. "Go with it. Relax and let me have fun. It's just like sex. When you feel like jerking away, don't. Push against me instead."

He took her breast in his mouth, loving how it puckered against his tongue. Her hips rose a bit, pushing against his fingers as he moved over her silky wet skin. He felt her withering, felt her growing wetter with every stroke of his finger against the tender little nub. But every few minutes she'd pull away, fighting instead of going with it. She didn't know how to let go. Neither had she completely opened her legs for him. He moved to nibble on the curve of her neck. "Think about what I'm doing. How I'm touching you, where I'm touching you."

"I can't. I'm not good at this," she insisted.

"Shhh. We're just getting started. And you're good all right. Bet you taste good, too." He trailed kisses over her belly as he slipped to the waiting treasure. He'd be damned if he let her down. Lacy would go all the way over the edge, even if it took all day.

Positioning himself between her half-opened knees, he kissed the inside of her thigh. "Make room for me," he said. "Let me see you, all of you. No hiding." He slowly pushed her legs farther apart and she let him with no resistance. "That's it." He lowered his face to her, breathed in her scent, and nearly lost it with wanting to rip his pants off, to bury himself inside her and rock against her, to rock hard until his body burst with release.

He gritted his teeth. Later. He'd find his own release later. He lowered his mouth to her. The moment his lips touched the tender pink flesh, she jerked away from him. "Relax," he whispered, and pulled her back.

"I can't. We should just stop. I'm not going to be able to—"

"Relax. It's going to happen." He kissed and savored the honey of her want. "You *do* taste good," he said, and had to smile when he realized the Christmas music still blared in the background.

"Ohhhh," she said, as he laved her with his tongue.

He wrapped one arm around her leg to hold her in place. "See how important the tongue is?" he whispered, and, sliding two fingers inside her, he suckled and licked until he felt her giving in to the moment. Her hips suddenly started shifting. Not to jerk away, but in that slow up and down motion, the dance of pleasure, of release. She made a throaty little noise and her thighs tightened around his neck. He pressed a hand under her soft bottom, holding her against him as he took her closer to that home run. Then he felt her let go. Her sex convulsed around his fingers. She cried out at the same time the first lyrics of "Grandma Got Run Over By a Reindeer" came over the stereo system. He pulled his mouth away, his fingers still stroking, and raised himself up on his elbows.

He smiled at the sight of her. She had her neck arched back and her bottom lip sucked into her mouth. Her fists clutched handfuls of the white sheet and her entire body trembled. A light purring noise continued from her throat. He'd never known a woman who needed this as much as she did.

When her whimpering stopped, he moved to lie beside her, wiping her moisture from his chin. He frowned when he found her eyes shut. "Where are those baby blues?"

Her lids fluttered open, and he saw the passion filling her eyes. He smiled at her, running his finger down her cheek. "Didn't think I could do it, did you?"

Her face reddened. "I didn't think I could do it."

He grinned, not because it was funny but just because it felt right. A lightness entered his chest, and Chase recognized it as happiness. His life was a mess and he was . . . happy. Damn, it had been a long time since he'd felt this.

"You are so beautiful." He kissed her then, moving his tongue over her lips.

"See how good you taste," he whispered into her mouth.

She hesitated as if the boldness of his words stunned her. But she didn't withdraw, and she allowed him to continue kissing her. Pulling back, he slipped one of his still-damp fingers into her mouth, letting her taste herself further. She brushed her tongue over his finger, and the action made the crotch of his jeans shrink two sizes.

Feeling as if he would burst, he pulled her to his chest and ran his hands over her naked back, over her curvy waist, and lower to the roundness of her buttocks. He wanted to grind himself against her, to find his own release, but something kept him from it. This was for her. And amazingly, he didn't feel cheated. Well, a certain part of him did, but he could wait.

"You ready to go again?" he whispered in her ear.

"Oh, no!" she said, and flushed red.

He laughed and spotted an innocence in her he hadn't seen in a woman since he'd been in high school. Something told him Lacy hadn't known very many lovers. "Come on, one more time. I thought you were an expert on multiple orgasms," he teased.

She shook her head. "But if you want, I could . . ." She moved her hand to his zipper. "It's only fair."

He grabbed her wrist. The offer should have had him shucking off his jeans. His sex throbbed with want, but something stopped him. Maybe it was her innocence. Maybe it was just that this felt different. Maybe she wasn't the only one holding back. He pushed the thought over a mental cliff.

"I'll get mine when we can go all the way," he said. "Which better be soon." He nuzzled her neck, but he felt her tense in his arms. "What's wrong?" he asked.

"Nothing," she lied, and buried the left side of her face in his shoulder.

They lay there without speaking, her head pillowed on his chest. All three cats joined them on the bed. The gray feline stayed on the edge of the bed, as if thinking of escape. Chase stared at the creature and it stared back with fear in its eyes. But Chase also saw the cat's need to be with people, to be loved. Glancing down at the woman curled beside him, he realized Lacy and the animal reminded him of each other. Both of them had been hurt, let down. And damn, if he didn't understand how it felt. Life could be brutal.

Lacy had her eyes closed, but he could tell she wasn't asleep. Lowering his cheek to her temple he whispered, "So, how was it?"

"How was what?" She opened her eyes and reached over and stroked the white cat.

"If you have to ask, it scares me."

Her lips shifted into a smile. "Let's just say it was worth shaving my legs for." Even joking, her voice sounded a little shy.

He glided his hand over her hip, past her thigh to test the smoothness of her calves. "Mmm," he said.

Time moved with a slow uphill climb. Not that he really minded; he had a naked woman in his arms for goodness's sakes. But this was the cigarette-smoking time, and as a nonsmoker he'd never really known what to do with it. Oddly enough, he'd never hung around this long with Jessie or the others he'd bedded in the last year to feel this what-do-we-do-now stage. With his late wife, well, there had been no awkward moments with Sarah. Just rightness. And when Lacy turned her head and her cheek pressed a little deeper into his chest, the moment's awkwardness seemed to slip into oblivion.

"Is that really the first time you came without going all the way?"

She didn't answer immediately. "Yes."

"Not even with the tongue? Oral sex?" He leaned on his side to see her face, to see if she spoke the truth.

"I . . . I just never got there. Terrible lovers, I guess. Or maybe it was me."

"Definitely not you. And don't be so hard on those other men either." He grinned. "They just can't compete with the best."

Her laugh sounded along with the music of "Jingle Bells" and her ringing chuckle struck him as more soul-soothing than the familiar song.

He traced a finger around the curve of her ear.

"You know, I don't think I've ever watched a woman come to 'Grandma Got Run Over By a Reindeer.'"

She chuckled again. "When and where did you get so good at that?"

"In high school. In the back of my father's Impala. I'd do anything to get in a girl's pants, even if it meant leaving mine on."

She sucked on her lip for a second. "Well, it was so good, I'll bet you didn't ever get much further with those girls. I mean . . ." Her blue eyes twinkled with laughter. "Why go to bat if you can still hit a home run without taking a chance of striking out, or hitting a foul ball."

He grinned. "Oh, but you haven't seen me use my bat. I never strike out or hit a foul ball. I'm a really good hitter. Just wait and see." He touched the tip of her nose.

A soft chuckle escaped her lips, but the tension came again into her body. Chase ignored it. Whatever reservations she had about going all the way with him could be dealt with. She'd given him this much; eventually she'd give him more. He kissed her and wondered how soon he could get his hands on some condoms. *Not soon enough,* the tightness in his pants seemed to communicate.

"You really are beautiful," he whispered, and his gaze moved down over her breasts, her flat stomach, the tapered curves of her waist and the soft triangle of hair between her legs.

She noted his gaze and reached for the sheet.

"Oh no." He laughed and pulled it back. "I told you the deal: I pleasure you, and I get to look." He rolled on top of her, took her hands in his and raised them above her head.

"So I'm going to walk around naked?" she asked.

He grinned. "That or I can handcuff you to the bed. Have my way with you whenever I want, as many times as I want. Practice my . . . batting average."

She smiled, and then her gaze moved to his shoulder and she frowned. "It's redder." She pulled free and touched his arm. "Did you put more alcohol on it?"

"Once," he said, turning his head, and seeing she was right; the wound did look redder. "You don't have any more antibiotics, do you?"

"You should go to the doctor," she said.

"You be my doctor," he said seductively. But as his mouth lowered, the doorbell rang. He growled and dropped his face into the curve of her neck. "Probably your FedEx guy back to beg for sex." He sat up.

Her eyes glittered with mischief. "Since I can't get dressed, I'll have to answer it naked," she teased. "I'm sure Hunky wouldn't mind. I think he's been hoping I'd do that for over a year."

"Funny."

Chase got up and threw her jeans on the bed. The doorbell rang again. Fabio started yapping somewhere down the hall. As Lacy slipped her legs into her soft denims, Chase went to the window.

"Shit!" he said. He moved back, his heart thudding against his sore ribs. "It's Zeke."

# FIFTEEN

Zeke ran his palm over the gun in his shoulder strap and knocked again. Pressing closer, he heard a dog yapping. He hated dogs. Then he heard music. He leaned close to the door. Christmas music? Frowning, he punched the doorbell two or three more times. He was freaking tired of this game.

In spite of dragging the lake, Kelly's body still hadn't been found. Exhaustion pulled at Zeke's nerves, making him jittery. If he wasn't careful, he would make a mistake, do something stupid, draw attention to himself.

He needed to calm down, to get his head together. To find Kelly. To kill him and be done with it.

Lacy snatched up her shirt and slipped it over her head. "I'll get rid of him." The soft cotton brushed against her nose and chin as she wiggled into it.

Chase grabbed her by the elbow, held tight. "No! Just stay here. He'll leave."

"He'll just come back later." She pulled free.

"Yeah, but I'll be gone by then," he said, raking a hand through his hair.

The thought of him leaving smacked Lacy in the face. But why? Wasn't she going to give him his running papers? Oh, mercy, maybe sex without sex was no different than sex with a bat. Was it starting already? One orgasm and she'd caved? Was she falling hard and heavy for this guy?

The doorbell chimed again. Fabio's bark grew intense. "I'll answer the door and say I haven't seen anything," she said.

"Lacy, you're the world's worst liar." Chase raked a hand over his face. "Zeke will know that—"

"I am not!" she snapped. *And I'm not falling for him! I'm just concerned.* "I can lie as well as the next girl."

"You can't. You really suck at it." He rolled his eyes as if exasperated.

"Am I really so bad?" She took a deep breath.

He nodded. The doorbell rang again, only this time it came with a loud rapping on the door. "Police," called a voice.

"Fine. I'll treat him like my mom." She took off out of the room, ignoring Chase's objections, ignoring the reasons she wasn't willing to let him do the talking. She stopped by her studio and collected her camera and hung it around her neck. Props, she thought, in case the man asked why she'd taken so long answering the door. But if she managed to pull this off right, the man wouldn't get the opportunity to ask a question.

The doorbell continued to ring. As she moved down the hall, she picked up Fabio, who still wore his reindeer horns. "Just a minute," she called out as she pulled open the door.

The man, wearing jeans and a black polo shirt, scowled at her. Then he caught sight of Fabio's horns and appeared taken aback. Fabio immediately went into his serious growl. Lacy's heart went into a spasm. It was the man's gray eyes: cold, empty. Pure evil, she thought. He made Hannibal Lecter look like someone you'd invite over for dinner.

"May I help you?" she finally managed to say, praying the man couldn't see the fear in her eyes.

He held out a badge. "Name's Zeke Duncun, with the HPD. We're looking—"

"Oh, my." She'd almost forgot her rules: ask questions before they do, answer the question before they can, and *never* shut up. "I'm not in danger, am I?" she blurted out.

"Danger?" The man blinked. "No, not unless you—"

"I'll bet you're here about that crooked cop who they think is dead?"

He nodded. "Yes—"

"You don't think he's around here, do you?" Fabio continued to growl. Lacy's heart continued to tremble. Whatever she did, she couldn't let Zeke take control of the conversation. She'd learned as a child that her mother could see right through her untruths. Back then, she'd just assumed it was her mother's maternal intuition and not that she sucked at lying.

"No. We're just checking. Have you—"

"Should I evacuate? I'd hate to have to leave, but if I'm in danger, I would."

"I'm sure you're safe. But have you—"

"Have you seen anything that would make you believe I'm in danger? I mean, the area is usually so safe. My grandmother lived here for years. Ten years, to be exact. She gave me the house. I've been here for almost two years and I haven't once been afraid. Well, except for that time that I heard noises in my attic. Turned out to be just a raccoon. Can you imagine, I'm all panicked and all it turned out to be was a raccoon? Have you ever dealt with raccoons?" She paused, told herself to breathe but couldn't manage it.

The man shook his head, obviously annoyed at her constant chatter. "I was just checking to see if—"

"Do you think I should get some friends to come and stay with me?" she asked. "Not for the raccoons, but for any other danger. I have friends who could come—"

He held up his hand as if to silence her. "I—"

"I'm so happy you stopped by. I feel so much safer knowing the police are in the area. I think I'll go call someone and see if they won't mind coming to stay here with me for a few days." She grabbed the door as if to close it. Not enough to make him suspicious, but enough to give him the idea of leaving. Her throat knotted.

"Why don't you take my card in case you do see something?" He frowned at her. Fabio snapped at the man's hand.

Lacy took the card. "Thank you."

He backed up, scowling again at Fabio. "Are you sure you haven't seen anything?"

Lacy swallowed, faced with the question, faced with having to lie. She considered what he might do if he discovered Chase hidden in her bedroom. If he'd tried to kill Chase once, he'd probably try again. He probably wouldn't stop with just Chase.

She blinked, and decided that lying was too risky. She'd throw him a curveball. Heck, she'd just hit a home run without ever batting, so surely she could toss this no-good slime bucket a curveball. "You mean raccoons? I haven't seen raccoons in over a year. But there were some squirrels hanging around."

He stared at her as if considering finding her a straightjacket. Then he turned and left.

Lacy shut the door, set Fabio down and then slid down the wall until her butt hit the cold tile floor. Dropping her forehead onto her knees, she let out the breath she'd been holding since opening the door.

Zeke started back to his car. Damn woman was nuts. A freak. He opened his car door, got in, and shoved the keys into the ignition. Then he hesitated. "Was she really crazy, or was she hiding something?"

He jangled the keys, trying to think. She hadn't let him inside. Every one of the other locals had invited him inside. Why hadn't she? He gazed back at the house, and suspicion started knifing at his empty stomach.

Knees still drawn to her chest, she inhaled and tried to work the knot out of her stomach. Fabio, sniffing around her feet, suddenly growled at the door again. The knock came less than a second later. Lacy jumped up, her heart pumping in her throat. She opened the door and faced Zeke Duncun. Again.

"Yes?" To her own ears, her voice sounded terrified. Oh, Heaven help her.

He held up his cell phone and studied her intently. The gray of his eyes had grown colder and suspicion lurked in his gaze. "I'm out of minutes. Do you mind if I come in and use the phone?"

"Minutes? Out of minutes." Lacy stared at Zeke and tried to sound normal, but her voice cracked and she just couldn't do it. Fabio growled from around her feet, and Lacy heard his teeth snapping.

She grabbed the dog before those teeth could snap a plug out of the man's ankle. As she stood again, the coldness in Zeke's eyes turned her blood to the consistency of a cherry slush. She could not let him inside her house. But if she didn't, he would suspect her of hiding something, and then God only knew what he might do. He'd already shot Chase once. The taste of fear formed on the tip of her tongue as she eyed the loose fit of his shirt. Was that where he hid his gun?

Blinking repeatedly, she could think of only one really good lie to keep him at her threshold, but then she realized if she truly had a deadly and rare African disease, she'd probably have a quarantine sticker on her door. That left no options. Oh, heck, she hating being without options.

"Sure. Come on in." She prayed Chase could hear her. Prayed he wouldn't do something stupid like storm out with his gun blazing. And she prayed harder that Zeke didn't intend to search her house.

Zeke's gray gaze followed her as she took a backward step. He pushed the door closed. "So, do you live—"

"Don't you just hate cell phones?" Swinging around on her heels, she took another step deeper into her entryway. "I mean, they run out of minutes at the most inopportune time. One time . . ." She kept talking, knowing that as her mouth moved he couldn't ask questions. Fabio continued to growl. She continued to chatter and realized she was beginning to sound like Sue. Oh Lordie, this was bad.

"And then there was that time I ran out of gas and minutes at the same time." Her gaze shifted to the hall where her singing fish again hung. When all this was over, she was going to get herself a better weapon.

Two steps away from moving into the living room, she paused. Would he see the blanket and pillow on the sofa and know someone had stayed here? What about the two plates on the kitchen table? Oh darn, she'd have been better off going with the African disease story.

"Of course, I wasn't as scared as I was with the raccoon. I mean . . . have you ever seen a rabid raccoon?" She crossed the threshold into the living room and relief unknotted her stomach when she saw that Chase had removed the bedding from the sofa. Her gaze darted beyond the living room and lit upon the clean kitchen table. Chase Kelly got points for being neat, though not quite as many points as he'd won in the bedroom. How many points did a home run count for anyway? The thought buzzed around her head like a bee on Ritalin. Lordie, how could she be thinking of home runs when she had a cold-blooded, gray-eyed killer a foot behind her?

"I swear he was foaming at the mouth a little. His eyes were all . . ." With Fabio tucked up under one arm, she grabbed the phone from the counter with her free hand and handed it to Zeke. "And his claws, did you know that raccoons have sharp claws? I didn't, but then . . ."

He took the phone, glaring at the growling dog,

then his calculating snake eyes scanned the room. He opened his mouth to speak.

"Would you like something to drink?" she asked before he managed to get words out of those thin, unappealing lips. "I have soda or tea. Actually, I don't have tea made, but it only takes a few minutes to make. Have you ever noticed how many types of tea there are? There's raspberry tea, honey tea, herb tea, and then there's—"

"No, I don't want any tea." He held up a finger to silence her.

But it was going to take more than a finger. "How about coffee? Do you drink coffee? I have decaf and flavored. I—"

"No coffee!" he snapped and shook his head. "You know what? I think I can wait to call later." He dropped the phone on the counter.

"You sure you don't want tea?" She followed him back through the living room.

To the door. All the way to the door, she chanted in her mind. But he didn't make it that far.

He stopped before he got to the entryway and stared down her hall.

Stared down the hall that led to her bedroom.

That led to Chase Kelly.

# SIXTEEN

Lacy's heart fell, landing somewhere around her bladder, and she had to pee, too. "It would only take a minute to make some tea. Did you know how healthy tea is? I read . . ." Oh jeepers, this man had pure evil stamped all over him and she was offering to make him tea. *Please let him leave.*

He started moving again toward the entryway, and she offered a thanks Heavenward.

"If you see or hear anything, you call me," he said, his tone about as friendly as a pet rock.

"Oh, I will. I'll call you first thing." *Right when Hell freezes your evil gray eyes shut.* When the door closed behind him, Lacy's knees almost buckled. She dropped Fabio and walked into the living room, sank onto the sofa, and pressed her palms against her closed eyes. When the phone rang, she nearly jumped out of her skin.

"Hi, Lacy. It's Eric." The loudspeaker played the message. "I noticed you were due to pick up your flea spray, and I thought maybe I'd drop it off. We could do dinner. I know this great Italian place. And to make myself clear, yes, I'm asking you out on a date. I know you've turned me down only a million times, but I'm told persistence pays off. Anyway, call me."

Lacy ignored Eric and, practicing breathing exercises, she tried to get her heart to return to a normal rhythm. Visions of Zeke Duncun's cold, hard eyes filled her mind, then her thoughts turned on a dime and mentally yanked her back into her bedroom, with Chase spreading her thighs and . . .

Oh, Cracker Jacks, she'd just had the best sexual experience of her entire life and it hadn't included everything. Only one little problem existed. Chase seemed pretty sure they were just in the first inning of this game—and he was quite certain he was next up to bat.

What really scared her was she wasn't altogether sure he was wrong. If sex with no sex could be that exceptional, just how good could it be if she actually let him get to the plate? Well, she had already seen him in the batting cage, and he'd had formidable power and accuracy. The thoughts brought flashbacks of pleasure, and her lower belly tightened.

Then another thought exploded in her head. That short fleeting moment when the idea of Chase Kelly leaving had taken her breath. As if she cared for him . . . as if . . .

No! She didn't care for him. Couldn't care for him.

Zeke dropped his head against the steering wheel and gritted his teeth. Headache. Damn, his head hurt and all that chattering . . . He started his car, but before he pulled out of the drive, he took out his little notepad and wrote down the address. The lady came across as a total bimbo, should have been blond, but the suspicion prickling in his gut hadn't completely gone away. He'd come back later.

As he pulled away, he punched in the hospital number and asked for the ICU. "Yes, this is Officer Duncun. Just wanted a report on Stokes."

"He's the same," the nurse said. "His vitals are good, but he hasn't come to yet. Doctor came in earlier and assured Mrs. Stokes that this really isn't unexpected."

"Thanks." Zeke tossed out the politeness, hoping his frustration didn't color his voice. "Oh, one other thing. Is someone else there from the precinct?"

"Someone's been here the whole time. Would you like me to give you the number to the line in the waiting room?"

"No," Zeke said, and hit the button. It was time he found out what the crap those guys were doing.

Lacy heard her bedroom door swing open and slam shut. "That was stupid!" Chase's angry voice boomed as he made his way down her hall. "Do you have any idea how stupid that was?"

*Yup. Pretty stupid.* If she'd insisted he leave this morning at breakfast, she wouldn't be in this situation. She wouldn't know how good he was with his tongue or his fingers. And her insides wouldn't be turning to jelly as she thought about him going all the way with her.

He dropped down beside her. "Are you okay?" Concern tempered the anger in his green eyes.

"I'm fine." She stood up before he could touch her. "I've got some work I have to do. Invoicing, bills and stuff. Help yourself to a video." She opened her cabinet where all her videos were stored. Then she took off down the hall, pushed open her office door, shut it and locked it. If she'd had a hammer and nails she might have used them. Not to keep him out, but to keep her in.

Chase watched her disappear into her study. He knew she was running away. A part of him wanted to chase her down, the part that responded to the enticing sway of her hips. But the other part of him insisted he let her go. He had his own fight-or-flight case raging inside him.

The few minutes waiting in her bedroom had been Hell with the heater stuck on high. He'd wanted to storm out, beat Zeke to a pulp, and get answers. And he might have, if he hadn't been afraid Lacy would end up hurt. Then the thought of how easily Zeke could hurt her had made Hell's temperature rise.

Standing, he paced the length of the sofa, feeling like a trapped animal, feeling useless, impotent. His sex stirred, as if wanting to protest that last adjective. He had to do something, figure this out. There had to be a reason Zeke was doing this.

There also had to be a reason that the thought of Lacy being hurt had cut a river of pain into his soul. A reason those feelings reminded him of another time.

The phone rang. Chase continued to pace as the sound system played the voice.

"Hi, Lacy. It's Eric again. I . . . Okay, I'm impatient. I was hoping you'd answer this time. That restaurant serves the best shrimp marinara that you've ever eaten. And their desserts are sinful. Please say you'll come. Be sinful with me. We can even share."

Chase clenched his jaw. There had to be a reason he wanted to send FedEx have-sex-with-me Hunky to

Timbuktu and a reason the idea of Lacy being sinful with Eric made him so hot he felt certain his bare feet left singe marks on the hardwood floor. These edgy, too-damn-close-to-jealous emotions had to pass.

It's just the anticipation, he told himself. Once he had her, the confusion would pass. But damn, if he wouldn't sign over his checkbook right now for a box of condoms.

An hour later, Zeke walked from his cubicle and knocked on the captain's door. "Yeah?"

Zeke shouldered-open the door and felt his blood pressure inch up a notch as he spotted Jason Dodd sitting near the man's desk. Zeke nodded brusquely at both men, but Dodd didn't acknowledge his greeting.

"Any news on Stokes?" Zeke asked.

"No." The captain's gaze flipped between Zeke and Dodd, reading, weighing.

Zeke clutched the doorknob tighter. "Nothing found at the lake, either?" He eyed Dodd. The man didn't look away from the accusations Zeke visually flung at him.

"I thought that was where you were," the captain said.

"I was combing the area. Thinking Kelly may have forced his way into someone's home."

"Chase Kelly wouldn't do that," Dodd said. "No more than he would have shot Stokes."

Zeke zeroed in on Dodd. "Then who shot him?" He wanted to know just what Dodd had told the captain. Better to know than to guess.

Dodd leaned back in the padded office chair. It squeaked with the movement. "Guess we'll have to wait until he wakes up to tell us."

"Are you making accusations, Dodd? If so, say it to my face."

Dodd stood so fast that his chair rolled across the room. "Okay. I'll say it to your face. I'll yell it into your freaking ear if it makes you happy!"

"Stop this shit!" The captain launched from behind his desk and caught Dodd's arm. "Damn it, guys. I don't have a clue how things are going to play out here, but until then I can't have my men at each other's throats."

"Chase Kelly was on the take." Zeke jabbed a finger at Dodd. "If this bastard says differently then maybe it's because he's afraid of what else we will uncover."

"Now who's making accusations?" Dodd spat.

"At least I'm doing it to your face."

"If you want to know what I think, why don't you just ask me? I'd be more than happy to meet you outside and have a little talk."

"I said stop it!" The captain moved between them. "Unless both of you want your asses suspended, you'll stay out of each other's way."

Dodd shook off the captain's grip and pushed through the door. Zeke watched him storm off, then he took the opportunity to move inside and ask his own questions. "What's he saying?"

"He wasn't saying anything. I called him in here. If Kelly was dirty, I'm finding it hard to believe that Dodd didn't at least suspect something. And I know IA is going to be all over his ass, too. It's my job to check this out."

"And what did he say?"

"He denies it. He seems certain that Kelly isn't the bad guy. And frankly it's hard to . . . Oh hell, Kelly's been flipping out lately, but honestly, I would have never—"

"You don't believe me?" Zeke asked. "You're going to take some suicidal maniac's word over mine?"

"I didn't say I didn't believe you. I'm just saying, oh hell, I don't what I believe. But the thing you said the other day about Dodd being in on this isn't ringing true. He cares about Kelly, maybe to the point he can't admit the man could have fallen off the edge. They partnered together for over seven years and it—"

"Which is why I'm guessing he's dirty. A partner knows these things, damn it."

The captain shook his head. "I don't think so." The captain's brow rose. "You were partnered with Kelly. Why did it take him shooting one of our own for you to catch him?"

Zeke felt the accusation all the way to the ulcered lining of his stomach. "Don't tell me you and Dodd are trying to push this on me."

"I'm not saying anything. But I'll get to the bottom of this, Zeke. I promise you. If I've got a dirty cop under me, I'll find him out."

"What are you doing?" Lacy asked when she stepped out of her office several hours later. She'd spent the time listening to the yin and yang of her conscience debate the wisdom of pulling Chase Kelly back into her bedroom and giving him a list of all the things she'd like to try: sex in the shower, sex on the floor, sex . . . *Stop thinking like that!*

Chase had several pieces of notebook paper strewn over her coffee table. He looked up and, when his eyes met hers, she saw raw sexual need reflected there. Cutting her gaze back to the papers, she took a second to catch her breath and considered heading right back into the study.

"I'm doing a time line. Hoping I can figure out the missing piece of this damn puzzle."

"Oh." She sat down on the sofa, keeping several feet between them, and scanned his notes. He had days listed on the tops of the papers, with hours going down the side and notes written beside them. She read on, seeing he'd listed everything from where he'd had breakfast to with whom he'd eaten lunch.

"You have a good memory." Tilting her head, she saw his frustration in his expression. "I don't think I could remember all that."

"You could if you tried," he said. "But it hasn't helped and I still have too many holes." He pointed to one of the sheets, which hardly had any writing on it.

"Maybe if I read it back to you," she suggested. She picked up the papers.

He shrugged, and Lacy leaned back and folded her legs beneath her. "On Tuesday, February 16, you woke up around six A.M., stopped off for coffee at Bee's diner. Went into the office around eight A.M." She hesitated and met his gaze. He studied her intently. The look in his eyes made her want to scoot over—like, all the way into her bedroom. "You don't have anything filled out for midmorning. Maybe nothing important happened. Maybe you sat at your desk and played solitaire."

Chase shook his head. "I never play solitaire."

She looked back at the paper, then gazed up at him. "You had lunch at a Mexican restaurant." She cut her eyes to him. "You wrote, 'cute waitress with a nice ass.' "

A smile pulled at his mouth. "Some things I can't forget."

She frowned. "Right." She scanned down the page. "You don't have anything filled out for the afternoon either. But that evening you . . ."

With lightning speed, he took the paper from her hands. "You know what? This isn't going to help."

But she'd already read it. "Cooked dinner and had sex with Jessie." She read the words again as the paper left her fingers. She raised an eyebrow and tried to decipher the sudden green emotion doing cartwheels in her chest. How dare he . . . have sex-with-no-sex with her when he was involved with someone else? He was just like Peter, like Brian. Only, this time she wasn't the person cheated on, but part of the cheating team. Oh jeepers, she felt like pond scum.

She raised her gaze. "At least you can tell her you didn't take your pants off with me."

He set the paper down on the coffee table. Then, closing his eyes, he pinched his nose between his thumb and forefinger. "Lacy . . ."

Feeling a hot emotion building in her chest, she jumped up and walked to the kitchen. She opened the fridge, wishing she could crawl into the ice maker and cool off.

"Eat the tuna today and pick up a gallon of milk," the fridge said.

"Shut up," she snapped.

She glared at the mayonnaise, then frowned at the mustard. In a few minutes, she heard Chase walk in behind her.

"It's not what you think," he said.

"What do I think?" she asked, inwardly seething, and praying he couldn't see it.

"You think I'm involved." He came closer and she shut the fridge and stepped away.

"And you're not?" Skepticism rang so heavy in her voice, she mentally heard the words drop to the floor with a thud.

"No, I'm not."

"You cooked dinner and had sex with her, but you're not involved." For just a second she wondered if that was what Peter had told his secretary: *"I'm married but I'm not really involved."* And Brian: *"Yeah, I'm engaged to her, but it's not like we're involved or anything."*

"Right," he answered. "That's all it was. Dinner and sex."

"A one-time thing, right?" she asked, almost certain she'd seen Jessie's name written on several other pages. Would he lie to her now? Of course he would. All men lied. Just like all men cheated on their significant others. But she and Chase hadn't really cheated. Hadn't *really* had sex. Not by the political definition of sex, or rather, former President Clinton's definition. Maybe she wasn't total pond scum.

Chase looked blank for a second as if searching for words. "No. It wasn't a one-time thing. We . . . Look, we've met twice a week for the last three months. I cook dinner and we have sex. But it's not as if we're involved."

She felt her mouth fall open. "You meet with her twice a week for three months and you don't consider that being involved?"

His brow wrinkled. "No, I don't."

"Oh, really? Well, excuse me for having to ask, but this is one I haven't read in *Redbook* or *Cosmo*. What in your male pea brain qualifies as being involved?"

She crossed her arms and waited for an answer. Her foot tapped the floor.

*Tap.*

She shouldn't care how many women he had.

*Tap.*

She had no right to question him.

*Tap.*

She had no reason to be hurt.

*Tap.*

It sounded as if he'd told her the truth, even when the truth sucked. Even when it made him sound like a real bastard. But he hadn't lied.

*Tap.*

Didn't he win points for not lying?

*Tap.*

Wasn't uninvolved sex what she'd wanted?

*Tap.*

It didn't matter. The man was history. Just as soon as he answered, she was going to insist he take his "bat" and walk out of her life.

*And miss the best part of the game?* her devilish conscience whispered. *Do you really want to do that?*

Right now she would love to smack both her conscience and Chase Kelly. "So, do tell. How do you define *involved*?"

*Tap.*

*Tap . . .*

Chase watched Lacy's foot movements. Up and down. He could see the anger glowing in her eyes, and he felt pretty much peeved himself. Though he couldn't quite put a finger on why.

"It's 'involved' when you are committed to each other." He passed a hand over his face. "When you share pieces of your life with someone. When the person matters. When you care. And that doesn't describe Jessie and me."

And that's when it hit him with all the power of an eighteen-wheeler: He was smack dab in the middle of being involved with Lacy Maguire. He'd known her only two days and yet here he stood, up to his ears in involvement. The thought sent emotional red flags flying all over: fear, denial, exhilaration.

He needed time to catch his breath—time to deal with the tire tracks that the big-rig realization had left on him—but Lacy looked about ready to send him packing. That fight-or-flight emotion he'd felt earlier returned and shook his already run-over state of mind.

He could stand his ground, fight to make her see that Jessie truly wasn't important to him. Or he could leave while the leaving was good, get out before his heart got tangled up. Turning, he stormed out of the kitchen, grabbed his gun from beneath the sofa, and headed for the front door.

# SEVENTEEN

He made it all the way to the entryway before every instinct inside him screamed to stop. He swung around, stormed back into the kitchen and dropped his gun beside the phone.

Lacy stood by the kitchen sink, her arms wrapped around her middle, her blue eyes filled with indecision, hurt, and leftover fear.

"Jessie sees her ex-husband four days a week," he tossed out, deciding just to lay down the ugly truth. "She's planning on remarrying him next month. And when she does, I'll send her a wedding gift. Hell, she'll probably send me a wedding invitation. She knows I see other women. She doesn't care. Hasn't ever cared. What we had was . . . was convenience and casual sex. And it was all about to end anyway."

He raked another palm over his face, realizing how cold and uncaring his relationship with Jessie sounded. He'd used her. She'd used him. Then he accepted it as exactly that—cold and uncaring. And unsatisfying.

He'd drawn more pleasure bringing Lacy to climax and keeping his pants on than he'd ever found naked and buried navel-deep in Jessie. In two days he'd shared things with Lacy that he'd never shared with Jessie. He'd told Lacy about his parents and his sister.

*You haven't told her about Sarah.*

The thought hit him upside the head. *But I will eventually,* he answered back.

Hell, he'd even told her about his skunk. And while he hadn't even gone all the way with her, he'd mentally stamped her as his. He'd warned off Jason, and the vet and the FedEx guy could just go to Hell, because he wasn't going to give her up without a fight.

"You know what?" she asked, grabbing a glass from the cabinet. "It's not important. This entire conversation doesn't matter fiddlesticks. I don't even know why I asked."

"Yes, you do," he said. By God, if he could admit what was happening, then so could she.

The phone rang and Lacy reached over and jerked it up. "Speaking," she practically growled. "Yes, that will be fine."

Chase listened while his insides churned. Was it Eric again? Had Lacy just agreed to go to dinner and share a lustful dessert with her impatient vet? He paced the kitchen once and decided without question that Lacy Mcguire wasn't going to be sharing sin with anyone but him.

He moved past her again, the temptation to snatch the phone from her hands growing stronger, but one look at the squint of her eyes and he decided against it. He'd never considered himself a good reader of the female mind, but something told him he wasn't the only one having a difficult time facing this thing happening between himself and Lacy. If he pushed, she'd push back. And right now, the only pushing he wanted to do was with both of them naked in bed.

Chase rubbed his shoulder, which had throbbed since breakfast. Lacy put the phone down. She leaned her forehead against the fridge. Then slowly she turned to face him, opened her mouth to speak, and . . . stopped.

"Is it hurting?" she asked, gesturing toward his shoulder as he attempted to massage the ache away.

"Some." He saw the anger in her eyes fade to concern. He'd take concern hands down over her anger. So he grimaced a little harder than before.

She sucked in her bottom lip and seemed to consider her next words. "Come on. Let's clean it again."

Chase followed her into the master bathroom. The anger they'd shared seconds earlier seemed to have stayed in the kitchen. She motioned for him to sit down on the toilet. He pulled off his shirt and watched her collect supplies. When she had her things, she moved between his legs and leaned over him to place all of the medicines and bandages on the back of the toilet.

Her breast brushed against his cheek, and he fought the desire to turn his face around and press his mouth against her. Thankfully, she backed up before temptation ruled.

"It might hurt," she said, and pulled back the bandage.

He wrapped his hands around her hips, inched them down to feel if she'd ever put on any underwear. She looked down, and he thought she might ask him to move his hands. She didn't: a small victory. Then something clicked inside his head, and he realized that this really was war. And his enemies were drawing close. Hunky and Eric might want Lacy, but the real enemy was her ex-husband, whom Chase thought she still loved. It was the only thing that could explain her reluctance to sleep with him. She still loved her ex-husband. The thought left a bitter wrinkle in his brain.

She spotted his expression as she dabbed cream from a small yellow tube on the wound. "Am I hurting you?"

Chase smiled at the way she sucked on that bottom lip, as if it pained her to doctor him.

"I can't feel a thing." He let his hands slide to her backside. *Nope, no panties.* Just Lacy. He remembered how soft she'd felt in his embrace. He remembered exactly where his tongue had been and where it wanted to return. His pants were shrinking again and his shoulder wasn't the only thing throbbing anymore. He looked up at her lips and she opened her mouth to speak; desire and need echoed in her expression, and she couldn't mask it. She might love her ex but she wanted him. His breath hitched. He'd take what he could get. Was she about to cave? She inched a breath closer, then he remembered . . . they still didn't have condoms.

"It reminds me of my grandmother's toe."

"What?" His brain stumbled around her words. "What reminds you of your grandmother's toe?" A laugh worked its way from his throat, and he moved his hands around to cup the soft roundness of her bottom.

"Wait! I know, I know." She swung around, leaving Chase's hands desperately empty, as she rummaged through a bathroom drawer.

For just a second Chase allowed himself to hope she'd remembered a tucked-away condom, but even he wasn't sure how Lacy could mentally move from her grandmother's toe to prophylactics. Then again, he wasn't sure how any thought could have led to her grandmother's toe.

"Yes!" She held up a small piece of paper. "The doctor gave my grandmother a prescription for an antibiotic when she had an ingrown toenail that got infected."

"I'm still lost." He ran a hand over his chest.

"We can get the prescription filled and you can take it . . . for the infection."

Prescription equaled drugstore. Drugstore equaled condoms. He stood up and laced his fingers with hers. "Let's go."

Lacy's brows beetled as she stared at him. "You can't go. People would recognize you."

"Not necessarily." He winked. "Give me five minutes." Leaving her with another smile, he took off to the other bathroom, where he'd hidden the supplies Jason had brought over.

Lacy handed the prescription to Mr. Tien, her grocer's pharmacist. "Is that toe giving her problems again?" he asked.

Lacy brushed a strand of hair off her left cheek and stared over the man's head so she wouldn't have to lie looking into his eyes. "Yes."

"I thought she was going to stay in Florida for a few months." He set the prescription on the counter. "Did it get too hot for her?"

Lacy panicked, having forgotten that Mr. Tien lived only a couple of blocks from her grandmother's new condo and knew her grandmother personally. "Uhh, yeah. The heat got to her."

"Well, tell her I said hello. Or maybe I'll see her at bingo Saturday." He looked down at the paperwork. "It will be about ten minutes to fill this."

"Thanks." Lacy turned around and nipped at her lower lip. A security guard walked past. Could she get arrested for drug trafficking for giving prescription antibiotics to an HPD narcotic officer?

As she stepped away, she spotted the blond-haired man wearing a baseball cap standing a few aisles away. He looked up at her over the shelves of tampons and Depends. Sucking her bottom lip into her mouth, she noted his dark brown eyes and copper-colored mustache. He smiled, a soft knowing smile that hit a ten on the Richter scale of sex appeal. Her heart did a little dance—a dance of indecision. Was she or was she not going to have sex with him?

When Chase had told her he'd go with her to the pharmacy, she had thought he'd lost his mind. Why, his face had been flashed across television for the last two days. There was no way he could go out in public.

When he came out of the bathroom wearing a blond wig, a mustache, brown contacts and a baseball cap, she'd been stunned silent. "I'm told blonds have more fun," he'd teased her. And then he'd grabbed her arm and hurried her to the car.

For the first half of the ride, she'd worried that Chase's rush to get to the pharmacy meant his shoulder hurt more than he'd let on, but then she'd seen the devilish glee in his newly brown eyes. And it hit her straight in her solar plexus; his eagerness to go to the pharmacy had nothing to do with his shoulder and everything to do with another body part.

*And next up to bat is . . . Chase Kelly.* The words echoed in her head as she made her way closer to the blond Chase. And as she neared, her palms grew sweaty. Needing a second, she stopped and feigned interest in a display of heating pads.

She believed him about Jessie. Chase Kelly really was a no-good scoundrel who would sleep with a woman about to remarry her ex-husband and then attend the wedding. He was all about sex, no commitment.

No involvement.

Just pleasure.

Casual sex, he'd called it.

And wasn't that how she'd told herself she needed to look at sex? Wasn't he the perfect guy to school her in no-strings-attached sex? Even if she was wrong, even if the worst happened and she started hearing the wedding march, Chase Kelly would never agree to it. Why, when all this mess with Zeke ended, Chase would leave and never look back. There were too many pretty waitresses with cute asses, and too many hot dishes like Jessie for Chase to waste time on a vanilla wafer.

She took a deep breath. She could do this. It was the twenty-first century. She was a modern, worldly woman, and worldly women had casual safe sex all the time. All she needed were some condoms and a willing partner. Chase seemed willing. So now all she needed were some condoms and enough courage to go through with it.

Gut instinct told her Chase intended to buy protection. But as a worldly woman, she insisted on buying them herself. Besides, if she invested some money in this project, she'd be less likely to abandon it.

Lacy glanced around the pharmacy to find where they might have hidden the condoms. Luck would have it that they would be right in front of the counter where Mr. Tien stood filling her grandmother's infected toe prescription.

Squaring her shoulders, she walked in that direction, got within two feet of them, and then lost her courage. Hesitating, she stared down at the row of over-the-counter drugs with fake interest.

"Looking for something, beautiful?" Chase's whisper tickled her ear. Or was it his fake mustache?

"Yeah, I need some . . ." Lacy glanced around the drug section in which she'd chosen to stand: It would have to be the hemorrhoid section.

She heard Chase chuckle behind her as if he knew her intentions.

"Can you think of anything else we might need?" Humor laced his voice. "Besides milk and Preparation H?"

She shoved her elbow back and caught him in his side. He moaned, and not playfully. Remembering his injuries, she swung around. "I'm sorry. I forgot."

He pressed a hand against his ribs. "I'm fine." He managed to smile, but she could see she'd really hurt him.

"Really, I forgot." She touched his side.

He leaned closer. His mustache tickled her upper lip, and then he kissed her. Not the kind of kiss that came with tongue and heat, but one of the soft, sweet kind that promised all the heat and tongue she could want later.

"I'm fine." He passed a finger over her lips. "So, what do you say? We need anything else?" He motioned to the condom counter a few feet away.

She glanced over at the display of bright-colored packages. "Oh. I was . . . I was going to pick some up." Now there. She'd sounded about as modern as a woman could get. Didn't she?

"I'll get them." His eyes sparkled and his grin widened.

"No, I can get them." She remembered the worldly-woman speech she'd given herself a few minutes ago.

"I have money," he said.

"So do I," she answered. "I'll get them."

"Do you know what size I wear?" His eyebrow arched, a teasing glint in his eyes.

She blinked, and her gaze traveled downward before she could stop it. "They . . . I mean . . ." She raised her face. "You're joking. Condoms don't come in sizes."

He looked surprised. "You haven't ever bought any, have you?"

She blushed again.

He laughed and leaned in so close his body heat warmed her through and through. "They really do come in sizes," he whispered. "And that's not all. They come with ticklers, in neon colors, and some even come in flavors." His lips brushed hers ever so lightly. "Strawberry." He breathed against her moist mouth. "Chocolate." He kissed her softly. "Vanilla."

With a deep intake of air she fought the heat climbing up her neck. "Well, if they come in sizes, then you'd take a large."

He grinned and wrapped a hand around her waist, sliding the tips of his fingers into the band of her jeans. "And I didn't think you'd noticed."

She shook her head. "I didn't. I just figure if they do come in sizes, what man would ever admit to wearing anything but a large?"

His laugh echoed in her ear as he pulled her to his chest and kissed her again. Then, with one hand draped around her waist, he slowly moved her toward the display. Lacy looked up and sighed in relief when she saw Mr. Tien was busy with another customer.

Chase reached over and chose a box. Lacy studied it as he pulled it off the rack.

"Wait." She touched his arm. "That has twelve." They didn't need twelve. "Don't they sell them in—"

"Don't worry." He reached out again and snatched another pack. "I'm buying two."

Chase offered to drive her blue Saturn on the way back, and she agreed; she didn't know if she could focus on the road with the number twenty-four echoing in her brain. Did Chase Kelly really expect to have sex with her twenty-four times?

Oh, Lordie! One time, okay, maybe two, and she might be able to escape the let's-get-married curse, but twenty-four times and she knew she'd have him hog-tied and stuffed in the back of her trunk taking him to Grooms-R-Us to be fitted for his tux.

She stared at her sandaled feet, concentrating on her painted red toenails. Chase drove a little fast, and from the way the car took the road, she knew he'd turned onto the dirt road that led to her house. He seemed eager to . . . to play a little baseball?

Twenty-four! The situation couldn't get any worse. But then he pulled into her drive and she heard him mumble a few choice words. She glanced at him briefly, feeling her pulse race at the sight of him. Desire and the need to finish what they had started earlier seemed to radiate from every beautiful inch of his body.

"Who do you know that drives a purple Cadillac?" he asked.

Lacy jerked her head up and realized she'd been wrong. The situation had not only gotten worse, it had just gone to Hell in a handbasket.

# EIGHTEEN

"No!" Lacy cried and leaned back against the seat.

"Who is it?" Chase asked, unable to hide his annoyance. They had condoms, damn it! Twenty-four of them, and he had already formed at least seventeen fantasies on how he hoped to use them. And he hadn't stopped at seventeen for lack of ideas; he figured he should leave a few scenarios open for Lacy.

"Let's leave," she snapped.

Chase threw the car in reverse, but he hadn't hit the gas when Lacy's front door jerked open and he heard a voice call out.

"Well?" he asked, and glanced at Lacy, praying she'd tell him to floor it and head straight to an available hotel.

"How do you feel about suicide?" Lacy mumbled.

Chase glanced to the house, and an older woman with dark hair, wearing a purple suit that matched the Cadillac, came strolling toward the car. Running his fingers over his fake moustache, he frowned.

"Your mother?" he asked, but already knew the answer. The resemblance between the two was strong.

"Prepare yourself," Lacy said. "This isn't going to be pretty."

The look on Lacy's face held more fear than it had when she'd gone to answer the door to Zeke. "How bad can it be?" He glanced back up to see the purple-suited woman hotfooting it across the yard toward the car.

"Have you ever had your fingers slammed in a car door?"

"Ouch!" he said and wiggled his hands.

"When this is over, that will sound like a cakewalk." She got out of the car. "Mom, what are you doing here?"

Chase stayed in his seat and watched Lacy open the back car door and grab the two bags of groceries she'd bought. Lacy's mother stood five feet from the car, but Chase could feel her brown eyes on him, sizing him up and probably finding him unsuitable. Wasn't that what mothers did—found all their daughters' boyfriends unsuitable? Cutting the engine, he stretched his fingers over the steering wheel, not really eager to have them slammed in the car door.

Shoulders squared, he got out and realized Lacy might accidently introduce him by his real name.

"Hello," he said before Lacy had a chance. "My name is . . . Jason Dodd." His ex-partner and best friend's name slipped out easily enough. "You must be Lacy's mother." He held out his hand.

"It's a pleasure to meet you, Jason," she said, and a smile flickered across her face as she took Chase's hand. "It's absolutely wonderful, in fact. My name is Karina Callahan, since my daughter doesn't seem inclined to introduce us."

Chase's apprehension faded. The woman didn't seem nearly as bad as he'd anticipated, or maybe they just hadn't gotten to the slamming-door stage. He glanced at Lacy, who had her arms filled with groceries.

"You've never been shy, Mama." Lacy juggled the bags and propped one on her hip as she adjusted her hold. "I figured you'd cover it." One bag started to slip.

"Oh." Chase pulled away from Lacy's mother and reached for the bag. Before he got to it, the sack tumbled and spilled onto the grass.

Chase knelt down. Lacy, still with one paper bag in her arms, dropped to her knees, and so did Mrs. Callahan. He reached for the dozen eggs, which no doubt were shattered, and that's when Chase spotted the two bright red boxes of rubbers that had fallen right beside the woman's purple pumps. Damn. The door-slamming stage had arrived.

Fighting the insane laughter that bubbled up in his chest, he swallowed. Then he cut his gaze to Lacy to see if she'd noticed. The look of sheer horror on her face nearly did him in.

"My, my," Mrs. Callahan said.

Chase reached for the boxes, in hopes that hiding them would make this easier for Lacy. Before he touched them, the woman had picked them up, making a show of tapping the boxes with her long, painted nails.

Lacy dropped her other bag on the grass and

flopped down on her bottom. "Don't say a word, Mom!"

Chase's gaze went from Lacy to Mrs. Callahan. The woman's brown eyes turned to him. He braced himself to hear a long lecture and remembered the time when he was sixteen and caught by another mother in a girl's bedroom. At least this time he had his clothes on and wouldn't have to endure the speech with only a pink Sleeping Beauty doll in his lap.

Mrs. Callahan cleared her throat, moistened her painted lips and . . . smiled.

Chase stared, thinking it had to be a sneer or a scowl. But nope, those lips definitely curved into a smile.

"I could just hug you," the woman said, and she reached over with her free hand and pinched his cheek.

It was Chase's turn to fall over. And he did, right off his haunches and back on his butt. Lacy moaned and crawled over the crushed eggs and snatched the condom packages from her mother.

"I said, don't say a word." She dropped the boxes into the other bag with the milk, ice cream, and vanilla wafers he had insisted be added to their purchases.

Mrs. Callahan continued to beam at him. Words still wouldn't form on his tongue. Had the woman just basically thanked him for wanting to have sex with her daughter?

"What am I going to say, dear?" Lacy's mother asked. The woman's eyes raked his body.

Chase shook his head. He'd had numerous moms give him the once-over, but *never* quite like that.

Why, the woman had mentally stripped him naked. Karina Callahan was unlike any mom he'd ever encountered. Unsure how to proceed, he simply smiled and started repacking the spilled groceries.

Mrs. Callahan stood, and Chase appreciated the woman's grace and beauty for an older lady. She had to be in her fifties, but she not only looked well-maintained, but most of it appeared to be by nature and not by the hand of some plastic surgeon. No too-tight cheekbones or Botoxed expressions. A few well-earned wrinkles spanned her eyes, but the woman had held on to her beauty well. Chase moved his gaze to Lacy and knew she'd probably age as gracefully.

"Jason," Mrs. Callahan said. "How did you two lovebirds meet?"

"Not now, Mom. My ice cream is melting." Lacy helped gather the rest of the items before she stood.

Chase grinned at her and she frowned, reminding him of their conversations about mothers and daughters. Something about this woman drove Lacy wacky. And now Chase felt he had a clue why.

"Do you live around here?" Lacy's mother asked.

"Right outside of Houston." Chase stood and tried not to moan when his sore ribs protested.

"Well, that's only a thirty-minute drive," she said.

"It's not bad, mostly country roads." Chase gathered the bags from Lacy's arms and took a few steps.

"How long have you known each other?"

"Mom!" Lacy snapped. "Please don't interrogate Jason."

"I'm not interrogating him. Why, I'm just mildly curious." The woman continued toward the door.

Chase took a few more steps and nearly tripped

over the sudden realization. In all his excitement to buy condoms, he had left without his gun. He'd been at the store before he'd realized his stupidity. When nothing went wrong, he'd decided to give himself a break and not beat himself up about it. But now he had to worry. He reached over and pulled Lacy close. "My gun," he growled at her.

Lacy's eyes widened. "Good idea. You shoot her and I'll help you bury her in my backyard." She started walking again.

"Lacy!" He pulled her back to his side. "I think I left my gun on the counter by the phone. If she sees it, she'll really pepper us with questions. Keep her busy in the living room while I hide the gun."

Lacy rolled her eyes and started moving again. Chase walked faster and beat both of them to the door.

Arriving in the kitchen, he hid the gun with the pots and pans. When he turned to put away the groceries, Mrs. Callahan stood in the doorway, her gaze on the counter where the gun had been. He grabbed the milk and headed to the fridge.

"You have to be quicker than that," she said. "I already spotted the gun. It scared me for a second, but when I saw the way she looked at you, well . . ." Her smile widened. "Lacy tells me you're a police officer." She stepped into the kitchen.

Chase looked up from putting the milk in the fridge, confused as to why Lacy had told her that much. "Yes, ma'am."

"Do you always carry a weapon?" She turned back to the counter where the gun had been.

"Mostly," Chase muttered, now understanding Lacy's reasons. He opened the pantry and tried to decide where to put the potatoes.

"She keeps the potatoes here." Mrs. Callahan opened another small pantry, and studied him with a knowing grin. "You haven't been dating long, have you?"

"Mom, would you like something to drink before you leave?" Lacy stormed into the kitchen.

"I'm fine, dear." She continued to eye Chase. "Did you know that cop they think got messed up in selling drugs and was killed by his own partner?"

"I could make you some tea," Lacy offered, trying to distract her. "Have you noticed how many teas there are?"

One glance at Karina Callahan and Chase knew she didn't distract easily. He reached for another bag. "Yes, ma'am. I did know him."

"Do you think he was dirty?"

"He didn't seem like the type to go bad." Chase dropped the bag and touched his face to make sure his mustache was in place.

"Have you heard from Grandmother?" Lacy moved to stand between him and her mother.

Mrs. Callahan smiled and clasped her hands together. "I almost forgot to tell you the wonderful news. Guess who is getting married?"

"You barely know him, Mother."

Mrs. Callahan flipped her wrist out at her daughter. "It's not me. It's your grandmother. She's marrying that Floyd man she met at her line-dancing club." The woman chuckled. "Mother said the man can do the Dirty Chicken dance like no man she's ever met."

"Mom, surely you're not going to let her go through with this?"

"Go through with what, dear?"

"She has no business getting married at her age," Lacy said.

"Why, Lace. I see nothing wrong with an older person finding bliss in marriage."

Chase's gaze moved from mother to daughter as they verbally sparred.

"Mom, how much bliss is she going to find at eighty?"

A smile lit the woman's eyes. Chase recalled Lacy saying that her mother always spoke before thinking, and he tried to prepare himself.

Her gaze found him. "I'll have you know sex only gets better with age. It's only a few of the more yoga-like positions that have to be rethought. Isn't that right, Jason? I'll bet your parents still bang a head-board against the wall occasionally."

Chase stared, but he wasn't able to form a word. All he could think was that Lacy was right earlier: This woman truly needed to get herself one of those "thingamabobs," the filter between one's thoughts and words.

"Please, Mom," Lacy snapped. "His parents have passed."

"Oh. I'm so sorry. Do you have siblings?" the woman asked, never missing a beat.

"Mom!" Lacy growled.

"A . . . sister," Chase answered, still trying to get the vision of his parents banging a headboard against the wall out of his mind.

"You two close?" Mrs. Callahan asked, unde-terred by her daughter's tone.

"That's it, Mom. No more questions. Come on, I think it's time you head on out."

Right then Fabio came barreling through the doggy door and into the kitchen with loud shrill barks. Mrs. Callahan moved a little closer to Lacy. "My favorite dog," she muttered, leaving no doubt as to her true feelings. She glanced up at Chase. "Have you ever seen such a mutt? The dog should be arrested for indecent exposure—he's *that* ugly."

"But he has personality." Chase grinned.

"Well, with looks like that, you'd sure hope so," Mrs. Callahan said.

"I'll walk you out, Mom." Lacy touched her arm.

Mrs. Callahan dropped into a kitchen chair. "I'm not leaving until I hear the charming story of how you two met. And I know it's going to be a doozy." She glanced at Chase. "You see, my daughter has lived like a nun for far too long. So I know you just about had to take her hostage to get her to pay any attention to you. So come on. Out with it."

Chase looked at Lacy and suppressed a chuckle. "Why don't you tell her," he suggested.

"Why don't you?" Lacy squinted her eyes at him.

"You're a much better storyteller," Chase said.

"That's not what you said this morning." She cocked her head and he remembered telling her she couldn't lie worth a damn.

"So he stayed here last night?" Lacy's mother asked.

Lacy frowned and glared at her mother. "Okay, here it is, Mom. Do you remember Hunky?"

"Who could forget Hunky? I'm still wondering if I couldn't fit into one of those FedEx envelopes." Mrs. Callahan grinned.

Lacy cut Chase a look that said he was going to regret not doing the storytelling. "Well, Ch . . . Jason and Hunky were special friends."

"Whoa!" Chase held up his hand, not liking the emphasis she'd given the word *special*. He looked at Mrs. Callahan. "We met through Sue, Lacy's friend. At a dinner party."

"And?" Mrs. Callahan asked.

"It was . . . magical." He looked at Lacy and found the next words easily enough. "She took my breath away."

"It was my singing fish that did that," Lacy interjected, a touch of humor in her voice.

Chase grinned and their gazes met and held. "We haven't been able to leave each other's side since."

"Maybe if you hadn't used handcuffs," Lacy teased again.

"Oh, this is good." Mrs. Callahan giggled. "Tell me more."

"I don't think I've ever met a woman so delightful," Chase said. "Or beautiful." He felt lost in Lacy's eyes. The room seemed to go silent, and warmth washed over him.

"Well, I can tell by the way you two are looking at each other, it's time I skedaddle." Mrs. Callahan pressed a kiss on Lacy's cheek. "Enjoy him," she whispered, just loud enough for Chase to hear. Then she stepped over to him and reached up on tiptoes to kiss his cheek. "Hurt her and I'll feed you into a meat grinder," she whispered for his ears only.

Chase raised his eyebrows. "I'll be careful."

Lacy stepped outside with her mother, fighting the strange mixture of fear and light fluttering in her stomach that had begun when Chase told her mom about meeting her. Had he meant what he said? Had she taken his breath away?

"So, how serious is this?" Lacy's mother asked as soon as they cleared the front door.

"It's not," Lacy insisted, and sighed with relief when she saw that Chase had parked to the side, leaving room for her mother to pull out.

"Oh, yes, it is." Her mother reached over and squeezed her elbow. "I know that look you gave him. Take my word. I hear wedding bells." She grinned. "We could always fly to Florida and make it a double wedding. Why, shoot, if you'll give me a few weeks, I might be able to talk Harold into taking the plunge. Imagine all three of us walking down the aisle!"

Lacy stared at her mother. "Great, then we could be in divorce court at the same time, too."

"Please," her mother said. "It's taboo to think of divorce when you're in love. And you're in love. I can see it on your face, young lady."

Pulling into the hospital parking lot, Zeke raked his nails over his neck. No doubt, the stress had brought on a case of hives. "Freaking A!" He had to do something.

He jerked out his cell phone and punched in Bruno's number. Dodd had left the precinct again, but Zeke didn't see his car. Where had that fool gone? God, he hoped he'd run to see Kelly. As much as Zeke had hoped Kelly had died already, right now, he would love to have the pleasure of shooting them both.

"Tell me you got Dodd in sight or I'll break both of your knees and you'll never dance again."

"You know, a hello would do," Bruno muttered.

"I'm freaking—"

"I'm tailing him now."

"Where are you?" Zeke unfastened the top button of his shirt.

"First he went to Kelly's condo again. Then it looked as if he was heading to the lake, but he turned left on the old highway. I don't have a clue where he's going, but I'm on him."

"He hasn't made you, has he?" Zeke asked.

"You kidding? I'm good at this. Nobody ever makes me."

"Stay on him and call me as soon he stops." Zeke shoved his phone back into his pocket and got out of his car. Maybe things were turning around. Maybe Dodd was on his way now to see Kelly. Maybe Zeke would step into the hospital and learn Stokes had died. Yeah. Things had to turn around.

Her mother had left but Lacy continued to stand with her arms wrapped around her middle, staring at the house where Chase waited with twenty-four condoms. She was a worldly, modern woman, but she was a scared worldly, modern woman. *Are you going to sleep with him or not?* The question grew louder with each step she took toward the house.

She walked through the front door and shut it. She moved into the living room. Her palms grew damp. Chase stepped out of the kitchen. He'd removed his disguise. The old Chase was back. Dark, seductive.

"You're right, she needs to get herself a thingamabob." He smiled and his green gaze raked over her, up and down. It was just a look, but it spoke of promises.

He promised her pleasure beyond pleasure, he promised to be tender, he promised to be rough. He promised to be slow and quick. Soft and hard.

The phone rang. Neither of them moved to answer it. They stood there separated by a space of less than five feet. Then Sue's voice came across the sound system.

"Where are you? Don't you remember we agreed to meet early this week? The fajitas are getting cold. I knew I should have called you earlier. You slept with Peter, didn't you?"

Lacy blinked and looked past him toward the kitchen. Oh, Lordie, she'd forgotten this was Friday. Forgotten she was supposed to meet Sue and Kathy. But now that she remembered, she knew without a doubt that she had to go. Well, she didn't have to go, but she would. Yup, this worldly, modern woman was running away. Running scared.

She grabbed her purse from the sofa and walked past Chase to snatch her keys from the counter beside the phone.

"I've got to go. I forgot, I have to . . ." She didn't explain any further and he didn't ask. The look in his eyes told her he knew better than to try to stop her. He frowned, folded his arms across his chest and watched her step out.

"Damn!" Chase let out a deep frustrated breath of air when he heard the door shut. The minute Lacy walked out, the phone started ringing again. "Uh, Chase. You around?" Jason's voice echoed through the house.

Chase darted for the phone. "Yeah," he answered.

"I went by your place again. There are no books there except regular books. I'm about a mile from the lake; I'm going to stop by. Be there in about ten minutes."

"I'll be here," Chase said into the receiver. "See ya." He dropped the phone and went to look out the window to see if Lacy had really left. She had. But damn, what was it with this woman?

# NINETEEN

Kathy's florist delivery truck, nicknamed the White Elephant, sat in front of her mobile home. Lacy got out of her car. Her heart hadn't slowed during the five-mile drive.

She'd turned around and headed back to her house four times. But each time when she got to the road leading to her house, she thought of her mother's words, *"I hear wedding bells."* Then she'd remember Peter and her shattered dreams. If that wasn't enough to put the car in reverse, a mental image of an old man doing the Dirty Chicken dance with her grandmother would fill her head. Did she want to wind up like her mother and grandmother, collecting divorces like they were stamps?

Taking the porch steps, Lacy walked through Kathy's front door without knocking. Sue and Kathy stood in the kitchen.

"It's about time." Kathy brushed her long mane of red hair off her shoulder. "You better have a very good reason for being late. I'm hungry and you know I get cranky when I'm hungry."

"I thought you get cranky when you're horny," Sue said.

"Hungry or horny. What's the difference?" Kathy laughed.

Lacy dropped her purse beside the door and walked over to the kitchen table, where she plopped down in a chair. Without understanding why, her vision became watery. Then her eyes started leaking. She swiped at the drops falling onto her cheeks. "Must be allergies." Lacy sniffed, trying to hold everything in, but the dam had burst and the tears continued.

Kathy and Sue studied her and then exchanged glances. "This doesn't look good." Kathy pointed a finger at Lacy.

"I think she slept with her ex-husband," Sue said.

They stared at each other, then back at her. "Is this a wine night?" Kathy asked. "Or should we go with something stronger, like Jack Daniels straight up?"

Lacy hiccupped. "Congratulations, Sue, on . . . the letter from the editor." She wiped her face again, fighting for control. "I'm happy . . . for you."

"Yup." Sue shook her head. "She screwed Peter again."

"I haven't screwed anyone." Hiccup. "I can't sleep with anyone." She drew in a shaky breath. In spite of being best friends with these two for the last eighteen months, she'd never confessed her big secret—the family curse. "I can't ever have sex again. Never! It's a curse. My grandmother had it. My mother has it. I have it." More tears flowed down her face. "No more home runs. Not even without going to bat. I'm just praying it's the bat that sets this whole thing off." Lacy dropped her forehead against the table and continued to hiccup.

"I'll get the Jack Daniels," Kathy said.

Lacy heard chairs being dragged across the floor, and she raised her head.

"Okay, first tell me about this curse." Kathy pushed over a box of Kleenex. "Then explain home runs to me." She poured whiskey into a small glass. "I think I got the bat reference." Kathy grinned, as if humor would help. "Maybe home runs, too."

Lacy pulled out a tissue and blew her nose. "It's like this: insert male organ and out goes my heart. Bat in. Heart out. I'm destined to fall in love with every man I sleep with. And then I *marry* them. Then they screw the secretary or the professor. And then I get a divorce or give back the ring." She picked up the glass and took a small sip. The whiskey burned her throat and she coughed.

Finally able to speak, she continued. "I can't do it. If I do, one day I'll wake up and I'll be just like them. I'll be competing against Liz Taylor for the Most-Divorced award." She curled her hand around the tissue. "Right now my grandmother is planning on marrying some guy who can dance the Dirty Chicken. My mother's marriage file is so thick she had to pay movers to get it to the lawyer's office when she went for her last divorce. She changes husbands more often than she does purses."

Kathy laughed.

Sue shook her head. "What's the Dirty Chicken? Is it that one where they . . ." She started flapping her arms. "Quack. Quack."

Kathy laughed harder and stared at Lacy. "Okay. You win this week's horniest award. I mean, after that story . . ."

"I don't want to win." Lacy blew her nose again. "I won last week."

Kathy shook her head and poured herself a whiskey. "Look. It's time we stop being angry, bitter divorcées and move on with our lives. It's not healthy. We need to let go of the hurt and become normal divorced sluts like the rest of the population. We've got to learn to use men like they use us."

"Didn't you listen to what I said?" Lacy asked. "I can't use them without dragging them to see a justice of the peace."

"Well, you just have to go after the guys who would never agree to marriage." Kathy's eyes sparkled. "The bad boys, the kind who would run from commitment. Like my plumber, Mr. Stan Bradley. Which is a great idea." She pointed to Lacy. "You sleep with him and I'll get my toilet fixed for free."

Lacy wiped her nose again. If she was going to take a chance on a bad boy, she already had one. "What if I try to change his mind? I mean my mother managed it five times."

"But you're not your mother," Sue said, and poured herself a drink. "None of us are our mothers. Why, look at my mom. She's a hypochondriac. She lives for her doctors' appointments. Just the . . ."

Lacy and Kathy's eyes met as Sue continued to chatter, and both of them had to fight hard not to laugh, because Sue was more like her mother than—The truth of it hit Lacy. What was it Chase had said? The apple didn't fall too far from the tree. Oh, Lordie! Was she really destined to be like her mom and grandma?

"I propose a toast," Kathy said and raised her glass. "To us. Not being our moms and forever being friends."

Three glasses met in the air, clinked, and then they all swallowed the burning whiskey in quick gulps. Next came serious coughing, followed by some serious laughter. Kathy put on a Sting CD, *Songs of Love*, and in a few minutes Lacy's desire to sob had lessened. Sting obviously knew how to take the sting out of heartbreak.

Pulling the food from the oven, they ate warm flour tortillas, chicken fajitas with guacamole and pico de gallo.

"Okay," Kathy said, picking up a tortilla. "Now for the discussion." Her eyes twinkled with a devilish glint. "Is it length or girth?" She rolled the tortilla long then folded it. "What's your take, Lacy?"

"Please," Lacy said. "Can't we table this topic?"

The topic got pushed back to talk about Sue's new sandals, which had only set her back forty bucks. They were still picking at the food when a knock at the door interrupted. Kathy got up to answer it. Lacy and Sue listened as a male voice came from the door. For a crazy second, Lacy's stomach knotted and she thought it could be Zeke. Her gaze zipped to Kathy: at least this time, she could do all the endless chatter.

"Sure." Kathy spoke to the visitor behind the door and stepped back.

Lacy's stomach clutched, but then a dark-haired man, early thirties, wearing jeans and light blue T-shirt, walked into the room. Definitely not Zeke.

The visitor grinned at Lacy and Sue, and his blue eyes crinkled with smile lines. "Ladies," he said.

"Didn't mean to intrude on girls' night." He walked past them and headed to the back of the trailer. Both Lacy and Sue watched him walk right into Kathy's bedroom.

Sue and Lacy stared at each other, then turned to Kathy. "Should we leave?" Lacy asked.

"You're taking the length and girth investigation to the hilt, aren't you?" Sue asked.

Kathy burst into giggles. "No. But that's the plumber. Here's your chance, Lacy—go work off my plumbing bill, would you?" More snickers erupted.

"That's the guy who wants to clean out your pipes?" Sue asked. "I wouldn't mind cleaning out his pipes."

"Shh!" Kathy wrinkled her lightly freckled nose and glanced back down her hall. "He is cute, isn't he?"

Lacy shook her head. "Why is he here now?"

Kathy grinned. "He said he forgot his screwdriver."

"Likely story," Sue said. "He just wanted to stop by on the off chance you might need something screwed."

Lacy chuckled. "Did you say his name was Bradley?"

"Yes, why?"

Lacy shook her head. She wasn't certain, but that seemed to be the name of the plumber who had called this afternoon and said her grandmother had hired him last year to come and check out the septic tank. "I'm not sure but—"

Footsteps down the hall interrupted Lacy's words. "Found it." His smile was all for Kathy. "Looks like you ladies had a feast with Mr. Daniels?"

"With whom?" Kathy asked.

"Daniels." He pointed to the bottle.

"Oh," Kathy said. "We don't really drink. Just sample."

He grinned. "Don't sample so much that you're sick. Well, I should be going. You've got my number. If you need anything . . . anything at all, call me." His gaze stayed on Kathy, and Lacy noticed the heat smoldering in his eyes when he gave her friend's curvy body the up-and-down. If a look could serve up hot love, Kathy had just been treated to a double helping.

Kathy nodded, her freckled nose turning red. "Yes. And you'll mail the invoice, correct?"

"I could just drop it off sometime." Hope filled his voice.

Kathy began folding and unfolding a napkin. "Just mail it."

Disappointment filled his eyes. "Okay." As he turned to leave he asked, "Oh, where's Tommy?" He swung back around and pulled out his wallet.

"At his father's."

He took a step forward. Kathy backed up until she bumped the table with her hip.

"Well, give this to him for me. I promised I'd pay him for helping me today." He handed Kathy a five-dollar bill.

"You don't have to do that," Kathy said.

"I know. But he's a cute kid. And I keep my word." He turned and left without saying good-bye.

Lacy and Sue both stared at Kathy. Sue spoke first. "He doesn't seem like the bad-boy type. He seems . . . sweet and sexy. And he thinks Tommy is cute."

Kathy sat back down and poured herself another "sample" of Jack Daniels. "Which is exactly why I'm staying away. I thought my ex-husband was sweet. Look what he turned out to be."

"Thought we were going to be normal divorced sluts." Sue dropped a hand around Kathy's shoulders.

Kathy frowned. "I'll start being a slut tomorrow."

"So, becoming a slut is like starting a diet. It's always going to start tomorrow." Sue chuckled. "In that case, tomorrow I'm going to call that Dodd cop back and let him interrogate me. Maybe do a strip search. Who are you calling, Lacy?"

Lacy knew that the Dodd cop Sue spoke of was Jason, the one who'd groped her last night. "No one." She had a bad boy waiting for her at the house. Lacy stared down at her hands. Part of her wanted to tell Kathy that she should throw caution to the wind and take a chance on the plumber. But who the heck was she to offer advice like that? Oh, jeepers! What was she going to do when she got back to her house? Her vision suddenly became watery again.

When Jason didn't show, Chase dialed his friend's cell phone. No answer. He waited another fifteen minutes and then called again. This time, Jason picked up.

"Dodd."

"It's me. I thought you said—"

"Can't talk now," Jason snapped. "I'll call later."

Jason didn't like his friend's tone, but then again, if something was wrong, Jason would have told him. At least he hoped like hell that was the case.

Feeling like a caged animal, he got up and paced. Needing to do something, he decided to cook.

A few hours later, Chase had made pasta with

chicken and wine sauce, and when Lacy didn't show up he stored it for the next day. Then he pulled out the vanilla wafer box and snacked beside the fire he'd started in the fireplace. He wondered how late Lacy would stay out. He wondered if he should have tried to stop her. He went to the hall closet and pulled out the bedding. After shooing the animals off, he tucked the sheet into the couch. When she did get home, he wanted her to know that sleeping with him was her choice. Never mind that they'd bought two boxes of condoms. If she wanted him to stay on the couch, that was where he'd stay.

As eager as he was to make love to her, only fools rushed in. Patience always won out. Eventually she'd give in. Or not. The "or not" burned in his gut.

Chase slumped down on the sofa. Fabio and the two cats joined him. He stroked the red tabby and started the video for the fourth time. He'd been looking at Lacy's movie selections when he'd stumbled across a tape that truly interested him. Written in black marker across the back was her name. Chase had stuck it in, hoping it was what he thought. He hadn't been disappointed.

Someone, probably Lacy's mother, had had all the old home movies transferred onto a video, and for the last three hours Chase had gotten glimpses of Lacy's past. The video started with a silent black and white tape of a three-day-old Lacy coming home from the hospital. There was one of her smearing baby food over her face. Following that segment was one of Lacy as a toddler carrying around another orange tabby. Chase laughed as Lacy's diaper slipped down around her ankles and she simply walked out of it and continued on with the limp feline in her arms.

Then the tape showed a young, teary-eyed Karina Callahan with a young Lacy in her arms, both of them dressed in black. When the camera turned to the casket with an American flag draped over it, Chase figured it was the funeral of Lacy's father. From there, several of the segments didn't make sense. They appeared to be at weddings, showing brief glimpses of Karina dressed to the nines, but Chase figured he must be wrong, because he'd counted up to as many as four of the events. Between some of the formal affairs, the video showed Lacy growing up. There was one of Lacy trying to ride a bike. She had fallen, and Chase's chest actually ached when the camera showed her holding her arm and walking away from the camera, her lower lip trembling. The next clip showed Lacy wearing an arm cast, and Chase's gut tightened.

Time moved forward, the tape continued, and the Lacy on the screen was in high school. He saw her all decked out in her royal blue prom dress. Damn, she had been beautiful even then. But Chase didn't care to see that the young man she was with seemed to think so too. The guy couldn't keep his eyes off the front of her dress. And neither could Chase.

By far, the most difficult segment to watch was of Lacy's wedding. She looked absolutely gorgeous in her white wedding gown. And the love in her eyes when she looked at that asshole Peter made Chase see red. When the movie ended, he pushed rewind.

Impatient, Chase pushed the orange cat from his lap. Standing, he hit pause. A smile crossed his lips when he realized he'd stopped the tape right when Lacy's diaper had dropped. Walking to the kitchen, he grabbed the phone and dialed Jason's cell number. This was the third time he'd tried to call.

"Hello?" Jason answered in a hurry.

"It's me," Chase said.

"I'll call you right back, Shelly!" The line went dead.

Chase got an ugly feeling in his stomach. He paced around the living room for ten minutes. The phone rang. Chase started to pick it up but realized he couldn't until he knew it was Jason. Lacy's phone had rung constantly. Between her mother and Eric, Chase had gotten an earful.

"Chase?" Jason's voice echoed over the sound system and Chase hit the button to answer.

"Yeah?" There was a pause. "What happened?" Chase insisted.

"It's Stokes," Jason said. "He took a turn for the worse. The doctor has been called in. Sounds like they may have to take him back into the operating room."

"Did Zeke get to him?" Chase curled his hand into a fist, thinking of Stokes's family.

"No. We've had someone here the whole time. I've told them not to let Zeke go in by himself." Another pause. "But there's something else. Zeke is on to us. He was suggesting to the captain that I could be involved."

"Christ!" Chase snapped. "What's the captain saying?"

"You know the captain. He's a straight shooter. He called me in and asked me right out."

"What did you tell him?" Chase asked.

"I told him I didn't think you were in on anything. Told him that if I were a betting man, I'd bet my left ball on Zeke being the one who's dirty. Then I lied and said I hadn't heard from you."

Chase closed his eyes and told Jason about Zeke showing up at Lacy's. "I'm sorry for pulling you into all this," he added. "Listen, watch your back. Zeke means business."

"I know. When this is over, you owe me a beer."

"Make that a six-pack," Chase agreed.

They continued talking. Jason told him he was looking into the old cases that Zeke had worked. Then Chase complained about hitting a mental brick wall when it came to Zeke's reasons.

"What do you think we should do next?" Chase ran a hand over his face. "Is it time I came in?"

In the back of his mind, Chase thought of the possibility of actually going down for something he didn't do. He thought about the possibility of being robbed of any real chance with Lacy. His gaze went back to the child on the screen, her bottom bare, her arms wrapped around a kitten, and his chest grew tight.

He'd always believed that love grew out of time and respect. He'd dated Sarah several months before he'd been hit with it this hard. Then again, his time with Lacy had been so intense. Could this really be love? For just a second, thoughts of Lacy and Sarah in the same brain cells sent a thread of guilt needling through his chest.

"Not yet," Jason said. "Give it a few more days. I'll either call or swing by to see you tomorrow. Gotta go."

Chase put the phone on the charger and walked back into the living room. He'd just sat down when he heard someone at the front door. The sound of the key being fit into the lock echoed in the silence, but with Lacy's fake-poop key holder, which was totally unsafe, he couldn't trust it would necessarily be her.

He held his breath. Fabio dove off the sofa, barking and growling his way to the entryway.

# TWENTY

"Hi, Fabio." Lacy knelt down to give her canine the customary greeting scratch behind the ears. Then she gave one more for good measure. In truth, she would have loved to sit down in the entryway and scratch Fabio behind his big ears until he was bald. Anything so she wouldn't have to face Chase.

She heard the grandfather clock chime ten times, and each swish of the clock's pendulum heightened her angst. Never in all her life had her feelings felt this complicated. Needs, desires and wants struggled with wisdom, reality, and logic. She stared at Fabio, then heard footsteps. *He* appeared in the doorway, tall and sexy. And irresistible. The perfect bad boy.

Fabio darted into the other room. Lacy remained kneeling in the middle of her terrazzo floor, staring up at Chase and feeling overwhelmed. Her calf muscles began to pinch, but she didn't move.

"Have a good night?" he asked.

She listened, thinking she'd hear resentment or

sarcasm in his tone, but none tightened his voice. "It was fine." The need to explain filled her throat. "We meet every Friday. If I hadn't gone, they would have shown up here."

"I don't doubt it." He walked over and extended his hand to help her up.

She looked at the outstretched palm, knowing that even the least physical contact could be dangerous. And wonderful. Oh, how she wanted the wonderful. Trembling, she placed her hand in his.

He pulled her up, lacing his fingers through hers, and moved toward the living room. His hip brushed against her as they walked. Suddenly she became aware of the smell of burning wood. He'd lit a fire in the fireplace. It draped the room in softly flickering shadows. Then other smells, the hearty scents of food, teased her senses.

"You cooked?" she asked.

"Chicken and pasta with wine sauce. I didn't know how long you were going to be gone."

"I ate. I'm sorry," she said. His hand fit so comfortably, pressed tightly against hers. So warm, so right. Oh, Lordie, what was she going to do? *Take a chance*, an internal voice seemed to scream.

"I've already packed it up. We can have it tomorrow."

Her gaze went to the television. Splashed on the sixty-inch screen was an image of her at eighteen months old, her diaper down around her ankles and Sunshine, her first cat, in her arms. She recognized the shot from the tape her mother had given her for Christmas a few years ago. "You . . . you watched my family movies?" she asked.

"You told me I could watch any of your tapes. I hope you don't mind."

A strange feeling came with knowing he'd witnessed parts of her life. "I don't mind. I just don't see why it interested you."

"You interest me. And that tape is about you." He placed his other hand on her shoulder and his gaze flickered to the screen behind her. His lips spread into a smile. "That shot is priceless."

She met his green eyes and in the corner of her gaze she caught the bedding on the sofa. Questions started to form. And with them came an emotion that resembled disappointment. Had he already lost interest in her and decided to sleep on the sofa? Was she such a vanilla wafer that he'd decided just a little more effort to seduce her wasn't worth it? The emotion couldn't be disappointment. She was relieved. And devastated! Okay, she was bitterly disappointed.

The old saying, *He made his bed, now he has to sleep in it,* echoed in her mind.

Chase's hand moved beneath her chin and he turned her to face him. "We have to talk."

She shook her head and took a step back. "No. It's late. Your bed is . . . I'm going to just—"

"No!" He reached for her, wrapping one arm around her waist. "I know what you're thinking, and you've never been so wrong about anything in your entire life." He moved her to the sofa, pushed her down and then settled beside her. The sofa sighed. The firelight flickered.

"You don't know what I'm thinking," she said. "I—"

He kissed her then, as if he meant it to be a quick

215

kiss to shut her up. But the quickness got lost somewhere between his hand moving to her neck and his tongue stroking her bottom lip. She leaned into him and noted a sweet flavor on his tongue. He pulled back, as if it took some effort.

"Lacy." His breath came out with her name. "I made up the couch because I didn't want you to feel pressured. You ran out of here this afternoon like a cat with its tail on fire. More than anything in this world, I want to take you into that bedroom and make love to you twenty-four different ways. But I can't be the only one wanting it."

This was it, she thought, the moment of decision. "I'm scared." The truth slipped out unintentionally.

"Why?" He ran a finger over her cheek.

"Reasons," she said, and noted the open box of vanilla wafers on the coffee table. He really did like vanilla wafers.

"Give me a chance to put those fears to bed. Let me love you." He dipped his head and pressed his mouth to hers again. His hand moved down to the edge of her cotton sweater and then under and up to touch her bare abdomen. "Tell me you want this."

Her breath caught. But breathing seemed unimportant right now. She wanted this. His hands on her naked skin, his lips on her body, everywhere. Him. She wanted him on top of her, inside of her. She just couldn't want him forever. But so what if she did? If she couldn't control the forever desire, it wouldn't be the end of the world, because Chase wasn't the marrying type; he played the field, offering pleasure but never commitment.

She pulled back enough to mouth her question: "You're a bad boy, right?"

\* \* \*

Chase heard the question. It wasn't Lacy's words that gave him pause, but the way she asked them.

"Do you want me to be a bad boy?" He brushed his lips over the corner of her mouth, tasting whiskey and Lacy. The combination was intoxicating.

"Yes," she answered, her voice wispy with desire.

"Then I'm bad through and through," he whispered. Slipping his hand around her back, he unhooked her bra. "I'll show you how bad."

He leaned her back on the sofa and pulled up her shirt. Pushing her bra away, he took the sweet flesh of her nipple into his mouth. Her hips rose off the sofa and he moved a hand between her legs to cup her through her jeans. Moving against him, she pulled at the bottom of his T-shirt, and ran her hands over his abdomen. Her soft fingers trailed up to his chest, taking his breath away, then she hesitated.

"Have you been taking the antibiotics?" she asked.

He drew back from her breasts, grinned, and looked at her face, the orange firelight casting a soft glow over her features. Damn, she was beautiful.

"Yes, Doctor." Sitting up, he removed his shirt, then he unsnapped his jeans and unzipped them so when it came time to remove them, it would be easy work.

She lay perfectly still, her sweater bunched around her shoulders. He reached down and pulled it over her head. Her bra came off too, and he feasted on the sight of her, naked from the waist up. Her nipples were puckered tight.

He rolled the peak of pink flesh between his thumb and forefinger and watched her face. She sucked on that bottom lip and he moved his free hand to the snap of her jeans. "I want you naked," he said.

Her zipper moved down easily enough. He stopped toying with her nipple long enough to push down her pants. She raised her hips and her jeans slipped down her thighs, exposing the white silk panties covering that soft patch of dark brown hair. When he got the jeans to her calves, she tried to kick loose her shoes.

"No," he said, stilling her legs with one hand. "I'm going to get to them." He lowered himself briefly to kiss her breast, then kissed his way down her abdomen. Lingering a second around her belly button, he dipped his tongue into that cute little dimple. She let out a whoosh of breath. "You like that, do you? What about here?"

Slowly, he trailed his hand downward, running a finger under the band of her panties. She hissed and her hips shifted upward. He edged himself down a bit, so that his tongue could follow the path his fingers had just taken.

"Oh, that feels . . ."

"Feels what, Lacy?" he asked. "Tell me what it feels like."

"Good," she said.

"Just good?" He lowered himself again, moving his tongue over the silk-covered center of her sex. "Just good?"

"Wonderful," she moaned.

"I need more than wonderful, Lacy. I need details. What does it do to you? Tell me."

"It . . . it . . . I can't think now. Just do it!"

He chuckled. "Impatient, aren't you?"

"Please." She shifted upward, pressing herself to his mouth.

"Tell me," he insisted, and ran his tongue over her again. "Tell me, Lacy, and I'll give you what you want."

"It makes me wet and ache to feel more. It makes me ready for you. For anything. Now, please. *Do* it."

"Much better words," he said, and pulled the silk back, rewarding her with two strokes of his tongue. She was already wet and ready, and her taste filled his mouth. She released a long breath. He scooted down and slipped her sandals from her feet. Raising one foot, he ran a finger over the arch. Then, lowering her leg, he slipped her jeans the rest of the way off.

She reached down and started pushing down her panties. Reaching out, he caught her hand. "No. That's my job. Your job is to enjoy and be patient."

"I can't be patient. I want you so bad I'm going crazy." She sat up and crawled into his lap, straddling him, and pressed her lips to his. He dropped back on the sofa and let himself enjoy.

As the kiss deepened, she snuggled closer to the ache between his legs. She shifted herself up and down, purring the whole time. Her hands moved over his chest, scraping her nails over his nipples. Then her touch lowered. She slipped her hand into his open pants and wrapped her hand around him.

His response was automatic; he rotated his hips. His hard shaft slipped inside her soft palm. "Sweet heaven," he hissed, and pulled her hand away. "You're gonna make me explode before I ever get my pants off. I haven't done that since I was fifteen." He pushed her back on the sofa.

"Take me now," she pleaded.

"Not yet, Lacy. The first time should never be fast." He stood and pushed his pants down. Her eyes lowered. When her gaze widened at the sight of his hardened sex, a sense of male satisfaction brought a smile to his lips. "Think it'll do, sweetheart?"

She raised her eyes and even in the flickering firelight he could see her cheeks tint. "I . . . think so."

"You're not sure?" he asked, loving to tease her.

"I'm . . . I'm just wondering if we shouldn't have gotten the extra-large condoms."

He laughed; then, leaning down, he scooped her into his arms.

"What are you doing?" She pressed a hand to his chest.

"Taking you to bed."

As he started down the hall, she briefly glanced back. "You don't want to do it on the sofa?"

"Not the first time," he said. "I want you flat on your back and spread wide. I want to be able to get to every lovely inch of you. We can christen the sofa later. Right after the kitchen table, maybe."

"The kitchen table," she echoed, her voice raspy.

"You got something against table sex?"

"No!" she squeaked, then shyly asked, "Can we do it on the floor and in the shower, too?"

"Anywhere you want." He laid her on the bed, whisking off her panties and letting them flutter to the floor. "I'm yours to please." The hall light gave him just enough illumination to enjoy the view, but just enough darkness for romance.

He started by kissing her again, then moved down her body with a slow progression. He tasted every inch of her, from the tips of her fingers to her navel again. When he got to the moist juncture between her legs, he decided to save the best part for last, and he bypassed it.

She protested with some serious whimpering. Her whines stopped when he entered her with a finger, his mouth moving down to caress her thighs.

He'd gotten only to her knee when she began to moan, pushing up and down, his finger slipping in and out. He pulled it out of her before she crossed the edge.

"No," she cried. "I was—"

"Not yet. I want to taste you when you come." He moved between her legs, which she spread wide for him. He'd barely gotten a good start when she screamed out his name and grasped the sheets in tight fists.

He pulled himself up to her side, curled his arms around her and held on as she trembled. Reaching to the bedside table where he'd tucked away one pack of condoms, he fumbled with the box until he had it open. "You ready for me now?"

"Yes, but I already—"

"Oh, you're going to come again. I'll see to it!" He pulled his arm from her so he could open the box and tear off a packet. Once he had the foil off, he started to put the condom on, then decided otherwise. He placed the rolled plastic into her hand. "Would you?"

She raised up and he saw a second of hesitation in her eyes. "I've never . . ."

He guided her hand down and helped her. When the job was done, she didn't pull away. Instead, she took him in her palm and held tight as if measuring him, feeling him. She saw him watching her and smiled through the touch of embarrassment.

He remembered. "Is it length or girth? Did you girls figure it out?"

Her eyes widened and her cheeks brightened. His breath hitched in his throat. "Damn, you're beautiful!" He kissed her. The words *I love you* lay on the tip of his tongue, but he bit them back. Instead, he moved over her. Fitting his thighs between her legs, he settled his hips against hers. He pressed another slow kiss to her lips. Her lower body rose to meet him. His shaft, hard and ready, found her moist opening. He pushed deeper, easy, slow, and he gritted his teeth as her tight sex welcomed him inside, wrapped around him with slick feminine muscle.

"Oh, this is good," she said breathlessly, jutting out her hips to take more of him.

Wanting to make it last, he tried to keep the pace slow, but Lacy seemed to have other ideas. He'd barely gotten all the way in when she pulled back and pushed in faster. She moved her hands around his back, lower, to cup his buttocks, her legs parted farther and she wrapped her soft thighs around his waist. He couldn't have stopped her any more than he could have stopped time. So he went with it, meeting her stride, push for pull, holding on by a sheer, thin thread, determined to hear her cry out before he crossed over his own edge of bliss.

Just when he'd almost lost it, he heard the sounds coming from deep in her throat. She moved her hands to his back and dug in her nails. Her sex started contracting, pulling him to his own climax, and the noise rising from his chest sounded more animal than human and surprised even him. And just when he thought the ecstasy of the moment had to end, it got even better. Exploding with pleasure, he continued to pump inside her.

Unable to breathe, he almost let go and dropped

on top of her, but then somehow he found the energy to roll over on his side, pulling her with him, refusing to leave her body. This was what making love was supposed to feel like. Damn, how he'd missed it.

He heard her soft intakes of breath. He pulled her closer, wrapped his arms tighter around her. Then her little gasps grew louder and the realization hit him like a bullet to the gut: Lacy Maguire wasn't just trying to catch her breath. She was crying—a deep serious type of crying that bordered on sobs.

# TWENTY-ONE

He pulled back to see her face. "Did . . . did I hurt you?"

She hiccuped through her sobs and shook her head no. But her inability to speak took his fear to a new level. He cupped her face in his hands and studied her eyes. "What's wrong, sweetheart?"

She didn't answer, just continued to cry. He brushed the tears away with the pads of his thumbs. "You're scaring me, Lacy. Tell me what's wrong."

She buried her head against his shoulder.

He wrapped his arms back around her. "I'm sorry," he whispered. "Whatever I did, I'm sorry." He gently rubbed his hand over her back and called himself a bastard.

Several minutes passed. Her shaking lessened and so did the sniffles. He pulled back, brushed his hand over her cheek and forced her to look at him. "You okay?"

She nodded.

"Did I do something wrong?"

"No," she said. "I . . . I don't know what happened. I just lost it."

"Then . . . that was a good cry? Happy tears?" he asked hesitantly.

"I guess so," she said, then hiccupped again.

He ran a hand through her hair. "This is going to take some getting used to. You scared me to death, woman."

"Sorry." She sniffled.

"No. Don't you dare apologize. I just thought . . . thought I'd done something wrong." He kissed her chin, moving up her face until he'd kissed away her tears. Then he pulled her tighter. "That, my lady, was the most amazing sex."

She grinned, even as her eyes still held the remnants of tears. "Really?"

"You don't think so?" he asked, suddenly insecure.

"Well, yeah, but I'm not as experienced in . . . in sex. I'm sure that with all the casual sex you've had, this was just—"

Her words caught him off guard. "Casual sex?"

"Isn't that what you called sex without involvement?"

He opened his mouth to inform her straight out that there had been nothing casual about what they'd shared. But damn, if something didn't tell him that Lacy would balk about it having been something more. But, why? All sorts of possibilities ran though his head; then the answer he'd come to earlier stuck against his heart like hot bubble gum on the bottom of a tennis shoe. *Peter.* Was that why she'd cried? Because of guilt, because she wanted him to be her ex?

Brushing her hair from her face, he told himself

that possession was nine-tenths of the law. And right now he possessed. Her body still hummed from the two climaxes he'd given her. Her lips were still moist and swollen from his kisses, and the taste of her sex still flavored his tongue.

He would make her see things differently. Lacy Maguire would have a change of heart. He wasn't about to give her up without a fight. And Chase Kelly could fight damn hard when he wanted something this bad.

She fell asleep against him. He studied Lacy, wishing he knew everything about her. Yet even as his body sang with pleasure, his heart ached for Stokes. To think, he'd been making love while his fellow officer lay on an operating table fighting for his life: guilt knocked at his mind like an unwanted visitor. But even as guilt sought companionship, Chase knew nothing he'd done or not done could have helped Stokes.

Taking a deep breath, he sent out a prayer that the man would pull through, that his boys wouldn't have to live their lives without a daddy. Even though he'd been seventeen, Chase had felt like a small boy when he'd lost his parents. No kid deserved to feel that. Then he remembered Angie, Stokes's wife, and the memory of losing Sarah crowded his mind. *God, let the man live.*

Zeke leaned back in the hospital chair and stared at the hospital's white ceiling, ignoring the way his skin itched. A group of officers and detectives filled the waiting room, but no one talked. Silence hung in the room like death. Zeke hoped it was death. He prayed it was death. Perhaps he'd go to Hell for praying for bad things, but he'd worry about that after he got out of this Hell on earth.

In the corner sat Stokes's wife, silently crying, surrounded by her family. Zeke tried not to look at them, afraid they would look back, afraid of what they would see in his gaze. He no longer cared that they hurt. He just prayed that Stokes died. If the man died, it would be one less thing Zeke had to take care of to make sure he got out of this crap. And he had to get out. He deserved that gold watch, just as much as he deserved the two hundred thousand waiting for him in a Swiss bank account.

He hadn't planned on doing this. He and his old partner had been on a bust, and while the two other cops took after the runner, he and James had gone inside. Hundred-dollar bills littered the room, and James had looked at him and they both knew what the other was thinking. Before the other cops arrived, they'd had most of the money well hidden.

After that, taking got easier, and they took the bankrolls from dealers that they arrested. Then his old partner turned him on to several other ways to clear some nontaxable income. Some of the bigger dealers would pay big to have a few guarantees. Zeke had gotten good at looking the other way.

It was during one of those payoffs that Martinez had caught sight of him slipping a quick stack of bills into his pocket for letting some of the evidence of an overdose victim fall to the wayside. She'd just been a whore. As a matter of fact, Zeke had screwed her a time or two himself.

\* \* \*

Fighting the intrusion of wakefulness, Lacy rolled over, her body extremely tender in places that hadn't been tender in a very long time. It took her only a fraction of a second to understand the twinges of discomfort. Oh, goodness, they'd had sex three times during the night. And she'd hit six home runs! Four of them in the bed, one on the sofa, and one on the floor.

She opened one eye, trying to get her bearings, attempting to see if she was alone in bed or if Chase still rested beside her. She hadn't gotten her eye open all the way when wonderful smells assaulted her senses and she knew Chase was cooking breakfast. She could get used to this.

*No, you can't!* a voice called from her good-girl conscience.

Samantha moved closer, and Lacy sat up and stroked the cat. The feline looked up at her. Lacy could just imagine that, if the cat could talk, she would probably be giving her a good talking-to about trusting strangers.

"Don't worry," she told Samantha, brushing her hand over the cat's arched body. "This is only temporary. In a few days he'll be . . . gone." Her heart seized up. "It's only casual sex." She closed her eyes, remembering; it had been so amazing that she'd fallen apart. And then, unable to help herself, she'd tossed out those words *casual sex*, half trying to test her emotional strength after making love and half hoping he'd tell her she'd misunderstood.

He hadn't. And that was what she wanted. Right?

In spite of the fact that her heart felt like it had a snag in it, as if it had a little loose thread that could lead to a full emotional unraveling, she had managed to survive. She hadn't begged him to marry her; she hadn't started deciding on the type of cake she'd have at the reception or envisioning what their children would look like.

So what if after all three times that they'd made love, she'd lost control of her emotions and wept like a baby. Chase had begun to believe it was natural for her. Then again, maybe it was. Maybe this was just how she reacted to multiple orgasms. But what was important was that she'd survived. Not to mention she'd had sex unlike she'd ever had before.

"And I'll continue to survive," she told the cat. "I'm a worldly, modern woman. One who just so happens to fancy white cake with cherry filling at her wedding receptions.

"No!" She pressed a hand over her mouth and sent that thought backpacking into the black hole of her subconscious mind.

Shaking her head, she crawled out of bed and went to her bathroom, where she pulled her short, blue terry cloth robe from the hook behind the door. She went to the mirror, squared her shoulders and studied her reflection. "You look fine. You feel fine. Well, the tush area is a little sore, but you had sex three times. Really good sex."

"We could make it four." Chase's voice boomed behind her. "If the . . . tush area isn't too sore."

# TWENTY-TWO

Lacy swung around and felt her face flush at the sight of Chase standing at the bathroom doorway, wearing only his jeans and a proud smile. He reminded her of a model in a jean commercial, a bare-chested man looking too sexy in his jeans and knowing it.

He stepped closer and started to kiss her, but she pulled back and cupped her hand over her mouth. "Morning breath," she mumbled.

He kissed her forehead. "After all we did last night, I'd thought we were past the fear-of-morning-breath stage."

The heat in her face grew more intense and he chuckled. "Brush your teeth and I'll trade you a kiss for breakfast."

She nodded, and he disappeared out the door.

Chase stepped into the kitchen just as the phone rang. He'd tried Jason four times this morning, praying to hear good news about Stokes. His fingers itched to pick up the phone, but he held his breath and waited to hear the machine.

"Chase?" Jason's voice filled the room.

Chase snatched up the phone. "Tell me some good news."

"He pulled through," Jason said, a lightness in his voice that sounded like relief. "He's still not completely out of danger yet, but he's a fighter."

"Yes!" Chase raised a fist in the air. "That's great news. Now you keep him alive. Don't let Zeke get close."

"I'm not. Oh, I'll catch you later."

The phone clicked off. The abruptness told Chase that someone must have walked up, but the important message had been given—Stokes had pulled through.

Chase took a deep gulp of morning air. A few flashbacks from the previous night tiptoed through his mind. He smiled, as appreciation for simply being alive struck him. It was a damn good day.


When Lacy walked into the kitchen, Chase looked extra cheery. He kissed her and, with his mouth melted against hers and his hands on her hips, two-stepped her across the room.

"Hungry?" he asked when they finally came up for air. "I hope you like omelettes."

She nodded. His hand moved up and down her back as he guided her to the table where a hot cup of coffee waited, figure eights of steam rising from the top. As she dropped into a chair, feeling all tingly, he went to the stove. The phone rang again.

"Your mom called last night." He lifted a lid off a skillet and grabbed a spatula from her silverware drawer.

"You didn't talk to her, did you?" she asked, noting how comfortably the man moved in her kitchen. How comfortable it felt for him to be here. He fit into her life like a soft nightgown fit against her body on a cool night. Perfectly. He even liked her animals.

"I didn't answer." He glanced up after placing a beautiful half-moon-shaped omelette on the plate. "But she left a very long message." Chase grinned. "You know, she's a strange one. But she's not really that hard to take."

"You haven't gotten to know her yet." Lacy sipped her coffee.

Chase picked up another skillet and scooped what looked like fried potatoes onto her plate. Then he raised his gaze. Concern filled his eyes. "How bad was she?"

Lacy heard his question and the implication in his voice. "She didn't abuse me. It's not like that. She loved me. It's just . . ." She stopped talking when the voice on the line came over the loudspeaker.

"Hi, Lacy? It's Eric. Your favorite vet. Well, since you didn't call me back, I'm assuming you were out all yesterday. But how about tonight?"

Chase frowned and pointed the spatula toward the phone. "That guy is getting on my nerves!" Fabio barked right then, and Chase looked at the dog. "Fabio doesn't like him, either. He confided in me last night."

Lacy grinned. "Yeah, but that's because the man neuters dogs for a living." Joy swelled in her chest. Chase Kelly was jealous! Surely that meant something, didn't it? He placed a plate in front of her, twisted it around as if presentation mattered, then kissed her neck before returning to the stove to fix his own plate.

They ate, talked and laughed. Chase told her more about his sister, and about his new nephew he hoped to visit soon. As he talked, he rubbed his foot against her bare calf. Lacy couldn't ever remember being so happy. The phone rang again. This time it was Mr. Bradley, the plumber, informing her that he would be there a few minutes late. She noted that the voice sounded like the same man from last night. Lacy stared at her plate and remembered Kathy and Kathy's resistance to follow her heart.

She took another bite, and Chase's foot moved up to her thigh. When she glanced up, she wondered if Chase felt any of the things she felt—the rightness, the warm wiggles in the stomach. Why, he'd told her the sex was great. And now he was jealous. And he'd cooked for her! A man didn't cook for a woman when it was just casual sex, did he? The words she'd read yesterday echoed in her mind. *Cooked dinner and had sex with Jessie.*

Oh, Lordie. She glanced down at the omelette, her appetite gone, and the snag in her heart started slowly to unravel. She was nothing but another Jessie to him. Biting her lip, she pulled her leg away from his foot.

"What is it?" he asked, drawing her attention as he bit into his toast.

The butter from the bread made his lips glossy. A few crumbs clung to the corner of his mouth. She watched as his tongue slipped out to remove the gloss and crumbs.

"Nothing. I'm just full." She sat up straighter,

adding some starch to her backbone. She couldn't allow herself to care; Chase was just—

"You've barely touched your food."

"I ate more than half." She patted her stomach. "Wouldn't want to get fat. Then no one would want to have casual sex with me anymore." Rising, she walked to the kitchen sink, but she felt him staring, and the starch in her backbone became mush.

"This is about Peter, isn't it?" He came up behind her and placed one hand on each of her shoulders.

Make that very weak mush! "What's about Peter?" Lacy turned and stared up at him.

"This," Chase said. "You're pulling back. And earlier, you being afraid to sleep with me. Then the crying afterwards. It's about him, isn't it? You still love him."

"What? I mean, why . . ." Oh, she got the gist of his question, but how had he arrived at the assumption that she still loved Peter? "I haven't seen him in over a year."

"He cheated on you, didn't he?"

She blinked. "Yeah, he did. He banged his secretary in the elevator, and I probably wouldn't have known if some freak hadn't gotten hold of the elevator video and splashed it over the Internet." She didn't understand what had provoked her to spill that poison, but now that she had, she really didn't regret it.

Chase held up his hands as if frustrated. "Then let the bastard go. Forget him. He's not worth one moment of your thoughts. Not one!"

She pulled away and started running dishwater, but she couldn't stop herself from asking, "Is that what you told Jessie about her ex-husband—to just let him go?"

He took her by the shoulders and turned her toward him. "What does Jessie have to do with this?"

"Nothing," she said, and turned back around. "Just like Peter. He's not important."

"Fine," he snapped, and went to clean the table. They washed dishes without speaking. The silence grew awkward, but slowly it grew less heavy and just felt like silence. When she put the last plate away, Chase wrapped his arms around her waist and buried his face in her hair. "I'm sorry I mentioned Peter, okay? Forget I said anything. It's just . . . Damn! It's nothing."

Turning, she pillowed her head on his chest and listened to the beating of his heart. She probably had just a few days with him, and she didn't want to spend the time arguing. When he left—and he would leave unless she gave in to the idea of handcuffing him to the bed—she'd be picking up the shreds of her heart for a long time. Now, however, wasn't the time to think about that. She looked up. "Thanks for breakfast."

He kissed her. "How about I run us some water in that Jacuzzi of yours?" He smiled. "I hear it's good for sore tushes."

The soak indeed helped the soreness. They sat across from each other, their legs brushing up against one another.

"Come here, let me wash your back," he said, but the look in his eyes said something altogether different.

Lacy twirled in the water, ready for everything he

offered. A soft sigh left her throat when he soaped up a washcloth and glided it between her shoulders. Then the cloth disappeared and his soapy palms moved over her back, up and down, then around to cup her breasts. With a slippery touch, he gently rolled her tightened nipples between his thumbs and index fingers.

She felt his erection against her lower back; the place between her thighs began to pulse and beg to be touched.

"Do you think you're too sore to—"

The doorbell rang, interrupting his question. Lacy, jarred from want, jumped up so fast she nearly fell.

Realizing it could be Zeke—or maybe Sue, who would simply walk in—Lacy skidded wet-footed across her tiled bathroom floor. Snatching her robe up from where it lay, she poked her arms inside with lightning speed, tied the sash around her waist, and ran to the bedroom to peek out the window. "Jeepers!"

"Who is it?" Chase followed her into the bedroom, naked, droplets of water rolling down his body. His voice came out firm and concerned, but the evidence of what they'd been doing in the Jacuzzi was hard to miss. Real hard.

"The plumber." She straightened her robe, put her hand over her pounding heart, and took one, two deep breaths. Then, squaring her shoulders, she started out the door. "I'll tell him where the septic tank is."

She heard Chase call to her as she stepped out of the bedroom, but the doorbell rang again so Lacy decided to take care of one thing at time. Pulling at her collar to make sure nothing was exposed, she unlocked the bolt.

"Hello." She poked her head out the door.

Mr. Blue-eyed, lost-my-screwdriver-Bradley looked up from his clipboard. His brow crinkled. "Aren't you—"

"Kathy's friend." She smiled. "I thought your name sounded familiar. Do you know where the septic tank is?"

"Yes." He hesitated, as if he had something else to say. "Listen, about Kathy . . . Is she . . . available?"

Lacy didn't know how to answer. "Yes, she's single—but she's not really open to dating right now."

"How 'not open' is she?" he asked.

Lacy nudged the door wider and leaned against the jamb. "I couldn't say." She wished she could offer him hope, but she honestly didn't know how adamant was her friend's stand on the "no men" rule. A few days ago, she would have insisted she herself would never fall prey to a man's charms, and look at her now.

"Should I give it up as a bad idea or keep trying?"

Lacy considered her answer, then said, "No one likes a quitter."

Bradley smiled and tapped his pencil on his clipboard. "I'm going to pull around back. I'm just going to look. I'll come back later to clean it out. I'll knock and give you an invoice before I leave. By the way"—his eyes lowered and he smiled—"did you know you've got your robe on inside out?" He turned and walked away.

She looked down at her robe, then backed up. "Oh—how long do you think you'll be?" she called.

He didn't hear her and kept walking. Closing the door, Lacy ran into the kitchen to get a soda, then started back to the bedroom. The doorbell rang again. He's probably lost his screwdriver, she thought, and chuckled. Still smiling, she opened the door. Her smile dropped like lead and her breath hitched. It wasn't the plumber.

# TWENTY-THREE

"Peter?" The soda can slipped from her fingers, fell and started spewing all over the entryway.

"Hi, babe," he said, looking down at the soda can, which was spinning in circles. "Can I come in?"

Lacy stared down at the mess pouring over her tile, but her thoughts went to Chase in the bedroom. "Uhh."

Peter pushed his way inside and shut the door. "Shouldn't you get something to wipe that up?" He pointed to the floor.

She turned around and went to the kitchen, grabbed a roll of paper towels and then went back to the hall and threw a handful on the floor. "What do you want?" she asked, setting the roll of towels on the antique sewing machine beside her purse.

Her ex crossed his arms over his chest and stared at her. "Do you know you have your robe on inside out?"

*Oh, yeah, I was just making love when the doorbell rang.* She would give her eyeteeth right now if she could tell

Peter the truth. But with Chase in hiding, she wouldn't risk it. "Yes. I know. What do you want?"

He smiled. "Can't an ex-husband stop by for a visit?" He reached out and touched her damp hair. "Did I catch you in the shower?"

"No, I wasn't showering, and no you can't stop by for a visit." She pulled away.

The doorbell rang again. Thinking of the plumber, she snatched open her purse and grabbed her checkbook and a pen. As soon as she got rid of Mr. Screwdriver, she planned to send Peter packing. She opened the door and asked, "How much do I owe you?" She looked up from her checkbook.

It wasn't the plumber. Blond, with dark blue eyes, and built like a football player, Jason Dodd had the market on good looks. Not that he interested her; she preferred dark hair, less bulk and . . . Face it, she preferred Chase.

"A hundred thousand would buy me a Porsche," Dodd said, and his blue eyes crinkled with humor.

"Put it on your Christmas list," she teased back. "Oh. Come on in. But be careful. I just spilled some soda." She swung the door open and Jason stepped inside. She dropped her checkbook back into her purse.

Jason stopped in the middle of her entryway when he spotted Peter leaning against the wall. Lacy looked at one man and then the other, unsure how to proceed. The awkward silence forced words from her mouth.

She waved a hand between them. "Jason . . . Peter. Peter . . . Jason." Fixing her gaze on her ex, she stiffened. "Now, what was I about to tell you? Oh, yeah, it's time for you to go, Peter." She pointed to the door.

The stunned look on her ex-husband's face

brought a smile to her lips. He thought . . . he thought Jason was her lover. *Think what you want, you secretary-screwing lugworm.* This was one misunderstanding she wasn't about to correct. She even helped the misunderstanding along by shifting closer to the blond cop and offering him a flirty smile.

Jason took one glance at Peter's expression, and he held up his hand as if he seemed to understand some of the undercurrents of what was happening. "I'll wait right in here," he said, and stepped into the living room.

As he moved out of the entryway, the doorbell rang again. Lacy grabbed her checkbook and swung it open.

"Surprise?" Sue said, and pushed her way inside with Kathy on her heels. "We were out garage-sale shopping and decided to stop by for a pee break and to see if you wanted to go with us. We found the cutest bedroom suite—not that either of us needs one." Sue's mouth moved a mile a minute. "Saw the cars. You got company?" She stopped jabbering long enough to look around. Her eyes widened.

"Who's this?" Sue glanced to Peter and back. Then her friend's gaze moved up and down Lacy's body. "Did you know you've got your robe on inside out?" Then Sue's focus swung back to Peter. "Are you going to introduce us?"

Lacy looked at her ex-husband, and she realized what they would think. But now didn't seem like a good time to explain. "Sue, Kathy, this is Peter."

"I told you she slept with him," Sue said, glaring at Peter and then looking at Kathy. "I knew it. All those tears. I knew something was happening." She pivoted on her heels and gave Peter a scowl. "I just hope he didn't pull out before the job was done this time. Early withdrawals come with penalties."

"Maybe he's gotten on the little pill," Kathy said, with the same venom in her voice. Lacy's heart swelled with love. Only really good friends would rake an ex over the coals for you.

Peter's mouth dropped open as if he'd been slapped. Lacy nearly choked on her laughter; then the doorbell rang again. "What is this? Grand Central?" she muttered.

She swung open the door, and there stood the plumber, but he wasn't alone. Standing behind him was . . . oh, God!

"Mama?" Lacy squeaked. "What are you doing here?"

"What's my plumber doing here?" Kathy asked. The question brought Lacy's gaze back to her friend, and she stared at Kathy's wide-eyed expression. Peter cleared his throat and stared daggers at Sue.

"Uhh." Lacy's mind whirled.

Kathy pointed at the plumber and frowned at Lacy. "Did you get my discount?" she asked, a touch of jealousy in her voice.

Lacy shook her head. "No."

"What discount?" Mr. Bradley asked, his smile and all his attention directed toward Kathy. "What a surprise to—"

"For Pete's sake!" Lacy's mother shrilled as her brown eyes flitted to Peter. "What in Hell's highway is *he* doing here?"

Lacy turned back to Peter. With five people in the entryway and soda-soaked paper towels on the floor, she barely had room to turn.

"She slept with him," Sue accused, glaring at Peter

again. "I can't believe she slept with him. I think . . ." Sue's chatter continued, bouncing around the crowded space, causing Lacy's head to hurt.

"I did not sleep with Peter," Lacy snapped.

"Did you sleep with my plumber?" Kathy asked, over Sue's constant ranting.

"With me?" asked Mr. Bradley, clearly shocked. His voice sounded hoarse.

"You're sleeping with him, too?" Her mother's high-pitched voice seemed to echo in the hall.

"So you *are* sleeping with him?" Kathy asked.

Lacy's mouth opened, but she couldn't think any more, couldn't speak. Sue, God love her, was giving Peter the lowlife speech, Kathy kept asking about her relationship with the plumber, and her mother kept going on about Peter and the secretary on film in the elevator.

"Please tell me you didn't sleep with Peter, too." Her mother's voice rose above the chorus.

"At least I was married to her," Peter shot back, his voice rumbling with anger. "And hello to you too, Mrs. Callahan."

"Don't hello me, you . . . you elevator freak. How dare you show your ass to half of America and screw your secretary when you're married to my daughter!"

Lacy's mother pushed past the plumber and stopped right in front of Lacy. "Did you know you have your robe on inside out?"

"Yes. I know," Lacy said, trying hard not to scream.

"I'm not sleeping with her," the plumber told Kathy.

Sue started chattering about Heaven-only-knew-what, and Lacy had the urge to clap her hands over her ears. "Silence!" she yelled. Everyone complied but her mother.

Her mother's words rang out loud and clear. "I thought you were sleeping with Jason Dodd."

"With whom?" a voice boomed from the living room.

"With Jason Dodd," her mother repeated, turning to look at the man moving into the hall from the living room. "Who are *you*?"

"Oh my God!" Sue grabbed Lacy's elbow. "Why didn't you tell me you were sleeping with him? I mean, at least you could have *told* me." Now Sue's voice held jealousy, and Lacy wanted to fall to the soda-soaked, soggy paper-towel-laden floor and have a good cry.

"She's sleeping with whom?" Jason Dodd repeated, then his gaze shifted to Sue and he smiled. "Hi. We met—"

"Well, I didn't actually see them doing it," Lacy's mother continued, her glare superglued to Peter. "Unlike some people, they didn't do it in front of a video camera. But they did have two boxes of condoms. And I'll bet she enjoyed every one of them."

"Stop it!" Lacy snapped. "Stop this right now." When she had everyone's attention, she turned a complete circle, wet paper towels squishing under her bare feet. "Just for the record, I know I have my robe on inside out and there is not one guy in this room with whom I've slept in the last year."

"I didn't sleep with her last year either," the plumber told Kathy.

And then the chatter began all over again.

"Stop!" Lacy called out. She turned to the one person she wanted gone first: "Peter. Get out of my life."

As Peter moved for the door, Lacy turned to the plumber. "Mail me the invoice. Good-bye." She waved him to the door.

The plumber glanced back at Kathy and said, "I'll call you." Then he followed Peter.

Lacy swung around to face her mother. "It was nice to see you, Mom. Now leave."

Her mother huffed rather loudly. "Call me tonight," she said, and peevishly added, "We need to talk about you seeing Peter." Then she tossed her purple shawl over her shoulder and left.

Lacy took a deep breath and faced Sue and Kathy. "Let me make this clear: I haven't had sex with anyone that either of you has remotely thought about having sex with. Now, go pee if you must, then go, and I'll call you later."

Sue and Kathy skipped the potty break and started for the door. Wiping her sweaty palms on her inside-out robe, Lacy turned to Jason Dodd. He watched Sue and Kathy walk out, his gaze mostly on Sue.

When the door shut, he faced Lacy and grinned. "Two boxes of condoms, huh? I bet I was good."

The sound of Jason calling his name brought Chase scrambling to unlock the bedroom door.

"Hey." Chase stepped back. Jason, a smile widening his face, walked into the bedroom. "Did you hear any of that?" He glanced around, focusing on the unmade bed.

"Some," Chase replied, feeling his frustration peak at having to stay hidden behind closed doors like a wanted criminal. Especially when there were men outside hovering around the woman to whom he'd been about to make love. "Sounded like there was a party going on. What's that guy, Peter, look like?"

"A dweeb." Jason grinned. "But if you really want to see for yourself, we could probably find his ass and other parts of him on the Internet. Or at least that's what his ex-mother-in-law seemed to indicate." Jason pressed his hand over his abdomen and laughed. "That was comedy at its best."

"I thought I heard Lacy's mother's voice." Chase leaned a hand against the wall, unable to appreciate the humor right now. "Who else was there?" he asked, ignoring his friend's hysterics.

"A plumber. Who was accused of sleeping with Lacy." Jason glanced at the unmade bed. "Then again, it looks as if—"

"The plumber?" Chase pushed a palm over his face. "First there's a FedEx man, a vet, her asshole of an ex-husband, and now a plumber?" Chase felt confident Lacy wasn't sleeping with the plumber, or with any of those men, but just how long was the want-to-sleep-with-Lacy line? "It's insane. Freaking nuts."

Jason held up his hand. "Hey. It's me she's cheating on. And after I invested in two boxes of condoms, no less!"

"I heard that part." Chase walked back across the room and this time couldn't help but smile. "I borrowed your name."

Jason laughed. "So my name had a little fun, huh?" At Chase's frown, Jason continued. "Well, I don't really think she's sleeping with the plumber. And she swore she hasn't slept with Peter in over a year. I think the plumber has a thing for the redhead. Not that I blame him. Both her and that Sue woman are fine specimens."

"They still here?" Chase asked, knowing Lacy was probably dying from embarrassment.

"No," Jason answered.

Chase went to the front window to see if all the cars were gone. They were; all except one. "Are you driving the station wagon?"

Jason nodded. "What? I don't look like a station wagon type?"

Wanting to see Lacy, Chase turned and walked out of the bedroom. Lacy stepped into the front hall at the same time. He met her halfway and tilted her chin up to see her face. "You okay?" Her cheeks were bright red.

"It was a three-ring circus. Like something that would happen on a sitcom," she answered. "It was terrible, awful, it was—"

"It's all right." He pulled her close.

"No, it's not all right. My mom thinks I'm sleeping with four different men." She dropped her forehead onto his chest, took a deep breath and then glanced up. "Which probably wouldn't bother her if one of them wasn't my ex-husband. She was part of the free love thing in the sixties, but has a definite rule about *not* sleeping with your ex-husbands. Both my girlfriends think I'm having sex with the men they wish they could sleep with if they weren't so scared to let a man get close. My plumber now thinks I offer myself to get discounts. Everybody thinks I had sex twenty-four times with . . . him." She pointed to Jason, who was stepping into the hall. "And during this whole episode, I'm wearing my robe inside out."

Chase bit back his laugh. "I tried to tell you about that." Leaning down, he kissed her cheek.

Jason cleared his throat. "Before you two get started on number twenty-five, I need a few minutes."

Lacy blushed even brighter and, pulling out of the circle of Chase's arms, started toward her bedroom without looking at Jason.

"Lacy?" Jason called as if in afterthought.

She turned around and met his smile.

"When you referred to the men your friends wanted to have sex with, I wouldn't happen to have been one of them, would I? Because if I can help one of them out, well—"

"Shoot him, would you?" Lacy said to Chase.

Chase grinned and watched her go. When he turned back, Jason was studying him with a sappy smile plastered on his face. "What?" he asked.

Jason clapped a hand on his back. "I haven't seen you look at a woman like that since . . . in a long time." He sighed. "Too bad she and I are already an item."

"Funny," Chase snapped. "What is it you need to talk to me about?" Then a dire possibility hit. "Is Stokes okay?"

The smile vanished from his friend's face. "He's hanging on, but it's touch-and-go. He stopped breathing last night."

Chase walked into the living room and dropped down onto the sofa. "And you're not finding anything, right?"

"I haven't covered everything yet," Jason offered, but his voice rang with frustration.

"Meanwhile, my staying hidden makes me look guilty as hell." Chase dropped his face in a palm and squeezed his temples.

"I did find one thing sort of strange," Jason admitted, sitting down beside him. "When I was going through the files, one of the cases you two worked had a bunch of pages missing from the report. Remember the Brandy Lakes case? She overdosed, and you and Zeke never did make an arrest."

"Yeah, I remember." He looked up. "What's missing from the report?"

"Just those pages. I guess they could have fallen out or something, but . . . I thought it might be worth mentioning. Maybe it would trigger something for you."

Chase took a deep breath. "I'll see what I can recall, but if my memory serves me right, there didn't seem to be anything suspicious about Zeke at the time. Of course, no matter how hard we tried, we couldn't seem to follow the drug trail. I remember the fact frustrated the hell out of me."

"Give it some thought," Jason said. "Meanwhile I'm going to stay away for a while. Don't call me anymore. I'll call you in a couple of days, or sooner if I come across something."

"You really think Zeke is on to you?" Chase asked.

"Yeah. Someone followed me today. Big guy. Flashy dresser."

"Bruno," Chase said. "*Dancing* Bruno," he added, remembering the incident on the bridge.

"Anyway, I parked my car at Shelly's place, jumped out a window, and borrowed her mother's station wagon. I say the less we communicate right now, the better." Jason stood. "I'll be in touch. Oh, here's Shelly's number." He pulled out a piece of paper from his jeans' pocket. "If you need me, call me here and leave a message. I'll get back to you as soon as I can."

"Who's Shelly?" Chase asked.

Jason raised a brow. "My soon-to-be ex-girlfriend."

"What did she do?" Chase laughed. "Mention the R-word?"

"How did you know?" Jason shuddered, then smiled. "Relationships."

"You're pathetic, Dodd."

"Yeah, tell me something that half the female population of Houston doesn't know."

"Ever thought of settling down?" Chase asked.

His friend glanced down the hall. "I might, if you didn't snatch up all the good ones before I could get my hands on them."

"Don't go there," Chase warned.

"Don't worry. I didn't try to steal Sarah, did I?"

"Yeah, you did," Chase said.

"Oh, yeah. I guess I did, but at the time I didn't know who she was."

A few moments later Jason left, and Chase sat back on the couch and tried to digest all the information he'd received. Stokes wasn't doing well. Zeke was on to them and having Jason tailed. Which meant that now Chase had put Jason's life in danger. Some of the files were missing from the Lakes case. Peter was a dweeb, and Lacy had sent him packing first. Did that mean she didn't care? Or was she just practical, afraid he might stumble across the fact that she had a new lover—a cop who just so happened to be wanted by the police—hidden in the bedroom?

He leaned back and closed his eyes. Things weren't looking good. The more time that passed, the more he realized Zeke truly might get away with framing him. Damn! Double damn!

\* \* \*

Zeke lay in bed, staring at his bedroom ceiling with the same intensity he'd maintained at the hospital. Sleep evaded him; instead, his gut turned over and pumped acid like an Iraqi oil rig. He finally sat up, grabbed the antacids from his night table and chewed them into chalky oblivion.

Each moment intensified the painful truth. Stokes had held on. Kelly hadn't shown up either dead or alive. Dodd, as slippery as oiled fish, kept losing Bruno. Piece by freaking piece, his life was coming unglued.

"Screw it!" He jumped up, jerked on his jeans, grabbed his gun and left the house. The least he could do was comb the area by the lake. Maybe he'd find Kelly's body washed up by now, or at least some freaking clue. And maybe Zeke would just take a freaking leap off the bridge himself.

Lacy rolled over, lacking Chase's warmth, feeling as if half of her was missing. When she'd fallen asleep he'd been spooning with her, kissing her shoulders until she drifted off. She sat up and glared at the clock. Almost three in morning. Where was he? She petted the three cats and Fabio at the foot of the bed. All of them had been very good about giving up their side of the mattress to a stranger—though, oddly, Chase didn't feel like a stranger anymore.

Stepping off the bed, she realized the tinges of soreness had returned between her legs. She remembered they had made love two more times after Jason left. Once in the afternoon while they waited for the dinner he'd cooked the night before to heat up in the oven. She'd never chop carrots on that counter again without remembering. The second time, after they'd gone to bed. She'd been almost asleep, curled up on her side, when his hands slipped between her thighs. His slow strokes had her moving with him. His sex, hard and ready, pressed against the back of her legs. She had started to roll over, but he moved in, the whispered words tickling her neck.

"No, stay like this. I want to take you like this." And he had.

Smiling, she ambled down the hall to the living room, expecting to see him sitting on the sofa. He wasn't, and when she found no lights on, there was a tug at her heart. Unraveling pain and fear made her clutch her hands into fists: What if he just up and disappeared one day? She walked through her house, room by room, and found each one hollower than the last. The emptiness harkened her back to her life before Chase had shown up.

She went to the front door and found it locked. Leaning against the wooden frame, tears begin to well into her eyes. He hadn't even said good-bye.

Chase walked the woods. Unable to sleep, cabin fever had grabbed him by the throat. He had needed to get outside, to breathe in fresh air. Now as he paced between the pine trees, stepping on moonlit shadows, thoughts of Zeke, of Stokes, gripped at his sanity. Then his thoughts turned down another path. Sarah.

Loving her.

Losing her.

Then, losing himself to the grief. He'd been so lost that he'd played at living, went through the motions and dared it all to end. It had taken having a gun to his head to wake him up. No, it had taken more.

It had taken the gun and Lacy.

Images of her flashed in his mind. Missing her, he wanted to be next to her again. To feel the way her body fit against his. To hear her breathe.

He headed back to her house, was about to cut through the trail to her front porch, when a car pulled into her drive. Zeke's car. Damn it! He reached for his gun, only to remember he'd failed to bring it with him. What was wrong with him? He was getting careless. Falling back into the shadow, he hunched down beside a tree. If Zeke went to the door, Chase would have to act. With or without a gun, he'd die before Zeke laid a finger on Lacy.

Think, think, think! His gut clenched, his chest ached. Then Zeke's car started backing out. Chase fell back a few feet in case the headlights hit his edge of the woods.

Only after the car's taillights grew small did Chase breathe. But the realization hit him like a hot poker. Staying here put Lacy in danger.

Lacy sat on the sofa, staring at nothing, her vision blurred. When she heard something at her front door, she jumped up and hotfooted it into her entry-way. The door swung open. Chase took a step inside and then jumped back when he saw her.

"What are you doing?"

"I woke up and you weren't there." She tried to blink away the tears, but from the look on his face she hadn't blinked fast enough.

He stepped closer and caught a tear with the pad

of his thumb. "I needed to get out for a second. Cabin fever. Then . . ." He paused. "I didn't mean to . . . upset you."

She shook her head. "Allergies." Wanting to run from the emotions playing handball with her heart, she turned on her heels and left him.

Her footsteps echoed in the hall as she fled, but she could feel his gaze on her. And a part of her prayed he'd follow, wanted him to wrap his arms around her and force her to admit what she didn't want to say. That she cared. That she didn't want him to leave. Not tonight. Not tomorrow. Could he stay forever? She even slowed her steps, but nothing. Chase wasn't coming. He wasn't the forever kind. She had to accept that.

# TWENTY-FOUR

Chase fought back the desire to follow Lacy and force her to admit the truth. She'd thought he'd left and she'd been crying, which meant that whether she liked it or not, she cared. He didn't go after her.

Closing his eyes, he tried to calm the panic still buzzing inside his chest. Five minutes ago, he'd been prepared to come in, grab his things and leave. But then it hit him; leaving wouldn't stop Zeke from coming back. And if Zeke returned and Lacy, with her inability to lie, wasn't able to convince him she hadn't seen Chase, then Zeke might hurt her. Leaving or staying, Chase had already put Lacy in danger. If he stayed, at least he'd be around to protect her.

So he would stay. But he had to keep his head. He couldn't make her promises. Hell, no. This wasn't casual, but where would it lead? What could he offer her? If something didn't turn around, Chase Kelly was either going to have to decide to make a run for it or turn himself in. If he did that, there was a very good chance that he'd be doing time. Either way, he didn't want to take Lacy down with him.

So now, no matter how much he wanted to tell her what he felt, he couldn't—not until he knew what the future held.

Lacy was still awake when, almost an hour later, Chase slipped into bed beside her. She didn't speak, and neither did he. Seconds ticked by like those of a clock low on batteries. She drew in a deep breath and caught his scent—an outdoors-type of aroma of wind and trees. His own inhalation followed hers and filled the dark room with a strange type of anticipation of what would happen next. Not just in the next few minutes, but regarding the next step of the relationship.

She felt him roll onto his side. The gentle sway of the mattress had her chest aching. He'd be gone soon. There would be no one making her mattress dip. Sure, the cats and Fabio, but they didn't count.

"Can't sleep?" he asked.

"No," she mumbled, but swore she wouldn't cry or beg him to never leave. She'd gone into this knowing it wasn't permanent, a lesson in sex without commitment. And Chase Kelly had sure as heck given her a crash course in sex. It was the *without commitment* clause that had caused the hiccup.

"Me, either." He brushed his nose against her cheek. "Can you think of"—his tongue dipped inside her ear—"anything that might help us sleep?"

"We could play chess," she said. "That always puts me to sleep."

"Did you say, 'play with your chest'?" His hand

whispered up under her shirt. His words, naughty and seductive, filled her ear. "I can do that."

Her nipples reacted instantly, pebbling against the soft pass of his warm palm. Oh, God, she loved his hands. She closed her eyes and tried not to moan aloud. "We're behaving like a couple of rabbits, you know?"

He laughed. "Are you suggesting a new position?"

"I don't know." She pressed her cheek onto the down pillow to look at him. Even in the dark, she could see his green eyes and melt-me grin. "How do rabbits do it?"

"Rabbit-style," he whispered, and kissed the corner of her lips. "Don't tell me you've never done it rabbit-style?" Then he pulled back. "Wait a minute." His hand moved out of her shirt and he bounced off the bed.

She raised her shoulders and watched him leave the bedroom. "Wait for what?" she asked the empty room.

He must have switched on a light, because a warm glow chased the darkness from the hall. Then she heard the spray of the shower in her hall bath turn on. Had he decided to take a cold shower in lieu of finishing what he'd started?

Suddenly, he appeared in the doorway. Naked and . . . hard. "Come with me."

"Where?" Not that it mattered. She'd follow him to Timbuktu, barefoot and through shards of glass. She rose up on her elbow.

He crooked his finger at her. "Didn't you mention something about wanting shower sex?"

"I might have," she said, her voice tight with want, her gaze homed in on his erection, which pointed to the ceiling. An empty, achy feeling filled her loins. Okay, she really was a rabbit.

He stepped closer to the bed, caught her hand and pulled her to her feet. "Are you game?"

"I might be persuaded." Jumping up and down with eagerness wasn't sexy, so better to play a little hard to get—a rabbit with a tad of a conscience. She followed him to the bathroom.

"Then let me see what I can do to persuade you." He twisted the round knob on the bathroom wall and the light lowered to a romantic level. Taking a step closer, he reached down to her waist, caught the hem of her shirt and whisked off the flimsy top.

He focused on her breasts. Reaching up, he stuck his finger into his mouth. The digit came out shiny and moist, and went straight to her nipples, where he drew lazy circles. Lacy's knees weakened, and she leaned against the bathroom sink.

Kneeling, he caught his thumbs in the elastic band of her short boxer-type bottoms and, with a slow hand, he lowered them. The soft cotton gliding down her thighs sent warm tingles spiraling through her. Cupping and raising her ankles one at a time, he slipped the shorts from beneath her and tossed them aside with her T-shirt. He didn't rise up. Instead, his gaze met hers again, and he held it. Her heart started to pound harder.

She stood completely naked, while he knelt in front of her. Five percent of her felt the situation embarrassing, but the other ninety-five percent was totally turned on. Maybe she was only ninety-five percent rabbit. She held on to the bathroom counter, listened to the cascading sound of the shower, and waited to see what he'd do next.

Shifting forward, he pressed his face to her abdomen. Lacy's breath caught. As if he were in no hurry, he touched the inner side of her right ankle, then trailed his finger up, up, over the inside of her calf, past the knee, higher to the inside of her thigh. Liquid heat pooled between her legs with anticipation. Okay, she was definitely a hundred percent rabbit.

His hand inched higher still. He was almost where it ached most when he stopped his slow ascent. She widened her legs, hoping he'd understand the invitation. His hand didn't move.

Instead, he kissed the top of her mound. Kissed her like he'd kissed her lips, full mouth and . . . He dropped down an inch. His tongue dipped inside the folds of her sex, found the tiny sensitive nub and flicked across it. Lacy gasped, closed her eyes, and leaned back against the counter even more.

"Lacy." His voice broke through the sexual haze befuddling her mind. "Eyes open, remember?"

She obeyed his request. He glanced up at her.

"Watch me." He trailed his tongue over her two more times, and she obeyed and kept her gaze locked on him as he masterfully brought her more pleasure than she'd ever known. When he pulled back, his gaze found hers again.

"Persuaded yet?"

All she could manage was a nod.

He smiled—a smile so sexy it should come with a warning label that read: I'm a bad boy, but you're going to love it.

"Ready for a shower?" But even as he asked, he slipped a finger inside her, and her weight shifted against the counter. She didn't need shower sex; bathroom sex was good enough.

His finger dipped inside two more times before he withdrew it completely. Then he stood up, took her hand and drew her into the tub, behind the shower curtain where steamy warmth seemed to be waiting.

The spray of warm water fell against her neck, and she watched as he slipped on a condom. With that done, he found the soap and slid it up and down her chest and then his own. Then he took her by the shoulders and pressed her back against the shower wall. The white tiles hadn't heated to the temperature of the water, and the cold sent a chill through her, which somehow made everything even more erotic.

"Shower sex is very . . . memorable," he said. "Two positions work best." He reached down, caught her legs and raised her feet off the large ceramic tub. He used his weight to keep her pressed against the wall.

The slippery feel of his chest brushing over her breasts had her nipples puckering even tighter.

It took one shift before he had her positioned. He bent his knees slightly, then jutted his hips up. His hard shaft stretched its way inside her. Deep. Then deeper. The sweet, hot feel of him had her wrapping her legs around his waist and writhing.

She let out a soft moan, which was accompanied by his low growl. He flatted his forearms under her arms to help sustain her. Then he began to rock faster. Out. In.

Higher. She went higher.

She heard his breathing hasten, grow raspy, felt the power of his release. She followed.

So lost in the rhythm, lost in the mind-blowing orgasm, Lacy didn't even try to catch herself when

Chase lost his footing. He pulled her against him, no doubt in an effort to protect her as they slid down. His butt hit the ceramic tub with a wet thud. She landed splayed out on top of him.

She raised her face off his soapy chest.

"You okay?" They both spoke at the same time.

Lacy caught her breath, the heavenly tremors of a climax still making her quiver. But he was no longer inside her.

She tightened her thighs once as the sensations faded, then rearranged her legs so she wasn't kneeing him in the groin. "I'm fine." The spray of warm water hit her back. "We probably shouldn't have . . . Are you sure you're okay?" She eyed his injured shoulder. She really should have stopped this; he wasn't physically fit to be—

"Yeah." He gave her a half-grin. "Other than the fact that I'm going to have a major purple bruise on my ass."

Right then, the worse case of giggles hit her. "Well, you said shower sex was memorable."

Suddenly he was laughing, too. Lacy wasn't sure how long they stayed there—naked, stretched out in the tub, the shower spraying them with warm water, and laughing. It was long enough for her to realize that no amount of time with Chase Kelly would ever be sufficient. She wanted him forever.

The next morning, Lacy woke up first and watched Chase sleep. Good heavens, God had created perfection in this man. As Lacy studied him—the shape of his ears, the way his belly button was a mixture of an outy and an inny—she found herself doing the big no-no: imagining a little boy with Chase's ears and lips and her nose. Or a little girl with his bright green eyes and her curly hair.

Oh yeah, she had it bad all right. But it was hopeless. Her only chance of coming out of this without a ring on her finger was if he truly wasn't the marrying kind. And even then, she wasn't above trying to change his mind.

She quietly slipped out of the room, passing the bathroom with a big smile filling her chest. She stopped and let the shower memory fill her with giddiness, and a touch of embarrassment, then she continued to the kitchen to make them breakfast. The time had come to show him that he wasn't the only one who could cook around here.

She made a coffee cake with a butter glaze. Feeling almost lightheaded with sexual bliss, she cracked the last of the eggs and left them in a bowl. Then she sauteed some onions, peppers, and mushrooms that she planned to cook with the eggs when he woke up. Going through her freezer, she found berries and sprinkled them with sugar and set them out to defrost.

When he didn't stir, she peeked in on him. He still slept soundly, and she decided to let him rest. She went to the living room, turned the television on mute, and sat down on the couch. Flipping through a magazine, she stopped to consider the various hairstyles on the models—styles that would work for a wedding. Yup. It was hopeless. What was it about sex that led her straight to wedding fever?

In a few minutes, Lacy looked up to see *NewsFlash* play across the screen. She grabbed the remote control and turned up the sound.

A TV reporter stood in front of the river. She wore

her hair up, and Lacy considered how that style would look with a veil. Realizing she wasn't listening, she tried to focus on what the blonde said.

The reporter continued talking, and Lacy tried to catch up.

". . . here at the Canvas Lake."

Lacy's sat up straighter. They were talking about Chase's case.

"We were just informed," the reporter continued, "that Houston P.D. detective Chase Kelly's body has just been found."

Zeke stood in the mud, watching the boat and the men bringing the body up. He'd been on his way back to visit the crazy tea-woman's house when he'd heard the news that they had found a body.

Pulling his coat closer to shield himself from the February cold, he waited like a kid on Christmas. *Let it be Chase Kelly.* What were the odds? Fifty-fifty. Kelly wasn't the first to take the plunge from that bridge. Of course, the first one had been dead at the time.

Pushing an impatient hand through his hair, he squinted to see what was happening. He saw Officer Candace look over the edge of the boat as if to identify the body. The man suddenly slung himself over to the other side and lost his breakfast. Even from where he was, Zeke could hear his retching. "Is it him?" he yelled.

One of the other officers looked over and called out, "It's him."

It took biting the inside of his cheek for Zeke to keep the smile from appearing on his lips. About damn time things had turned his way. Now all he had to do was get rid of Stokes. Maybe Lady Luck would take care of that, too. Maybe the man would die on his own. Yeah, maybe.

Lacy dropped the magazine, her breath caught, and she stared at the television in horror. Leaping up from the sofa, she ran into the bedroom, pushing the door open so hard it sounded as if it splintered against the wall. Chase lunged out of bed, wide-eyed and looking ready to kill. "What?" he asked.

"They said . . ." The words lodged in her throat. She grabbed the bedroom TV's remote from the bed-side table and finger-jabbed the on button. A Fruity Pebbles cereal commercial played.

"Said what?" He ran a palm over his chest, thread-ing his fingers through the soft mat of hair.

"They said they . . . found your body."

His brow pinched tight. He raked both his hands over his face this time, one after another. "You must have misunderstood," he said, his eyes still puffy with sleep.

Lacy felt inclined to agree with him. They couldn't have found Chase's body. All six-foot-plus of it stood beside the bed, deliciously naked and slightly aroused. Maybe she'd misunderstood. But then the news returned. They showed Chase's face on one portion of the screen and a news reporter's face with microphone on the other. "We're told that Chase Kelly's body will be transported to the morgue."

She glanced at Chase, who stared at the television, his eyes wide with shock. She watched his Adam's apple bob up and down.

Slowly, a sleepy grin tilted one corner of his

mouth and his gaze met hers. "You know what?" He ran another hand over his chest. "I feel pretty damn good for a dead man."

The phone rang. Not thinking about it being her mother, Lacy snatched it up. "Yes?" she answered.

"Lacy. It's Jason. Is . . . is Chase still there?" His voice was gritty with emotion, telling her a lot about the friendship the two men shared.

She looked at Chase. "Yes, and he's still breathing, too."

His deep sigh filled the line. "So you've seen the news, huh?"

"Yup," she said.

"Can I speak to him?"

She handed the phone to Chase. "It's Jason."

Lacy hung around to listen, but half the conversation gave her zip, zero. Chase hung up, and she looked at him. "Well?"

"He was as shocked as we were. He's going to head out to the morgue and see if he can get any answers." Chase moved around from the edge of the bed and pressed a kiss to her forehead. "Ever have sex with a dead man?" He smiled.

She grinned back. "No, but after learning what good sex is, my only two other lovers should be shot for their lack of skills."

He laughed. Then he had her cradled against his naked and still-living body, kissing her. When he came up for air, he lifted his head and inhaled. "Something smells good. You cook?"

She grinned and nodded.

"But cooking is *my* job." He brushed a hand over her cheek.

"You get a day off for being dead." She tossed him his jeans, took him by the hand and pulled him to the kitchen.

They spent the day waiting for the phone to ring, with the television on mute. Chase had gotten out his time line papers and made a bunch of notes about the Lakes case. If he put the two things together, maybe he'd find a connection. He also kept his gun by his side. If Zeke returned, he wouldn't be unprepared.

Lacy gave him space, with just the right amount of interruption. She fed him, brought him antibiotics with a light snack, and kissed him whenever she saw he was becoming frustrated.

After lunch, Chase kept going back and forth from one set of papers to the next. Lacy walked up, a basket of clothes in her hands. "Take your pants off, big boy."

He looked up. God, he loved her. "Sex, sex, sex. The more I give you, the more you want. Can't you think about anything but that?"

She chuckled. "Give me your jeans so I can wash them."

"I'll take mine off if you'll take yours off," he bartered.

"No. You're busy." She motioned to his papers.

The way she said *busy* made him wonder if she felt ignored. Well, he'd fix that. "Busy? Let's see, it's bang my head against the same brick wall . . . or have sex with the hottest chick in Texas. Hmm, let me think." He scratched his head. "Okay, sex wins." He waggled his brows. "Take your pants off."

"No, seriously. I don't want you to think I'm the

type of girl who . . . who would be hard to live with. You need to work."

He frowned at her. "The thing getting hard is not you." He stood and made a show of unbuttoning and unzipping his jeans. She rolled her eyes at him.

He took a step toward her. "Besides, I don't like being turned down."

She took a teasing step away and shook a finger at him, but the sexy smile on her lips was provocative. He snatched the basket from her hands. Dirty laundry flew up in the air. Lacy giggled and made a run for it. He caught her in the hall and that was where he got her pants off, where he made love to her—in the middle of the hall floor with all four of her pets watching. Even Samantha was getting used to having him around . . . or maybe the feline just had a thing about watching. He didn't care; right now he just wanted to enjoy being with Lacy. For a dead man, he couldn't complain about a thing.

Afterward, Lacy snatched up his jeans and wiggled herself back into her sweats. She looked totally content, sexually satisfied. "Crazy, what a woman is willing to do just to get her man to wear clean clothes."

Lying buck naked on the floor, he rubbed his knees where he was sure to have friction burns. Her words vibrated through his mind. She'd called him "her man." Chase both wanted to dance a little jig and deny it at the same time.

After finding the sweats he'd worn earlier, he went back to the couch and started going through his notes again. He wanted this solved, damn it, so he *could* be her man.

\* \* \*

"What the fuck do you mean it isn't him?" Zeke growled at the homicide detective unfortunate enough to give him the news. "Candace identified him. He fucking looked right at the body and said it was him."

"Yeah, well, he was wrong. The man they fished out of the river might look like Chase Kelly, but it wasn't him. He's Hispanic. It isn't Kelly!"

Zeke closed his eyes, feeling as if his world were crumbling.

"We're running fingerprints on the floater, and maybe they will tell us something."

It wouldn't tell Zeke crap that he didn't already know. He knew God damn well whom they'd fished out of river; he'd put the bullet between the kid's eyes himself.

He jerked around and started down the hall.

"Where you going?" the detective called. "I need to ask you a few questions."

Zeke didn't answer; he didn't stop. But he did know where he was going. To Hell. But first he had to make sure he didn't go alone. Stokes, and then Kelly. Oh, no, he wasn't going to Hell alone.

# TWENTY-FIVE

That afternoon Lacy came running through the living room, a small digital camera in her hands, chasing the white cat that now wore a Mrs. Claus outfit.

"Sweetie Pie!" Lacy called, but the cat darted beneath the sofa. She dropped the small camera beside Chase's leg, then got on her knees and peered under the couch. "Sweetie Pie, I'll give you a can of Fancy Feast . . . if Chase will share." She looked up at him and grinned; then her attention went back to the cat. "Come on, baby. One more shot is all I need."

Chase picked up the camera. Something tickled his memory. Then, in a flash, things started meshing. "Damn. That's it!"

"What's it?" She popped up.

His mind spun. "Pablo Martinez. Why didn't I remember that before?"

"Remember what before?" she asked.

He ran to the phone. His hands went to his pockets, only to realize that he now wore the sweats. "My jeans? Where are they?"

"In the washer. Remember? We had sex and then I took them."

"Damn!" Chase made a mad dash for the laundry room, praying he could still read the number on the scrap of paper. "Damn, damn!" he cursed as he jerked open the washer and pulled his jeans out of the soapy water. Water rolled off the denims and onto the floor. "You didn't check the pockets?"

"Sorry, the hall sex must have left me a bit rattled." Her eyebrow arched with a bit of annoyance.

He carefully retrieved the paper, which was smeared but readable.

"Who are you calling?" she asked, and he saw the frustration in her eyes.

"Just a minute." He punched in the number.

The phone rang and then a recorder came on. He gritted his teeth. "Call me, Jason." He slammed down the phone.

"What is it?" Lacy asked. The tightness in her voice made him turn around.

"It's Martinez. That's the connection with the Lakes case and the last few days."

"Who is Martinez? And what's the Lakes case?" she asked.

Chase ran a hand over his face. "He's an informant. Half-loco kid, thinks of himself as a James Bond type. He likes weird gadgets, mini tape recorders and . . . your camera reminded me of him. He always has these tiny cameras around. He had one about the size of a matchbox, said he uses it to get pictures of deals going down." Chase paced the kitchen. "He called me last week. Said he had something for me. Wanted me to pick up something at our normal spot."

"Your what?"

"I didn't pay much attention to him. I mean, the kid's nuts. Usually what he hands over is trivial, like a street kid selling a joint, but there was one case that he actually gave us something. It led us to a dead girl. Brandy Lakes was her name. But things didn't pan out. It was squirrelly. And . . ." Chase stared at the ceiling. "Oh, hell!"

"What?" Lacy snapped again.

"He . . . he's the same size as I am and has dark hair."

Lacy blinked. "And that's bad?"

"It is if he was just pulled from the lake."

"Oh, you think . . . That's terrible."

Chase nodded. "Yeah." He took off for the bedroom. Lacy followed. He grabbed his T-shirt and pulled it over his head. "I need to borrow your car."

"Where are you going?" she asked, her voice strained.

"I've got to get whatever it is Martinez left me."

"Where . . . where did he leave it?"

"At a gym locker. He gave me one of the those key cards after the Lakes case. Said he rented it to be our drop-off spot. Said he'd contact me and leave information there. I don't even know what I did with the freaking card."

Chase dug his wallet out of Lacy's drawer and started tossing things out. Some of the papers were smeared from his dunk in the lake.

"What gym?" she asked.

"Crap!"

"What?"

Chase grabbed his things and stuffed them back into his wallet. "The card has to be at my place."

"So just wait on Jason."

"I can't wait. I've wasted enough time."

"Wasted?" The hurt in her voice made him look up, but damn it.

"Lacy, I don't have time to answer questions right now. I really need to get this behind me. Then we can sit and talk about—"

"But it's dangerous. Zeke could be waiting for you. He's probably watching your place right now, hoping you'll go back there. That's what they do in the movies. And then, like an idiot, the hero walks right in and gets—"

"This isn't the movies. Can I borrow your car?"

"You're going to get killed," she said. "I can't let you do that."

"I'm not going to get killed. Please, give me your keys."

She chewed on her bottom lip. "Let me go. Let me go to your place. He won't be looking for me."

Chase glared at her. "He knows what you look like. You had the bastard in for tea, remember?"

"He knows what you look like even better. I could . . . I could put on a hat or something. Wait. I know. I know. I saw this on *Charlie's Angels*. I know what I can do."

Chase took her by the shoulders. "Lacy. This isn't a damn *Charlie's Angels* episode!" He took a breath and tried to calm himself. "Just give me your keys. Please."

"No." She held up her chin, tilted at that defiant angle that both endeared her to him and made him madder than hell.

"You're not going," he said, not withholding the sharpness from his tone.

"I won't give you the keys."

He stormed around her and headed for the living room, where he knew she'd left her purse. She dogged his steps down the hall.

"And if you take them from me, I'll follow you. I'll—"

"You don't have another car." He snatched up her purse and turned it over, spilling everything out on the hardwood floor.

"I'll . . . I have Zeke's card. I'll call him."

Chase grabbed the keys and glared up at her. "You're going to tell him I'm going to my apartment? You want me dead?"

"No. I'll tell him I know something. He'll come here and then . . . then he . . . he won't be at your place waiting on you."

Chase stared at her. "So he'll kill you instead. Was that on *Charlie's Angels*, too?"

Her eyes took on a glint of blue steel. She was serious. The damn woman was serious. She would call Zeke. Put herself in danger. She cared that much about him that she'd put herself in harm's way.

She gave her shoulders a little shrug, squaring them off as if preparing for battle. "Are you going to take me or not?"

Chase kicked her purse across the room. "Lacy, don't do this."

She settled both her hands on her small hips. "*You* did it. You got me mixed up in this and now it's too late."

Zeke's eyes burned right along with his stomach as he walked down the hospital hall. Mrs. Stokes and her two boys stepped around a corner and appeared

273

right in front of him. The acid gusher in his gut spewed into high gear.

"Say hello to Mr. Duncun," Mrs. Stokes told the boys. "Tell him how much you appreciate all he's done for us by staying at the hospital. Getting help to your daddy so fast."

The boys looked up at him and said their thanks in small voices. Then Mrs. Stokes reached out and touched Zeke's arm. Oddly, Zeke realized how long it had been since another human had touched him. Purposely touched him. He'd paid a few whores to screw him, but this wasn't sex, this was one human touching another. Kindness he didn't deserve. Emotion, like electricity, raced up his arm.

"The nurse told me you've called at least a dozen times a day. I just want you to know how much it means."

Zeke managed to nod, even though he felt a part of him was frozen inside. And he realized that part had been frozen for a long time. Since his wife left, since the judge had given custody of his kids to his wife. Since he'd watched another man walk into his home, mow his lawn, and take his son to father/son day at school.

"I'm . . . glad to . . ." He felt sick to his stomach. The hope had returned to her eyes again and it hit him so hard he couldn't breathe. Hadn't the doctor warned them last night that things didn't look good? But the woman still hoped. Was she a masochist, or had someone actually given her good news?

"How is he?" He forced the words out.

She smiled. "Better. He even came to for a second. It was short, but he looked right at me." Tears welled up in her eyes.

Acid welled up in Zeke's gut. "Well, I . . . I should go." His hurried escape across the hospital floor rang in his ears.

Lacy walked into the trailer that served as Kathy's florist shop. The bell on the door jingled.

Kathy looked up from arranging a vase of yellow roses and frowned. "What's wrong? Lose my plumber's phone number?"

"Do you really believe I had sex with him?"

Kathy clipped off a rose leaf. "No. But Sue's pretty sure you slept with her cop."

"Well, I didn't." Lacy leaned against the counter.

Kathy pulled out a rose and snipped its stem. "Then you had sex with Peter?"

Lacy rolled her eyes at the question. "No."

"Then whom were you having sex with?" Kathy leaned on the counter.

"Maybe I didn't have sex with anyone."

Kathy pointed her scissors at Lacy. "You had your robe on inside out. And you're a terrible liar."

Lacy sighed and decided to give up lying altogether. "Okay, I was having sex, but not with the plumber, not with Jason Dodd, and not with Peter."

Kathy's eyebrow arched upward. "You had the FedEx guy hidden in the bedroom?"

"No!"

"The vet?" Kathy asked.

"No!" Lacy said. "Look. I promise you I'll spill my guts later. Right now I need a favor."

"What favor?" Kathy slid the rose back into the vase.

"I need to borrow the White Elephant and . . . and

one of your delivery uniforms and a large vase of flowers."

Kathy cocked her head to one side and stared at her. "And this is because . . ."

"I can't tell you." Lacy took a step closer to the counter. "Please, Kathy. Just trust me on this. I'll only be a couple of hours, and I'll leave my keys so if you need to make any deliveries, you can use my car."

Kathy made a face. "Why do you—"

"Please?" Lacy dropped her keys on the counter. "No questions. It's top secret. I can't discuss it now. Just do it."

Kathy's nose wrinkled. "When did you go James Bond on me?" She tossed her long red braid over her shoulder and sighed. "Fine. But the White Elephant comes back in mint condition. Not a scratch on it. I just had it painted and my logo airbrushed on it. Cost me almost two thousand dollars."

"Mint condition. Got it." Lacy smiled and ran around the counter and gave her friend a hug.

Kathy shook her head. "Something tells me I'm going to regret this."

Something told Chase he was going to regret this. Seriously regret it. Damn. If Lacy got hurt, he'd never forgive himself. But the woman wasn't lying; he'd seen it in her blue eyes. If he didn't bring her with him, she would call Zeke. Freaking nuts—she was loony! Lacy had truly lost touch with reality. He'd fallen in love with a lunatic.

He had to admit, though, her idea of getting the floral delivery truck and pretending to deliver flowers to his condo building had merit. Maybe when this was over he'd start watching reruns of *Charlie's Angels*.

When Lacy walked out of the florist shop wearing a pair of coveralls and a hat, and carrying a large vase of yellow roses, his heart dropped and his fear kicked in all over again. He'd rather die or rot in prison before she got hurt. Damn, why wouldn't she listen to him?

"Let's go." She opened the driver side door and dangled a pair of keys in front of him.

He got out and stared at her over the top of her car. "Lacy? Please stay here. I'll take the truck and flowers and I'll do it, okay? If something happens to—"

"No." She slammed the door closed with her hip.

"You're not being reasonable. Damn it!" Chase's gut knotted as he moved to walk beside her.

She handed him the vase and unlocked the truck door.

"Let me drive," he said.

"No." She pulled the keys close to her chest. "If something happens to the White Elephant, Kathy will grind me up and use me for fertilizer."

"I don't give a rat's ass about this truck." He crawled in the passenger side. "It's you I'm worried about." He slammed the door. "This isn't a damn episode of *Charlie's Angels*!" he repeated.

She turned her head, her expression unconcerned. "Where do you live?" she asked, and started the engine. Suddenly her mouth dropped open. "I can't believe I'm sleeping with a man and I don't even know where he lives."

Zeke drove to his apartment feeling numb inside. He sat in the car staring at nothing. Hope leaked out of him like air out of a day-old balloon. He pulled his gun out, laid it on his lap and eyed it. Then slowly he picked it up and pointed the barrel at his temple.

His hands started to shake and he called himself a fucking coward. He could take other lives. He could kill, but he was too weak to take his own life. To end his misery. Damn it! He deserved to die.

He pushed the gun into his mouth, tasted the cold metal against the back of his throat. His stomach heaved and he threw his gun down on the floorboard. Wiping his mouth, he slung his head back against the headrest, biting his lip until he tasted blood.

The fury building in his chest clawed at the self-pity that had bedded down there for the last few hours: This was Kelly's fault. He reached for his keys and started the car. He'd find Dodd and beat the truth out of him. If Kelly was alive, Dodd would tell him or he'd die.

Pulling his cell phone from his pocket, he dialed. "Where's he at right now?" he asked when Bruno answered.

Bruno hesitated. "He just went inside Kelly's condo again."

"Fine. I'll be right there." He hit the off button and slung the phone to the floorboards with his gun.

Maybe Kelly and Stokes weren't the only ones who'd be joining Zeke in Hell. Jason Dodd could come, too.

# TWENTY-SIX

Lacy punched in the security code as Chase called it out to her. He'd insisted she drive around the condominium parking lot four times to make sure he didn't see anyone watching. She finally parked the car and cut off the engine. "Where's your condo key? And where will I find the key to the locker?"

"Change of plans, I'm going in." Chase raked a hand over his face, and gave the parking lot another glance.

"No. Someone will recognize you."

"Lacy—"

"Tell me I'm not right, Chase. Do you really think you'll get inside without someone calling the police?"

She saw the truth of her words hit him and she pressed: "Please. No one will think twice about me walking in. I'll go in and out. Nothing to it." But even as she retained a calm front, Lacy's stomach danced a tango. Jeepers! She didn't know how Chase did this kind of thing every day.

"Lacy, please." He brushed a hand over her cheek. "Stay here. I'll go."

"And if you get caught now, what's going to happen? You'll go to jail before you can prove what Zeke did. You know I'm right." She closed her eyes to the warmth of his touch. She loved him. The realization would have sent her heart racing if it hadn't been already dancing to keep up with her stomach.

"The key." She held out her hand. "We're wasting time."

"It's unit two-fifteen." His jaw clenched, but he dropped the key in her palm. "The key card is bright blue with 'Ace Gym' written on it. It will be either in a basket on my bathroom cabinet or in the top left drawer of my dresser in the bedroom. You go in, get it, and get out. I'm giving you three minutes and then I'm in after you."

"Ten," she insisted. "Give me ten."

"Five."

She reached down for the vase of flowers sitting in the console between the two seats. The smell of roses filled her nose. Opening the door, she gave him a quick smile.

"In and out, Lacy," he warned as she closed the door.

She nodded and held the vase of roses in front of her face. Reaching the stairs of the condominium, her heart pumped fear through her body, making her tingle, giving the hairs on the back of her neck a reason for a standing ovation. But deep down, Lacy had to admit she felt gutsy and a little bit high. A real Charlie's Angel, she thought.

The bottom floor of the building had people strolling around. Lacy got in the elevator, her face shielded by green sprigs of baby's breath. The elevator doors started to close, then out of nowhere a hand appeared between them. Lacy bit her lip, relieved when two women hurried inside. Giving them personal space, Lacy took a step back.

A brunette with big brown eyes stepped in beside her, and a tall blonde, sleek and sophisticated and wearing a pink silk suit, took the place in front of her.

"Oh, hi, Jessie," the brunette said, touching the blonde on the arm.

*Jessie?* Was this make-dinner-and-have-sex-with-her Jessie? Lacy peered through the roses to get a better look, but with the woman's back to her, she could only see a cascade of hair. Nice hair.

"Hi," Jessie answered. "How's the job search going?"

"Terrible," the brunette answered, and then cut her eyes to Lacy with interest. "You wouldn't be delivering them to condo four hundred, would you? I could use a sweet gesture. Or a job would do."

Lacy shook her head. "No. Sorry."

"How about two-thirty?" The woman named Jessie chuckled and slowly turned to face Lacy.

"Sorry." Lacy lowered the flowers to get a good look, and silently prayed the woman had a hook nose or short chin.

"A girl could hope." Jessie shrugged and smiled.

Yeah, Lacy thought. A girl could hope, but some hopes were futile. Jessie didn't have a hook nose—not even one unbecoming feature. She looked like a magazine model. No wonder Chase visited her twice a week. Lacy blinked and tried to deal with the emotions playing havoc with her heart.

"I heard you're moving out next month and putting the condo up for sale," the brunette said as the elevator came to a stop.

"My ex and I are retying the knot," Jessie said.

*But you're still sleeping with the man I love twice a week.* Lacy's grip on the vase tightened.

"Well, congratulations," the brunette answered as the doors opened. "Oh! Did you hear about the cop who lives on your floor? They think he's dirty, and now they think he's dead."

"Yes, I heard. That's terrible." Jessie frowned, as if disturbed by Chase's apparent demise. But only slightly disturbed? Lacy bit her lip. Was that how little Jessie cared about Chase? She wasn't going to attempt to defend him or at least go teary-eyed at the possibility of him being dead?

*You don't deserve him.*

"Later." Jessie walked out of the elevator.

Lacy suddenly realized she was supposed to get out, too. Staring at the roses, she pushed past the brunette. She moved fast down the beige-carpeted hall, listening to the padded footsteps of Jessie moving the opposite way. "Two-twenty. Two-nineteen." She read the numbers on the door aloud, grateful she'd actually turned the right way. Finally, at the end of the floor she found unit 215. A door opened and closed down the hall. Jessie's door.

Lacy's heart picked up speed. She closed her hand around the key, and glanced back to make sure no one was watching. Her breath caught in her throat as she unlocked the door and slipped inside. With the vase of flowers held to her face, she shut the door.

Her gaze moved about the condo. Chase's condo. She took in its ransacked condition—the tan leather sofa set at an odd angle, a metal entertainment center lying flat on the floor with stereo equipment scattered everywhere. Someone had been here . . . could still be here. She glanced back at the door and fought the urge to run.

Swallowing her fear, Lacy listened to the silence, assuring herself she was alone. Realizing she couldn't waste time, she set the vase of flowers down on a smoked glass coffee table and darted past the mess on the floor to the hall.

She pushed open the first door, and peered inside a bathroom decorated in yellow. Items from the cabinet littered the floor. A noise, a light creaking sound, sliced through the silence. Lacy knelt and wrapped her hand around the first thing she could. Staring at the toilet plunger, she decided it offered more protection than a fish.

Slowly standing, she backed up against the wall. Hesitating, she listened. The noise had seemed to come from the unit upstairs, and she relaxed, but she wasn't ready to give up the plunger yet.

The door next to the bathroom led to a small room with a desk and a computer. Papers and office supplies covered the beige carpet. Lacy took a few more steps. The closed door at the end of hall had to be it: Chase's bedroom. She prayed the items weren't so scattered that she couldn't find the key card to the locker. Shaking, she looked at the knob. Every closed door seemed to tease her with the possibility of someone being on the other side. She gripped her plunger and nudged open the door. The light squeak of the hinges made her pulse race.

Her gaze went straight to the king-sized brass bed centered on the far wall. Pillows and blankets lay tossed across the mattress. Lacy couldn't help but wonder if Chase brought Jessie to his place. If he made love to her here. The ache of jealousy pricked her heart as she envisioned the tall blonde wrapped in Chase's arms on that very bed.

Pulling her attention from the ruffled blankets, she looked around. Drawers from the oak dresser lay scattered on the floor. She frowned. It might take her a while to find the key. Stepping inside, she knelt and picked through the items, hoping to spot a bright blue card.

She turned over a picture frame. Shards of glass fell from the eight by ten. Behind the last remnants of broken glass, the picture caught her attention. Lacy's heart stopped beating. She stared at the picture of Chase decked out in a tux and . . . a woman dressed in a wedding gown. The frame slid from her fingers, landing near the toilet plunger.

Staring at the image, Lacy couldn't believe it. Why hadn't he told her he'd been married? The question hung like a slab of slaughtered beef in the freezer of her heart. Then a cold and terrible thought surfaced. What if . . .

"No." She shook her head. He was having casual sex with Jessie. He couldn't be married, too. But she couldn't stop herself from looking around, checking for signs of a wife.

She spotted the jewelry box on the floor near the edge of the bed. Earrings and a pearl necklace lay scattered beside it. Her stomach clenched. Forcing herself to stand, she grabbed the plunger and rushed to the closet. When she spotted the eight to ten dresses and pastel-colored sweaters hanging beside an array of men's shirts, she felt sick to her stomach.

She closed her eyes as her vision became clouded. No wonder Chase hadn't wanted her here. As she turned back around, her toe hit the edge of a drawer. There, beside loose change and a box of large condoms, lay a blue card with *Ace Gym* written in bright purple letters.

She picked it up, curling her fingers around it. Feeling numb inside, she headed back down the hall, through the living room and out the condo door.

Six minutes. Chase sat in the passenger seat of the van and stared at his watch. One more minute and he was going in. He grabbed for the door at the same time he spotted Zeke's car pull into a parking spot on the other side of the lot.

"Damn!" Chase reached for his gun on the floorboards, his gaze glued to the entrance of his building.

The front door swung open and Lacy came hurrying out, carrying a . . . a toilet plunger? Where the hell were her flowers to hide her face?

Keeping his gaze mostly on Lacy, he turned the key in the ignition. The van motor sputtered to life. He glanced back in Zeke's direction and saw the man stepping out of his car.

Lacy kept walking toward the van. Zeke took a few steps from his car, stopped, and stared at her. Chase knew the exact moment Zeke recognized her, because his posture changed and he reached to check his gun. "Double damn!"

Even from inside the van, Chase heard Zeke call out. Lacy either didn't hear it or pretended not to, because she continued toward the van, bearing the toilet plunger like a sword.

Chase's breath caught as Zeke hesitated. Then Zeke stared after Lacy as if second-guessing himself. Chase's hold on his gun tightened.

Two cars away, she paused, as if noticing the running engine. Zeke called out again. Lacy swung around. She saw Zeke, shrieked and lunged for the van door. Zeke bolted after her.

"It's Zeke!" She jumped up in the driver's seat, slung the plunger and card key at Chase. A second later, she jerked the van into reverse.

Zeke appeared in front of the van. "Stop!" He raised his gun.

Chase dove across his seat. He snatched Lacy's arm and jerked her down. The bullet crashed through the windshield, missing Lacy by only inches. She stared at him, her eyes round with fear.

With no time to assure her, he slid beneath her upper body until he sat on the edge of her seat. He pushed his foot on top of hers to hit the gas. With one hand, he pressed her into his lap. He used the hand with the gun to turn the wheel.

The van had moved only ten feet away when another bullet crashed through the windshield. This one exited through the passenger window. Lacy screamed and attempted to sit up.

"Stay down!" Trying to drive, perched on the edge of his seat with her upper body across his lap and her legs crowding the floorboard, was near impossible.

Lacy jerked up. The sudden movement caught Chase off guard and he fell between the seats. Lacy took hold of the wheel. Chase rose up just as the van crashed into a parked red Buick.

"Oh, Lordie," she muttered.

Thrown back on the floor, Chase scrambled back into his seat. "Move." He kicked her foot off the brake and hit the gas pedal. She jerked the wheel and slammed into a curb.

"Jeepers!" she shouted, and bounced against him.

Another bullet hit the side of the van. Lacy yanked the wheel back to the right.

"Let me drive," Chase snapped.

"No!" Another bullet slammed into the back of the van. The noise caused her to jerk. When she did, she hit a black sedan. "Please tell me those aren't real bullets!"

"Let me drive!" He clasped his hand around her arm to jerk her away, but she had a death grip on the wheel. As the van screeched in a turn, the bumper caught a light pole.

"Kathy is going to kill me!"

"Move!" Chase looked out the window and saw Zeke running back to his car.

Lacy hit the brakes as she approached the exit gate, but Chase stomped his foot on the gas. The sound of wood cracking and grinding metal rang loudly as the van screeched through.

"Oh, Lordie!" Lacy squealed again. "I'm dead for sure! Dead! Dead!"

"Turn right," Chase snapped, half sitting on the edge of Lacy's seat. "Turn, damn it."

Lacy jerked the wheel right. The tires screamed and the smell of hot rubber rose from the street through the shattered windows.

"Now turn left." Chase shot a glance over his shoulder, then stared at her. "Turn!"

"Kathy's going to kill me." Lacy pulled her foot off the gas.

"Zeke is going to do it for her if you don't drive. Now go or get out of my way."

She glared at him. "I am going."

He glared right back. "Faster." He rammed his foot on top of hers again.

"Stop!" She jumped and the van veered to the right. "I can't drive with you doing that."

"Then let me do it," he insisted.

"No." She slowed down when the light turned yellow.

That did it; Chase latched onto her elbow and slung her across his lap so he could take the wheel. She landed hard on her knees between the two seats. She muttered something, but he ignored her. He'd apologize profusely later; right now he had to make sure he got her out of danger.

"I was driving," she snapped as she crawled into the passenger seat.

"And doing a lousy job of it," he said. "Buckle up."

His grip on the wheel tightened. He took a sharp turn at the light and spotted Zeke's car peeling out onto the street behind him.

"Shit." He pushed the gas pedal to the floor. Tires screeched again. In the distance he heard sirens. "I knew I shouldn't have let you do this. You had no business getting—"

"Why, because I might learn you're married?" she yelled. "That's why you didn't want me to go inside, wasn't it?"

He digested her words, but kept his gaze between the road and the side mirror where he saw Zeke's car racing after them.

"I'm not married." Chase jerked the wheel, taking

the next corner so sharply that the van leaned on two wheels.

"Oh, God." Lacy slammed into the door.

"Buckle up, damn it!" Chase could hear sirens and he accepted the hopelessness of running. The only thing that concerned him now was Lacy's safety.

"Liar. I saw the picture and clothes in the closet."

Her accusation caused him to flinch. He made another right as the van struggled to stay on the road. Behind him, he heard more tires burning rubber in an attempt to keep up. When he glanced back in the side mirror, hope flooded through him. Racing along beside Zeke's car was Jason's Mustang, the siren flashing from the dash.

Chase turned to Lacy. "That's Jason back there. As soon as we get to a good spot, I'm going to pull over. I'm going to step out of the van. You stay in your seat and keep down. You got that?"

Tears rimmed her eyes. The hurt he saw in those beautiful baby blues coiled like a rattler in his stomach.

"Why did you lie to me? Why did you do this?"

He stared back at the road. "I didn't lie, Lacy. My wife died. I just . . . I kept some of her things around. I wasn't ready to let her go. I didn't even think about you seeing her things." He shot his gaze left, then right. The street was empty. The time had come to call this game to an end. He gave the side streets one more glance, not wanting any civilians to be involved.

"I'm pulling over." He turned to her and saw from her expression that she believed him about Sarah. Relief flooded his chest.

She jutted her chin out in a familiar stubborn angle. "I'm getting out with you."

His relief went up in smoke. "No!"

"Yes!" She swiped the tears from her cheeks. "The cops won't shoot you if I'm there."

"It's Jason," Chase said. "He won't shoot me."

"Zeke's there! He'll shoot you, Chase. You said he would."

Chase gritted his teeth. "Jason won't let him shoot me."

"I'm getting out with you," she insisted.

"God damn it, woman! You're not getting out of this van!" Chase slammed his foot on the brakes. The siren wailed louder. Tires squealed behind them. "Don't you dare move." He pointed a finger at her. "I mean it. You keep your ass in that seat."

In the distance, Chase heard Zeke call out, "He's got a gun! Watch him!" Jason yelled back, but he couldn't make out the words. Chase opened the door and threw his gun as far as he could.

"I'm coming out," he yelled. "I'm unarmed."

Offering her one more glance, Chase wished he had the time to offer her a kind word, a gentle touch. The luxury didn't exist. He stepped from the van. He slammed the door shut and took a deep breath, not knowing if it would be his last. In spite of what he'd told Lacy, he knew Zeke preferred him dead. Throwing out the gun might make Zeke hesitate, but honestly it would be easy for the man to shoot now and try to excuse his actions later.

Chase kept his hands high and took two more steps, wanting to get away from the van—away from Lacy.

"Stop right there, Kelly!" Zeke shouted.

"No!" Lacy screamed.

Chase cut his gaze around, his breath coming up

short. Lacy had one leg out of the vehicle, that damn plunger wielded in her hand like a weapon. "Get back in the freaking van!" he yelled, glancing at Zeke.

Jason's voice boomed out, "Put your gun down, Zeke."

"You bastard!" Zeke screamed, raising his gun.

"Don't do it," Jason yelled. "It's over, Duncun."

"It's not over." Zeke's tone was so cold, Chase prepared himself to take the bullet. But God damn it. He wasn't ready to die.

"You're going to pay for this," Zeke said. The ice in his voice now echoed his expression.

"Put the gun down." Jason pointed his Glock at Zeke.

Chase glanced at Lacy and stepped farther away. His eyes shot back to Zeke.

The man sneered. "I wanted to see you in Hell with me. But I know how to hurt you more."

Before the bastard moved, Chase knew what he planned to do. "No!" He threw himself at Zeke.

Zeke swung his gun around, aimed toward the van, toward Lacy, and fired.

# TWENTY-SEVEN

Everything happened so fast, all Lacy could do was grip her toilet plunger and try to keep up. Guns were drawn, pointed. Words were spoken, then Chase yelled out and she saw him lunge forward.

A loud pop sounded at the same time she heard the familiar metallic *bing* of the White Elephant taking another bullet. Then came the grunt of two bodies colliding. Chase and Zeke fell to the street, their legs and arms swinging.

They rolled right, then left. Chase ended on top. Zeke held his arm up in the air, gun clasped tight. Chase gripped his wrist with one hand while his other hand pounded Zeke's face. Zeke punched back.

The two men rolled. Zeke ended on top this time. His gun hand was extended, held there by Chase's strong grip.

Lacy's gaze zipped to Jason, who was standing only five feet away, scowling. His gun was aimed, but it moved a half-inch this way, then a half-inch that.

"Do something!" Lacy screamed, but even as she

said it, she knew why he didn't fire. The risk of hitting Chase was too great.

Her gaze flew back to Zeke and Chase. As if in slow motion, Zeke's arm lowered, the barrel slowly moving down. Down. Down toward Chase.

Lacy rushed forward. Her first swing brought the plunger down across Zeke's head; the second hit smack dab on his balding forehead. That blow must have momentarily stunned him, because Chase gained control and twisted on top.

Too bad Lacy couldn't stop mid-swing. The plunger's third strike bounced off Chase's face.

Suddenly, in the blink of an eye, Jason Dodd was in the middle of the scuffle. Lacy danced from one foot to the other, plunger held up like a bat, trying to find her target, the snake-eyed Zeke, in the middle of the three-man scuffle.

She swung, heard a grunt. She wasn't sure who she'd hit, but Jason Dodd cursed. She swung again and got Zeke on the ear.

The clink sounded of a gun being dropped onto the pavement just as more sirens and screeching tires echoed around them.

Chase, blood oozing from his lip, lunged up and grabbed Lacy by the shoulders. He gripped her tightly as his gaze flew up and down her body. "You weren't hit. You weren't hit," he repeated, as if talking to himself.

Lacy waited for him to pull her against him; instead he let her go, held out his hands, and clutched his fist in front of her. "Do you fucking see why I told you to stay in the van? He could have killed you."

"He didn't," Lacy said, and swallowed her need to cry.

Jason Dodd's voice rang out. "We've got him," he yelled to the officers getting out their patrol cars.

Chase watched Lacy pull the plunger to her chest and hug it as if it were a damn teddy bear. Then he swung around and watched Jason handcuff Zeke. Chase's hands shook as he fought the need to crush his fists into Zeke's face.

Jason, his knee pressed into Zeke's back, looked up at Chase. "Stokes regained consciousness," he said. "He gave this asshole up."

Zeke jerked his head back. "He must be in on it, too! He—" Zeke spluttered to a stop when Jason gave his face a shove into the pavement.

Only when Jason stood up and two officers hauled the red-faced and furious Zeke off to their patrol car, did Chase really believe. He drew in a shaky breath and wiped the blood from his mouth. Remembering what had brought on the injury, he spat the taste of blood, rubber and toilet water from his tongue.

Then his gaze went back to Lacy. She stood by the van door, that damn plunger still clutched to her chest. He shook his head, furious at her for not listening—more furious at himself for allowing her to be put in harm's way.

He marched over, now within an arm's reach of her, and noticed the chalky color of her skin. With her face washed white, her blue eyes spoke volumes on what she'd been through. She dropped the plunger, and he saw her chin quiver. His heart seemed to follow suit.

"You are the most stubborn, hardheaded woman I've ever met," he growled; then he wrapped his arms around her.

She leaned into him, circled her arms around his

waist and held on like a woman who never intended to let go. Chase closed his eyes and let his hard body absorb the soft feel of hers. He was certain nothing in the world had ever felt so good.

"It's over," he whispered.

Lacy sat in the small room, turning the half-filled coffee cup in her hands. Every few minutes she'd look at the four walls and wonder who watched her. Every cop show she'd ever seen had either two-way mirrors or some way of watching the person squirming in this type of room.

For the last hour, she'd done her share of squirming. She'd spoken to two different men and given them a blow-by-blow account of how she'd ended up with Chase Kelly. Of course, she didn't tell them everything. She didn't want to cause trouble for Chase, so she'd altered her story a little, omitting the fact that she'd resisted helping him in the beginning, and leaving out that she hadn't been able to resist him later on.

The door squeaked on its hinges, and Jason Dodd walked into the room. "You okay?" he asked

Lacy stood and held up her cup. "Whoever made the coffee should be arrested."

"I'm sorry. Starbucks is just around the corner." He smiled and hesitated. Then he gave his jaw a pass with his hand. "You know, I've never considered a toilet plunger a lethal weapon until now."

She forced a smile onto her face. "Sorry. I was aiming at Zeke."

He reared back on his heels. "I know." There was a pregnant pause. "I had someone bring the van around front." He dropped the keys into her hands and offered a good-bye smile that came with a nod. "You can go now."

"What about Chase?" She gripped the keys.

"IA will have him here for hours. He said to tell you to go on home."

"Why are they keeping him?" She folded her arms over her middle, hoping to stop the nervous tickle in her stomach. "I thought Stokes cleared him."

"He did. But there's still the question of the drugs they found at his place."

"But Zeke put those there," Lacy insisted.

"I know that and you know that, but they don't."

"Then we'll tell them. Where are they?" Lacy started for the door.

Jason caught her by the arm. "They won't listen to us, Lacy. Chase is just going to have to convince them. It will take a while, but he'll come out of this. The best thing you can do for Chase right now is to go home. He told me to make sure you did just that."

Lacy sucked in her bottom lip, remembering Chase telling her it was over. Did he mean they were over? Oh, she didn't want to believe it. "How long will they keep him?"

"I wish I knew. They could drag this out for days if they decide to be jerks. They've got someone going over to the gym to see if Martinez left anything that could clear him."

"I'll just wait then." She started back to her chair.

"You should leave. You can't do anything sitting here. Chase has got to work this out himself."

She looked up, and a thousand questions formed, lined up in her mind like soldiers. She swallowed, afraid to ask, afraid she'd learn something she didn't want to know. But she had to know. "When did his wife die?"

Jason's eyes widened. He hesitated, as if he questioned the wisdom of answering. "A little more than two years ago."

"How?" she asked.

Lacy spotted a touch of grief in Jason's eyes. That grief told her that he, too, had been close to Chase's wife. "A brain tumor," he said.

"That must have been difficult." She thought of what Chase must have felt, losing a wife after he'd already had to face the loss of his parents.

"It's been hard for him." A frown pulled at Jason's expression.

"He must have really loved her." She bit into her lip as her emotions began to swirl in another direction.

"They were good together. They had . . . Sarah was a good person."

"How good?" She felt stupid being jealous of a dead woman, but that's what she felt: jealousy, pure and simple. Okay, it wasn't so pure.

"You know, you probably should speak to Chase about this. He said he would call you." Jason glanced at the door and plastered another smile on his face, but the expression didn't hide the emotion in his eyes. Was it pity? Oh, God, it was. He pitied her because . . . because . . .

He cleared his throat. "And tell your friend Sue I said hello."

Lacy blinked, feeling another dad-burn allergy attack coming on. "Is he really going to call me? Or do you think he's just saying it to get me to leave?"

Jason opened his mouth and then closed it.

"Tell me," she demanded. "I'm a big girl. I can take it. He still loves his wife, doesn't he?"

Jason reached out and gripped the back of her chair. "He'd be a fool not to call you. And if the way he—"

"But *is* he a fool?" she asked. "Did he, like, swear or something to never care about someone else after his wife died? Is that why . . . why he dates women like Jessie?" Suddenly it made perfect sense. He dated women who could care less about him because he didn't want to care about them. "Tell me I'm wrong," she insisted.

Jason didn't answer. He didn't have to; the look on his face told her what she didn't want to know. She snatched her purse from the table and left before her allergy attack became Noah's flood.

She managed to hold back her tears as she walked through the police station. She didn't shed one drop all the way down the front steps. But when she saw the White Elephant parked out front, the windshield cracked, its bumper drooping, bullet holes marking the freshly painted words, *Kathy's Florist*, and dents running along both sides, the tears broke loose.

*"Not one scratch."* Lacy recalled Kathy's words, and she cried harder.

Now, the only decision left to make was if she wanted to be buried or cremated, because Kathy was going to kill her.

# TWENTY-EIGHT

Lacy parked in front of Kathy's trailer, hiccuping and wiping her eyes as she got out of the van. Knocking on Kathy's door, she heard her friend call out for her to come in.

Lacy took in a deep breath, stepped inside, and hoped Kathy went straight for the heart when she killed her, because right now her heart was hurting so badly that it would be a relief not to feel it anymore.

Kathy rose from the table where her boy Tommy sat with schoolbooks in front of him. "I was just starting to get worried." Her friend stretched and stopped midway through a yawn when she noted Lacy's tears. "What's wrong?"

Lacy hiccuped, and a new wave of tears filled her eyes. "Allergies," she said, gazing at Tommy. "Hi, guy."

Tommy grinned. "Hi, Lacy. How's your fish doing?"

"He's fine. Still singing." She tried to smile. "He's a good fish. Doesn't eat much."

Kathy shook her head. "Tommy, why don't you go watch televison in Mama's room?" She kissed the boy's forehead and then turned back around. "What's up?"

Lacy walked to the kitchen table, dropped down in a chair and tried blinking away the tears. "You're going to kill me."

Kathy dropped into the seat across from her. "So you *are* sleeping with my plumber."

"No." Lacy shook her head and sniffled. "It's the White Elephant."

"You're sleeping with my White Elephant?" Kathy grinned.

Lacy sucked in her bottom lip, then let it out. "Remember, you told me not to get one scratch on it?"

Kathy's brows pulled together. She looked toward the front door. "How bad of a scratch is it?" She pushed a carton of Kleenex toward Lacy.

"Bad. But you know I'll pay for it. Every penny. I swear I will." Lacy pulled out a tissue and blew her nose.

"Am I going to cry when I see it?" Kathy stood up.

"You probably shouldn't even look," Lacy said. "I'll drive it home and tomorrow I'll take it to be fixed."

Kathy took two steps toward the door and hesitated. "No one was hurt?"

"No. Just the White Elephant."

"Is it, like, just limping, or is it gasping for its last breath?

"Both," Lacy said.

"Is the damage in the front or back?" she asked.

Lacy winced. "Both."

"Left or right side?"

"Both." Lacy wanted to drop her head on the table and sob.

"Damage to all four sides?" Kathy put a hand over her heart. "How many cars did you hit?"

"I only hit two cars," Lacy explained, feeling an anxiety attack brewing inside her. "But it was shot on the other two sides."

"Shot?" Kathy's hazel eyes widened. "By bullets? Real bullets?"

"I hit a red Buick on the left side and the black sedan on the right, and then I ran through a security gate. The bullets hit the right side and the back. They took out the front windshield. And I think they did some damage to the bumper when it was towed to the police station. Oh, and the passenger window is history, too." Lacy's eyes filled with tears again. "I'm so sorry." She hiccupped.

"Po . . . lice station?" A stunned look appeared on Kathy's face. "Why was it towed to the police station, and who . . . who was shooting at my elephant?"

"It's a long story." Lacy blew her nose and her insides started shaking again. "Fabio found him by the shed last week."

"Found who?"

"Chase. The man I was having sex with."

Kathy laced her hands together and pressed them to her chin. "You had sex with someone your dog dragged in?"

"He didn't drag him. He just found him, and then I found them both. And he was shot and I thought he was going to shoot Fabio and then he handcuffed me to the bed and took my antibiotics for my female infection." She sniffled. "Then Sue came over and started talking about becoming lesbians."

"Are you having a mental breakdown or something?" Kathy's brows puckered. "Because I have some Prozac."

"No. I'm not having a nervous breakdown." Lacy shook her head. "But I fell in love with him."

Kathy's mouth dropped open. "You fell in love with the man your dog found and who handcuffed you to the bed and took your female infection medicine?"

Lacy nodded and hiccupped again. "Yeah. And now they're keeping him for questioning. Not for shooting that other cop. They know he didn't shoot him, but they still think he stole the drugs."

One of Kathy's eyebrows rose. "He didn't shoot a cop? But they're questioning him about stealing your antibiotics?"

"No," Lacy said. "They think he stole cocaine."

Kathy's mouth dropped open again. "So you had sex and are now in love with a drug dealer?"

"No! He's a police officer." Tears spilled down her cheeks.

Kathy held both her palms up in the air. "Wait! I'm totally confused here. He's a policeman?"

"Yeah. You know the cop they've been looking for?" Lacy asked.

"The cop?" Kathy's gaze went even wider. "The one whose body was found in the lake this morning?"

"Yeah," Lacy said. "That one. I'm in love with him."

Kathy reached over and took her by the shoulders. "You just hang on a little longer. I'm getting the Prozac."

# TWENTY-NINE

Chase felt like leftover mashed potatoes. His head hurt, his shoulder hurt, his ass hurt where he'd fallen in Lacy's shower. Everything hurt. He hadn't slept in over thirty-six hours.

He fit the key into the lock and pushed open his condo door. The sight of his place in shambles made him want to hit something, or better yet, someone. He'd love to take a swing at Officer Short, the IA investigator who had interrogated him for thirteen hours.

It wasn't as if they hadn't had proof. The book containing photos, witnesses, and detailed notes that the wanna-be cop Pablo had left in the gym locker incriminated Zeke up to Zeke's eyebrows. Oddly enough, Pablo had done a damn good investigation.

In his notes, Pablo had stated that he had stumbled across someone who suspected Zeke of selling cocaine—cocaine Zeke had ripped off from a drug bust. Pablo had accumulated quite a bit of evidence, but Zeke caught on and things backfired. Pablo found himself running for his life. That's when the man had left all his evidence in the locker, thinking Zeke wouldn't kill him as long as he knew the evidence was out there.

Of course, even with all of that evidence, IA wanted more. *"Just because Zeke is guilty that doesn't make you innocent,"* they had said.

Chase knew where to go. Big Bruno! As soon as IA turned Chase loose, he and Jason had searched and finally found Bruno in a club, kicking up his heels to some hip-hop tunes. Now Bruno would probably be dancing to the tune of about ten years. Zeke wouldn't get off so easy; the system generally came down hard on dirty cops, and Zeke had dirt embedded deep in the soles of his feet and under his fingernails, murder being the worst.

According to Bruno, Zeke shot Pablo and asked questions later. Pablo's last words were that Chase knew everything and would take him down.

Bruno's confession cleared Chase, but one of IA's questions kept slapping against Chase's brain. "How could you be his partner and not know he was dirty?"

The answer hurt, and it made Chase face the truth again. He'd lived in a vacuum these past two years, if he could even call it living.

Chase stepped over his toppled three-thousand-dollar stereo system and made his way to his bedroom. Hitting the light switch, he moaned at the mess. In a way, his slew of belongings mirrored his emotions right now.

His gaze shifted around and settled in the middle of the floor, on the picture of him and Sarah. He picked it up, staring at Sarah's face, at her tender smile. The ache in his heart doubled. It wasn't, however, the same pain that he might have felt last week had he stared into the picture. This pain had a different name. This wasn't about losing her. This was about saying good-bye. This was about admitting that life went on. About knowing how much love could hurt. It was about love being worth the pain.

And he loved Lacy.

He loved her with the same intensity that he'd loved Sarah. What if something happened to her? What if some freak accident or illness took Lacy? Could he withstand watching another person slip away? Could he stand upright with dignity and watch another coffin being lowered into the ground? The vacuum, the gosh-awful vacuum he'd lived in these past two years, suddenly felt like a safe house.

*"I saw the picture and I saw the clothes in the closet,"* he remembered Lacy telling him. Standing, he set the frame back on the dresser then went to the closet. He hadn't kept all her things, just those tied to the more special memories.

He ran his hand down the soft yellow sundress. She had worn it on their first date. The cotton, faded to a silky softness, slipped through his fingers. And right then he became snared between the past and future, caught between taking that last step into the real world, a very scary world, or going back to his vacuum where even the pain felt familiar. Familiar got points for being easy. Familiar he knew he could deal with.

Almost forty-eight hours and not one word. Lacy's mother walked into Lacy's bedroom with a tray carrying a tomato-basil soup and hot tea. "You don't have to do this," Lacy said.

"Yes, I do." Karina shooed Leonardo from the bed. "What kind of mother would I be if I let you go hungry?"

"I wouldn't starve myself to death," Lacy said. "I ate a whole gallon of chocolate mint ice cream at Kathy's last night. And then Sue brought over pizza with pineapple for breakfast."

Her mom set the tray down on the bedside table and edged down on the corner of the bed. "Oh, sweetie. Is there anything I can do to make you feel better? I could run to the store and pick you up another gallon of chocolate mint ice cream. Or maybe chocolate fudge? I could call my masseur and have him bring out a table and give you the rubdown of your life. Or I could hire a hit man to take that jerk out."

Lacy smiled through her pain. "I'm fine." Then, reaching up, she gave her mom a hug. The woman drove her crazy, but when the poop hit the fan Karina was always there, pooper scooper in hand.

She squeezed Lacy's shoulder. "You know, the only thing that hurts worse than a broken heart is seeing your child dealing with one. You're so special, and if that idiot can't see that, he doesn't deserve you."

"It's not his fault," Lacy said. "I knew when this started that he wasn't open to committing. I just thought . . . I thought I could keep my heart out of it."

"The heart is a strange thing, Lace. You can't control it. It loves when it loves." Her mom handed her the tea and tucked a curl back behind Lacy's ear. For just a second, Lacy felt like a child again, and she wanted to wallow in the safe cocoon of her mother's love.

But even that cocoon allowed a few feelings to

penetrate. Lacy looked at her cup and found the courage to ask the question she'd pondered for a long time: "Did you love them all? Did you love the men you married?"

Her mother's eyes clouded over. "I thought I did at one point or another. But the truth is, no, I didn't love them all. I liked them all and"—she grinned—"the sex was always great."

Lacy held up her hand. "Please, Mom."

Her mother ignored her objection. "No, you need to listen to me. Because sometimes I feel guilty about how my mistakes might have affected you. Did you know I'm seeing a therapist?"

Having sipped her tea, Lacy choked. "You are?"

"Yes." Her mom stared at her. "I'm not beyond admitting I need help, Lace." She let out a deep sigh. "Mr. Black, my therapist, is making me see a few things about myself that I would really prefer not to see."

"What kind of things?" Lacy balanced her cup in her lap.

"I loved your dad so much. We were young and . . . naive. We didn't know what it took to make a marriage. When we got the divorce, I thought I would die. I loved your dad like I've never loved anyone. And he loved me. It was that kind of love that fit, that felt like slipping on a silk glove. Perfect. But we were young and . . . let things come between us."

Her mother took Lacy's hand in hers. "We had half decided to remarry when he was sent to serve in Germany for six months. He begged me to make it legal before he was sent out, but . . . I wanted to take things slow, to be sure. I thought we could use the six months to figure out how to do it right. And then . . ." Her mother stared at the wall. "He was killed." She smoothed a wrinkle from her skirt. "The biggest regret in my life is that I didn't take that chance on us again. I let the opportunity go, Lace. So now whenever a man asks me to marry him, I . . ." She pressed a manicured nail against her lips.

"You feel as if you're making the same mistake," Lacy finished for her.

"I want love." Her mother's voice tightened with emotion. "And I don't want to let the chance get away." She cupped Lacy's chin. "But you're not me, sweetie. You can't make decisions about your life based on my mistakes. We can't even make decisions based on our own mistakes sometimes. We have to weigh our mistakes against our fears, and then let our heart and brain fight over what's right." Karina stroked a hand through Lacy's hair. "Do you really love this twerp?"

Lacy stared down at her tea, suddenly not sure how much of her refusal to call Chase was due to her believing he didn't want her, or her fear of marriage and of turning into her mom. "I think so, but I'm scared. It all happened so fast. One minute I thought he was going to kill me, the next I was fantasizing about getting him fitted for his tux. What if I'm fooling myself? What if we get married and then it doesn't work?"

"I knew your dad only five days when we got married, and he was the true love of my life. I'm not saying that this man is right for you. I'm just saying you shouldn't *not* try to work things out because you're afraid. Just like I shouldn't marry the next guy who asks just because I'm afraid."

Karina let out a deep breath. "If you think you love

him, you owe it yourself and to him to give it a fighting chance. *Hey.*" She gave Lacy's hand a squeeze. "I didn't raise a quitter."

Lacy chewed on her bottom lip and remembered what she'd discovered about Chase. "I'm not quitting. But . . . he still loves his late wife. He doesn't want to love again. He—"

Her mother touched her lips to quiet her. "His wife is in the past. I saw the way he looked at you. He's ready to move on."

Lacy gazed at her mother, wanting to believe, wanting to put her fears behind her once and for all.

Her mother cleared her throat. "I'm not saying you should marry him. But what would it hurt to drop by his place, to let him know that you're thinking about him? Maybe he's waiting on you to make the first move."

"You think so?" Lacy asked.

"Yeah, and if he turns you down, then I'll hire that hit man."

Lacy grinned and pulled back the covers. "You're right. I should at least go find out where I stand."

"That's my girl," her mother said.


After her mother left, Lacy pulled off her *Divorced, Desperate and Delicious* shirt and grabbed a shower. Feeling a mite desperate and wanting to feel a bit delicious, she dug deep into her closet, to the clothes from before her anti-men campaign. She needed something sexy, something that said *wow*, something that could compete with Jessie. A dark feeling of jealousy surged through her, but she ignored it.

A red fitted silk dress with a scooped neckline was about as *wow* as she had. Lacy grinned, deciding that some matching underwear would make the outfit say *double-wow*.

After drying her hair and banana-clipping it, she even put on a bit of makeup. A pair of red pumps, gold hoop earrings and a squirt of Red perfume added the final sparkle. Smiling into her mirror, she winked. "Watch out, Chase Kelly."

She knew there was a chance that Chase would turn her down, but she felt optimistic. One way or the other, she would deal with what happened. If Chase didn't want to continue seeing her, well, she would move on. She might tell her mother to go ahead and pay the hit man, but Lacy Maguire was finished hiding.

She drove through rush-hour traffic to get to his place. Like air from week-old balloons, by the time she cut off the engine her courage had seeped out. Her stomach hurt and her hands felt sweaty, but she forced herself to get out of her Saturn and walk up the stairs. Remembering the pass-code, she let herself in. As she moved to the elevator, a man walking past stopped and smiled, his gaze brushing over her in definite male appreciation. Her courage rose a notch. But her heart thumped against her breastbone when the elevator opened on the second floor.

She took a deep breath, stepped out, and started down the hall towards Chase's unit. Two more steps, and she heard someone whistling a lively and familiar tune. Lacy paused as the words ran through her head. It was "Grandma Got Run Over By a Reindeer."

She stopped and glanced over her shoulder. There, fifty feet from her, his back to her, Chase ambled down the hall. She opened her mouth to call his name, but her voicebox seized. He carried a bouquet of red roses in one hand and a plastic grocery bag in the other. He stopped, juggled the items in his arms, and knocked on a door. On Jessie's door.

Lacy froze. Sometimes, the truth was hard to swallow and it took her a couple attempts to get this bit of truth down her throat. The truth being that Chase preferred women who didn't care, and his returning to Jessie could only mean one thing. He really hadn't cared about her. Her lungs shut down and the snag in her heart started unraveling for good this time.

Jessie's door opened. "Chase? Oh, my God!" The woman's voice seemed to bounce down the hall and slap Lacy right between the eyes. "I've been worried sick. Oh, my, you brought me flowers."

Swerving around, Lacy repeatedly hit the elevator button. When it opened, she stumbled inside and punched the button at least four times to close the door. An allergy attack hit full force, but she fought back the tears, remembering her vow to move on. She hadn't gotten dolled up to go home and cry—she could always do that later. Some guy, somewhere, was going to enjoy the red outfit. And maybe even the red underwear.

Chase placed another log on the fire and paced the wooden floor in Lacy's living room. All four of her animals sat on the sofa and observed him, their heads turning left then right as he moved. He'd had the evening all planned out. However, his plans had a serious flaw.

When he had found her gone, he'd decided to surprise her. He'd pulled his car around back and started dinner, grateful for the time to figure out exactly what he needed to say. But that had been three hours ago. Now he'd practiced his speech so much that he felt sure even Fabio knew it by heart. Leonardo had gotten bored and sneaked into the kitchen and eaten the baby's breath that came with the roses. And dinner had long since grown cold. The grandfather clock struck ten times. Where could she be at ten o'clock on a Tuesday night?

Car lights sent a beam of brightness through the front windows. Chase stepped to the door and started to open it when he heard voices. He moved to the window in the dining room and peered out. His heart plummeted.

It was Lacy, wearing something far too sexy to be standing next to any man besides him. She stood on the front walk next to another man.

# THIRTY

Jealousy flooded Chase's blood like poison. He forced himself to breathe, to not react like an idiot.

"You didn't have to follow me, Eric," Lacy said. "I told you I was fine."

Chase scowled. So this was the impatient vet who'd wanted to share sin with his woman. *Maybe I should act like an idiot.*

Eric brushed a hand up against Lacy's arm. "What kind of guy would I be if I didn't make sure you got home safely?"

*A dead man if you touch her again.* Chase doubled his fist when he saw the man lower his face. Lacy turned her head, and the man's lips only landed on her cheek. Nevertheless, Chase didn't want the man's lips anywhere near her.

"Thanks for letting me hang out with you at the clinic." Lacy put her hand on his chest to ward off another kiss. "I should go in. It's been a long day."

Chase decided to give the man two seconds to get Lacy's send-off message before he offered his own send-off. Much to his disappointment, Eric shrugged and walked away. Lacy watched him drive off, then she turned to unlock her door.

She stepped inside and dropped her purse on the antique sewing machine. Standing a few feet inside the dining room, Chase didn't move, didn't make a sound. She must have sensed him, because she swung around.

"Oh, God! You scared the pee out of me!"

His gaze moved over her body, wrapped in red silk. The dress's neckline dipped low, showing off the soft swells of her breasts. The waist hugged her figure, and the hem of the dress fell an inch above mid-thigh, leaving all that leg exposed. Chase didn't know much about women's fashions, but he knew when a woman dressed like that she was on the make.

"You went out with Eric?" he asked.

Her eyes squinted with what looked like anger. But he was too busy dealing with his own fury to worry about hers.

"How did you get in?" She crossed her arms over her middle, causing the scooped neckline to lower.

"You went out with him?" he asked again.

"What business is that of yours?"

"I'm making it my business!" He waved a hand up and down. "Do you know what that dress says?"

She looked down as if needing a reminder of what she wore. "It says, 'get out of my house,'" she snapped. "No, wait. That's what I'm saying. Get out, Chase."

He ignored her. "It says, 'Take me off.' When a woman wears a dress like that she doesn't intend to keep it on very long."

"How would you know?" she said. "Does Jessie have one just like it?" Turning on her red-pump heels, she took one step then swung back around. "Call me selfish. Blame it on the fact that I'm an only child and I never learned to share. But I refused to share Brian with the professor, or Peter with his secretary, and I won't share you with Jessie."

Chase raked a hand over his face and stared at her. "Why are you bringing up Jessie?"

"You slept with her. I know I'm just a vanilla wafer. And that's what happens to vanilla wafers. But someday I'll find a guy who loves vanilla wafers so much that he won't need to go sampling other cookies."

Confusion filled Chase as he tried to decipher her meaning. "I was completely up front with you about Jessie." He took two steps toward her and got a whiff of perfume. Delicious. "You can't be mad about that now."

"Oh, I see." Her tone rang with fourteen-carat sarcasm. "You told me about her and so that makes it okay to sleep with her. Well, if that's the way it works, you knew about Eric, too. So put the key back under the dog poop and leave."

"You slept with Eric?" His emotions ping-ponged back and forth as he tried to make sense of the conversation.

"No," she said. "But if I wasn't such a lousy liar, I'd tell you I did."

"Then why the hell did you wear that dress?" he asked.

She kicked off one of her shoes. The red pump swished by his leg, landing in the dining room, and then the other came whizzing by and hit the litter box. *"Good kitty,"* the litter box's recorder played. *"Now cover it up."*

"You're right," Lacy said. "I intended to get laid tonight. But it just didn't work out. So tell me, did you have better luck than I did?"

He raked another hand over his face. "What's that supposed to mean? I'm not understanding something here."

She yanked a clip out of her hair. "Please, don't play me for a fool. I saw you, Chase." Her bare foot started tapping.

Her words sank in and he got his first clue to this puzzle. "You saw me where?"

She pushed her fingers through the dark curls, shaking them loose. Chase longed to step closer and help her. One or two runs of his fingers and he'd have her hair properly mussed for a night of serious lovemaking. A second or two more and he'd have that dress unzipped and puddling around her ankles. He wondered if she had on red underwear to match the dress. Damn, she looked sexy. Smelled great. But she'd dressed up for Eric; hadn't she? Her foot continued to tap on the floor.

She pointed a finger at him. So, Lacy was a toe tapper and a pointer. Chase watched that small digit start to shake. His mother had been a pointer, and if he'd learned anything, it was that when the finger came out, hell was about to break loose. But Lacy wasn't his mother and he could give her hell back.

He grabbed her by the wrist. Her blue eyes squinted tighter, and she started talking. "You had flowers and groceries. It was another . . . another cook-dinner-and-have-sex-with-Jessie night. Never mind that she doesn't give a flip for you. Oh, but wait. That's why you like her!"

Understanding hit like a cool breeze in mid-July, and damn if it didn't feel good. "You came to my place tonight? You saw me knocking on Jessie's door? You know, I smelled your perfume when I got in the elevator."

"Congratulations, Columbo. You finally figured it out." She jerked her hand free and propped it on her hip.

"So this . . ." He waved a hand up and down. "The dress and the perfume, it was all for me?" He smiled and reared back on his heels a little, and took some time to enjoy the view.

Lacy couldn't believe Chase stood there all cocky and smiling. The nerve, the gall! How dare he find something humorous about this? She was definitely going to tell her mother to hire the hit man.

"What kind of flowers were they, Lacy?" He stepped closer. Fabio came barking into the room.

"You know what kind." She walked backwards into her living room, nearly tripping over her own feet as Fabio danced in her path. Oh, Lordie, but Chase looked good tonight. Dressed in khaki Dockers and a button-down blue shirt, sex appeal oozed from him. But he'd already oozed it all over Jessie. Still, she longed to touch him. She'd missed him, missed his laughter, and the devilish gleam in his green eyes. But the green-eyed devil was going to have to go, because sharing just wasn't her thing.

"Were they red roses?" He arched an eyebrow. "Like those?" He pointed behind her.

She swung around. Her mouth dropped open.

There, on her kitchen table, complete with candles and two plates, sat a vase of red roses. She heard him move behind her.

"Leonardo ate the baby's breath," he apologized, and his hands came around her. "I went to wish Jessie good luck with her husband and to tell her good-bye. Nothing else. Just good-bye." He pressed his lips to the back of her neck. "So, you expected to get laid tonight, did you?"

She bit her lower lip and turned around. "You . . . you didn't stay at Jessie's?"

"No, I came here and cooked chicken cordon bleu, rice pilaf, and fresh green beans with pearl onions. And . . ." His gaze shifted to her neckline. "I was kind of hoping to get laid, too."

He raised his gaze and frowned. "What were you doing all night while I was slaving away in your kitchen?"

"I watched Eric neuter a male cat." She grinned. "He had the third shift at the clinic. It was actually very interesting."

"Remind me to sleep with one eye open if I ever make you mad." He lowered his forehead to hers. "You didn't play doctor or vet with him?"

"No! There wasn't any spark." Her breath caught when his hand moved down to her backside and held her against the hardness filling his pants.

"What about now?" he asked. "Feeling any sparks?" He wrapped his arms around her waist, cradled his arousal against her abdomen, and started them slow dancing.

There wasn't any music, but it didn't matter. With Chase this close, she heard music. They made their own music.

"Feeling sparks?" he repeated, and his right hand moved up to caress the swell of her breast.

"That depends." She sucked on her bottom lip.

"On what?" His lips brushed across her cheek.

"Is this casual sex?" she asked.

He leaned his head back and stared into her eyes as if trying to read her. "You want it to be casual?"

"I asked you first." She closed her mouth to keep from saying that she'd take him any way he came, temporary or permanent. But good Lord, she wanted permanent.

"Casual is okay," he whispered, studying her eyes, then he tilted up her chin. "If I can casually tell FedEx Hunky, Impatient Eric, Peter and the plumber to go shoot themselves." He lowered his hand to the hem of her dress and moved it up and up, until he cupped her silk-covered bottom in his palm. "Casual is fine if I can casually sleep with you every night. And hell, since we're spending all our time together, I don't see why we can't just casually do the paperwork to make it legal."

He slow-danced her around the room, his body brushing against hers in all the right places. He breathed into her mouth. His tongue slipped between her lips. "You know, sooner or later one of those condoms might fail us and you might have a little Chase or maybe a little Lacy growing inside you. Paperwork just makes things like that easier." He pressed a palm against her lower abdomen, as if imagining her carrying his baby.

She ran her hands up to his shoulders. "And how would you feel about . . . about a little Chase or Lacy?"

"Ecstatic," he whispered in her ear. "I'm thirty-two, so I figure I'd better get busy." He ran his tongue along the curve of her ear. "What about you? Kids okay?"

She grinned. "I'm open," she said, unable to hide her excitement.

"Um." He pushed his thigh between her legs. "How open?"

She pushed against him. "Very open."

"I love you," he whispered, and his hand moved around her waist. "And for the record, I'm very fond of vanilla wafers. I don't believe in sampling other cookies when I have the perfect one at home."

She chuckled and pressed her face into the warmth of his chest. "I love you, too," she said, and her zipper fell open with Chase's help. The silk dress slid over her shoulders and down her body.

"Um." His head dipped to get a better view. "I was hoping you were wearing all red." He swayed against her.

"You really are a bad boy," she said, and stepped out of the dress encircling her bare feet.

He waggled his eyebrows, pulled her close, and continued to dance. "I even brought my handcuffs." His gaze lowered again to her body. "Wow, you look good." His tongue traced his bottom lip. Then his gaze continued to feast on her matching red bra and panties. "Victoria's Secret?" he asked.

She nodded, then cupped his face in her hands. "There's a lot of things we need to talk about."

His feet slowed and they finally stood frozen. "I should have told you about Sarah," he said, somehow reading her mind. "I think I just needed to say good-bye first."

"You loved her a lot," Lacy said, trying to control her jealousy. "Are you sure—"

"I did love her. A lot. But she's gone now, and she'd be happy for me. I love you. I don't want to spend my life in the past. I've never been surer about anything."

"Good." She smiled, then rested her head on his chest.

"What about the Peter issue?" His hands moved to her upper arms.

Lacy raised her head from the warmth of his shoulder. "I'm not in love with him anymore. I haven't been for a long time."

"But I thought—"

She pressed a finger over his soft lips. "It was never about Peter. I mean, he hurt me, and I guess that didn't help but . . . it was really about my mom, and my grandma." She took a deep breath. "They have a history of marrying and getting divorced. I don't want to wind up like them."

"Is it the married or the divorced part that bothers you?" His hands moved down her forearms to rest on her waist again. And they felt good there. The kind of good that she could get used to.

"Definitely the divorced."

"Good. Because when I get married—casually, of course—I don't get divorced." He kissed her, a soft touch of his lips to hers, a touch that spoke of commitment, of honesty, of forever. She knew she could trust him.

The phone rang. They ignored it. Her mother's shrill voice echoed through the sound system: "Lace? Are you okay? Do I need to hire the hit man to take out that cop? We could kill him for ten thousand or wound him for two. What do you think?"

He ended the kiss. "Jeez!" he said. "This is going to be my mother-in-law?"

Lacy smiled. "I told you . . . she's missing that filter thingamabob, and therefore she speaks before she thinks."

"I think," her mom continued, "we could choose if we wanted it to be an arm or leg."

Chase rolled his eyes.

"She really wouldn't hire a hit man." Lacy giggled.

"Well, I hope the hell not." He took a breath. "Tell me? Do they give thingamabob transplants? I'll even pay for it. Find that woman a doctor for goodness's sake."

Lacy grinned. "She's not *all* bad. She's the one who told me not to give up on you. And the bra and panties . . . she gives me a five-hundred-dollar gift certificate to Victoria's Secret every Valentine's Day. I have a drawer full of . . . surprises."

"Five hundred? I love her already," Chase said, and moved to the kitchen to pick up the phone. "Hello, Mrs. Callahan." He paused. "Yes, ma'am. I plan on that. No, ma'am. I would never do anything to hurt her. I remember. It was something about me and a meat grinder." Chase held the phone to his ear, but his gaze moved up and down Lacy's body with lusty appreciation. With a quick finger-wiggle, he motioned for her to come closer.

Lacy slid into him, running her hands up and over his chest. Slowly she undid his first shirt button, then the second. He folded his free hand around her back; then, lowering his head, he pressed his lips against the curve of her neck.

"Uh-huh," he mumbled into the phone. "Mrs. Callahan, I hate to interrupt, but . . . your daughter is standing here and I'm in the mood for a vanilla wafer." He paused. "Well, let me put it this way:

She's practically naked and all I can think about is banging a headboard against the wall. Can we discuss wedding dates another time?"

Lacy buried her face into Chase's shoulder and tried not to laugh. She failed, and her laughter spilled out on his shirt.

"Yes, ma'am." He hung up and met her gaze. "Your mother said for you to enjoy yourself." He kissed the top of Lacy's head.

Leaning back, she felt her laugh bubble up again. "I can't believe you told her that!"

"Hey, there has to be some advantage to having that woman for a mother-in-law. If she speaks without using a thingamabob, then I can give my own thingamabob an occasional break." He grinned and unhooked Lacy's bra. "Now . . . what were we doing before the phone rang?"

# Pet Tips from Christie Craig

Pets are an important part of my books because they are an important part of my life. They are furry, cuddly, love us unconditionally, and their very existence enriches us and brings us joy. Below are some tips to care for pets, as well as some tips from pets on how to take better take care of ourselves:

*Tips on Taking Care of our Pets:*

1) Pets need and deserve *TLC*. Tender loving care, yes, but they also need our time, loyalty, and commitment.
2) Keep them healthy by getting them vaccinated, by taking them to regular checkups and getting them plenty of exercise.
3) Get them spayed or neutered. Each year, millions of dogs and cats in the U.S. are put to death in shelters because there are no homes for them.

# DIVORCED, DESPERATE AND DELICIOUS

*Tips From Our Pets on Taking Better Care of Ourselves:*

Dog:

1) Speak up: It's a simple trick, but one that most of us humans should practice more often. It appears that we do a lot more rolling over than speaking up.
2) Latch your teeth onto what you want: When we're ready to growl because our wants and desires are falling by the wayside, we should latch onto our goals like, well, a dog with a bone.
3) Demand a walk every day: While a brisk stroll around the block may not seem as crucial to us as it is to our dogs, it can work wonders on reducing stress.

Cat:

1) Take a catnap: While our feline buddies are always working on their Zs, studies show that Americans are getting less and less sleep. Napping won't make up for sleep deprivation, but a short nap can prevent us from being too catty.
2) It's okay to be finicky: Both with what you put in your mouth and the people you allow in your life. And once someone is deemed trustworthy, demand a little lap time. Snuggling, hugging, are good for the soul.

For more animal tips and tales, check out my Web site: www.Christie-Craig.com

**Dorchester Publishing Proudly Presents the
Winner of the American Title III Contest!**

# Jenny Gardiner

Wham, bam, no-thank-you, ma'am. That about sums up the
sex life of Claire Doolittle. Not-so-happily married to Jack—
once the man of her dreams but now a modern-day version
of the bossy, dull Ward Cleaver of '50s sitcom fame—Claire is
at the end of her rope. Gone are the glorious days of flings in
elevators and broom closets. They'd once had a world of col-
or, of wanton frivolity. Now, life's black and white: a sitcom
in reruns. A not-very-funny sitcom. Cue an old boyfriend—
the "one that got away"—throw in a predatory hottie who's
set her sights on our leading man, and watch Claire's world
spiral out of control.

In the old TV show, the Beaver always got a happy ending.
Stay tuned.

**AVAILABLE FEBRUARY 2008!**
ISBN 13: 978-0-505-52747-9